AMNESIA

THE BOOK OF MALADIES VOLUME 6

D.K. HOLMBERG

ASH
PUBLISHING

A TRIAL OF VENOM

The jar containing the greenish eel venom felt warm in Alec's hand, as it always seemed to, regardless of the temperature of the room. There was something unsettling about that, though he wasn't sure why.

He dipped a spoon into the jar, coating it with venom. Holding the spoon over the paper, he let a few drops fall onto it. He had done it a few times, but each time, he had struggled to discover the secret—the connection between the eel venom and easar paper. He was determined to figure out how to make their own. Otherwise, they would be forced to depend on the university and whoever their supplier was to maintain their supply.

"I don't think direct application is what is required," Master Helen said.

Alec looked over at her. Her gray hair was twisted back in a tight bun, and she wore a gray jacket over her shoulders, keeping herself covered. It was probably for the best as there had been several times when the venom had splattered, and they didn't know what topical absorption might do.

"I thought varying the concentration might make a difference," Alec said. The piece of plain paper he had sourced from Mrs. Rubbles lay on a metal table in one of the classrooms. They were far enough away from where students might pop in that they could experiment without many distractions. They didn't want someone to spring in on them and begin asking questions. As it was, it was possible someone would notice that he had been spending quite a bit of time with Master Helen.

"I agree that was a good starting point. Neither the yellowish venom nor the oral venom seems to make a difference, and trying them together..." Master Helen began.

"Trying them together has been completely ineffectual," Alec said.

Alec sighed and turned away from the paper, jotting down a few notes in his journal. He was determined to keep track of their trials, prepared for whatever it might take to understand what went into the easar paper. "If we had a larger supply of the easar paper, we could afford to experiment on it, maybe break it down and determine what went into its construction."

"Unfortunately, our supply is limited. We certainly don't have enough to destroy the supply we already have."

Alec understood, but without it, they were stuck trialing it. "What if the eel venom is not a part of creating easar paper?"

"There is one fact that has managed to come out of the Thelns lands, and that is the eels play a crucial part in the creation of easar paper. We had known about the oral venom, but we had never extracted the yellowish venom you found. Now that we have, I think it's much more likely that we will find a way to create our own supply of paper."

Alec looked at the stack of different types of paper. If they were to be methodical, they would perform the same trial on every single sample. He just wasn't convinced that it would make a difference. In addition, they would soon run out of eel venom, and he didn't look forward to going out to harvest more. He could ask Bastan, and Alec was certain the man would help, but he would rather go about it a different way.

"Your father might know more," Master Helen said.

"He might," Alec agreed.

"You don't intend to ask him."

"Knowing what my father is, and what he has done, I don't know if I can."

"Your father was once a master physicker. He could be again."

"You would have me ask my father to return to the university?" Alec wasn't certain he would even consider it. His father had been away long enough, and had very distinct feelings about the university, at least he'd led Alec to believe he did. Maybe those feelings had not been real. His father had apparently concealed many things from Alec over the years, enough that he no longer knew whether the man had been telling him the truth about everything.

"Aelus Stross is a brilliant man. He should never have been allowed to leave. We have needed someone with his intellect, and I think of how much we've missed out on because of his absence."

Alec turned his attention to the next piece of paper. "Well, he's not here, so you can either continue to work with me, or you can pine for my father."

Master Helen looked over at him sharply. "Pine? I'm only suggesting that he might have insights that you lack, Physicker Stross."

"I have insights from my recent experiences. I think that's enough."

"You have insights from experience, but fail to have the necessary understanding of context, something that can only come with time."

Alec turned his attention back to the paper. "If you would prefer that we finish for the day, we certainly can," Alec said.

"If that would be easier for you, we certainly may, but I would be interested in continuing our research," Master Helen said.

"I'm not sure what else we can try. If we continue to reproduce these experiments on the different types of paper, it might help, but it might be that the paper itself isn't the key," Alec said.

"You think it is something more than simply adding the venom to paper?" Master Helen asked.

"I don't know, but it could be. It could be that the venom needs to be a part of *creating* the paper, not adding it to already milled paper."

"That would be unfortunate and would be much more time-consuming."

"But it could be more efficient. Think of it, Master Helen. If each page had to be treated, that would be a very slow process. But if making easar paper was no different from making regular paper, it could be incredibly efficient."

"Perhaps it would be more efficient, but it is much *less* efficient for us as we try to understand how to re-create the paper. If we have to go through the entire process of making it, it will take a significant amount of time."

"I can work with it and see what I can come up with," Alec suggested.

Master Helen straightened and wiped her hands on her jacket. "I had hoped this would be an easier process. After your discovery, I thought…"

"No discovery worth anything is easy," Alec said.

Master Helen snorted. "I suppose not. That doesn't change the fact that I wished it were. Will you keep the venom safe?"

Alec nodded. He had refused to allow her to take the eel venom, especially as he had been the one who had harvested it. There had been some argument about it, but ultimately, she had conceded.

Master Helen left, and Alec collected the various pages, stuffing them into his satchel. He needed to destroy them, not wanting to risk anyone getting exposed to the venom. Enough people had already been harmed because of the eel venom.

He put the cap on the jar and left the classroom. He debated going to the hospital ward. He always found some satisfaction in seeing the patients there and treating anyone that he could, but right now, he had no interest in that. He wanted to understand how to create easar paper so that he could better help Sam so that they could head to the Theln lands.

And maybe Master Helen was right. Maybe he needed to go and speak with his father, to move past the issues that they had. But doing so was difficult, at least for Alec. In the time since he had restored his father, he had not spoken to him much. He simply hadn't wanted to.

It was time for him to change that.

Alec made his way from the university, keeping his satchel with him. It was better that he kept the satchel and the jars of eel venom with him than to leave it behind in his room. The rooms were lockable, but that didn't mean someone couldn't break in. There had already been enough strangeness within the university for him to know better than that.

It was a bright, sunny day, and Alec made his way from section to section, walking quickly. He felt a sense of urgency. How long would Sam give him before she made a run for Tray? He was surprised she had delayed as long as she had, but that was partly because of Marin, and he didn't think she would wait much longer. Not when it came to finding Tray.

And Alec didn't disagree with her desire to search for Tray.

He wouldn't tell her about his interest in seeing what those who went to Theln lands—other Scribes—knew. There had to be something, especially since so many were compelled to remain behind when they went there. What reason would there be for that?

He would not suffer from a similar temptation. He knew himself well enough to know that while he might be able to learn something from them, there would be no reason for him to remain behind. That and the fact that were he to stay behind, he would miss out on having time with Sam. He wouldn't do that to her. He wouldn't betray her in such a way.

When he reached the Arrend section, Alec slowed. Everything here was familiar and comforting. He enjoyed his time here, even if it was something that he had outgrown. When he passed Mrs. Rubbles shop, he looked over at it fondly, remembering all the times she had helped him, along with the times that he had helped her. She was a friend, much like so many of the people in the section. It was why it was hard for him to return. Leaving for the university meant that he would never return here, and it meant he would never be able to help these people —people who were essentially part of his family—quite the same way as he once had.

His father's shop was closed, and no lights were on inside. Alec checked the door and was surprised to find it unlocked. He stepped inside, noting the jingle of the bells as he always did, and took a deep breath, savoring the smells within the shop. Everything about it was familiar, even if it wasn't the same shop as his childhood home.

"How can I help... Alec." His father stepped out of the back, his hair standing wildly, and a smudge of ink on his cheek. "I haven't seen you since you healed me. I thought you were disappointed with me."

"I am."

"Then why are you here?"

"I can be mad at you and still care about you," Alec said.

His father stared at him for a long moment. "I... I thought that maybe you would have decided otherwise."

Alec looked around the shop. Though it bore all that was familiar from his father's old shop, each time he came, there was an increasing sense of strangeness for him. No longer did this feel like *his* shop. Now it was his father's. Though it had always been his father's, Alec had been a part of it, and this had been his place, just as much as it had been his father's. So much had changed over the last few months.

"Can we talk?"

"You are always welcome to come and talk with me," his father said.

Alec made his way to the back of the shop and took a seat on one of the hard chairs. His father typically used them for assessments. The cot looked like it had been recently used, and there were sheets that were thrown back, leaving Alec to wonder who had recently come through here, and with what illness. He looked around, knowing that his father would have left a sheet of paper with notes, and maybe that was what he had been working on when Alec came into the shop. He found it on the table near the cot. The ink remained unstopped, and the pen he'd been using rested across the page.

"Have you seen any interesting cases lately?"

His father glanced over toward the table. "There's always someone who comes in with an interesting case, you know that, Alec."

"Sometimes, there are surprisingly interesting things," Alec said.

His father shrugged. "We don't get to choose who we treat."

Alec dragged his gaze away. The question he wanted to ask—that he needed to ask—came to his lips. "Did mother know?"

His father stared at him for long moments. After a while, he got up and made his way over to a small hearth, where he pulled a pot from atop the flames. He poured steaming water into cups and handed one of the cups to Alec. Alec took a deep breath, recognizing the heady scent of the tea his father preferred, much stronger than what he could find at the university.

"I was a physicker when I knew your mother," his father started slowly. He remained standing, pacing slowly as he started to talk. Alec had seen it many times before and had long ago grown accustomed to the way his father felt the need to pace in order to think. Sam was much the same way, though she had a little bit more agitation to her when she paced. "It wasn't until I left the university that I learned her other calling."

"Calling?"

His father nodded. "There are many uses for the knowledge we have, Alec. I have tried to use my training as best as I can, wanting to take the lessons I was taught when I was a physicker so that I could help as many people as I could. And I have. You may think less of me, but over the years, we have helped a great number of people."

Alec sat back in the chair, his eyes drifting closed. It was difficult to see the side of his father. This wasn't the man Alec had thought he was. His father had always been the healer, the ideal that he wanted to live up to, so for him to learn that his father might be something else—and someone else—it was difficult. Painful.

And yet... Alec couldn't deny that they truly had helped countless people over the years. Alec had seen it time and again. People who came to his father often had no one else to go to, and they had been desperate. His father had willingly offered his services, not charging nearly what the university would have charged.

Even recently, Alec was able to think of people his father had helped, like the woman who was laboring, her baby in breach. Had his father not offered his help, would that baby have survived? The child certainly wouldn't have made it had the mother gone to the university for help. Even if she had tried, would the university have been willing to help? And if they offered, could they have even helped her?

"Why?" Alec asked softly.

"You know why. You know there are costs to do what we do. From the supplies to the medicines to the ingredients I harvest. Everything I do is expensive. Why else do you think the university charges what they do?"

"So, you have become a poisoner in order to help others?" Alec opened his eyes and looked up at his father. "You have abandoned everything that you know so that you can claim you're helping others?"

"I haven't abandoned everything I know. The entire purpose behind what I have done was to work with those treatments. Don't conflate the two."

Alec looked at his father with incredulity. "How can I not? You're trying to convince me you have some altruistic reason behind the awful things you have done."

"Tell me, Alec, what have you learned in the time since you went to the university?"

It was a strange shift in the conversation, and his father stopped only a few paces from him, his arms crossed over his chest, the mug of tea resting on his arm. It steamed, sending little trailers of smoke toward his face.

"I've been learning healing. I have studied with the masters, and I have—"

His father shook his head. "No. You've learned that *at*

the university. What I'm asking is what you have learned in the time since you left for the university."

Alec frowned. "Do you mean Marin?"

His father shrugged. "Marin. The Thelns. The likelihood of other attacks. All of that. You have learned that there is a different threat within the city than you ever knew."

Alec leaned back, breathing out heavily. There had been a time when he would have believed the city was completely protected. Isolated as they were, with the ocean on one side, the mountains with the steam fields on another, and the swamp to still another, it was incredibly difficult for anyone to reach them. They were protected.

And yet they weren't.

Perhaps his father was right. That was the largest lesson that he had learned. Discovering there were others —and powerful others—who wanted to do harm in the city had surprised him. Discovering the Thelns and what they had intended still shocked him.

None of it was nearly as shocking as what he had learned of the princess.

That was something that he wasn't sure he should—or could—share with his father.

"What's your point?"

"My point is that you can have every intention to remain pure. I certainly did. When I was at the university, when I was learning what they were able to teach, I wanted nothing more than to help as many people as I could. The gods know that was why I went. I believed I would discover some great secret, truths that could only be learned by studying the body, but I learned something else."

Alec sat up. It was always difficult to get his father to talk about his time at the university. Maybe his anger was what was needed, some way to motivate him to share.

"And what did you learn?"

"I learned there are things that cannot be changed, Alec." His father breathed out heavily, and then he took a sip of his tea before sitting across from Alec. "When your mother… When your mother died." He swallowed, as if forcing back a lump in his throat. "Something changed in me. She was so good, and she was so proud, but…"

Alec leaned forward. "But what?"

"She hid secrets." His father looked up at him, and tears welled in his eyes. "I learned of them after she was gone, and only then. She wasn't from the city. I had always known she was from one of the more remote sections, but after she was gone, when I went searching for answers, I found nothing about her. That sent me searching for even more answers."

Alec couldn't breathe. "If she wasn't from the city, where was she from?"

His father met his gaze. "I can only speculate. You wonder why I spend as much time away as I do, why I have gone searching, often leaving the city to find various medicines, but it's not only for the medicines. I've gone searching for answers. They are answers I don't know I'll ever find, but I have to look. I have to know."

Did his father suggest his mother had come from Theln lands? Alec already knew the Thelns had people who were somewhat like Scribes. They were responsible for the Book. If that was the case, then why was she in the city?

Unless she was trying to keep tabs on the city.

That meant she would have been a spy.

Alec knew nothing of his mother. Everything he knew had come from his father. Knowing his father—or at least what he once had *thought* he knew—Alec had an idea of what kind of person his mother was. She would have been caring, much like his father. She would have wanted him to find himself, and knowing the affection his father still held for her, she would have wanted him to find love again.

Yet all of that was imagined.

"Why have you kept this from me?"

"Because you haven't needed to know."

"And why tell me now?"

His father set his tea down and leaned forward resting his elbows on the table. "From what I have heard, your friend is preparing a journey. If I know you—and Alec, regardless of what you want to say, I do know you—you will go with her. If you do, I want you to be as prepared as you can be."

Alec blinked. Did his father really know that he was thinking about going to the Theln lands?

"You would help?"

"Whatever else you believe about me, know that I care for you. Deeply. I would do anything to keep harm from falling on you, even harm you don't know is coming."

2

AN UNEXPECTED FIND

Alec stared at the table for a long moment before standing and walking into the front room, hoping to clear his head. He willed his heart to slow down, trying to get control of his mind as it raced. He wanted to know more. His mother was a total unknown to him, the person who had left his life far too early, leaving him only with questions about who she was.

The sounds of his father tinkering in the back of the shop were familiar. Alec had known those sounds his entire life. There was a part of him that was tempted to go back and begin to organize, to update the catalog of which medicines were low, so that his father could go harvesting, or could leave and purchase what was needed.

That wasn't his task, not anymore.

He needed to find Sam. If anyone needed to know about what he'd discovered of his heritage, it would be Sam.

And she likely wouldn't be surprised. He was a Scribe, and though his father wasn't—though he apparently had some potential toward it—he suspected now his mother had been.

What sorts of things would she have known?

What sorts of things could she have taught his father?

Alec got up and made his way to the back of the shop. He found his father swirling water, cleaning out one of the pots. "Was mother a physicker?"

"No. At least, I don't think she was."

"And yet, there were things you learned from her, weren't there?"

His father turned and looked over his shoulder. "Why?"

"You… you think she was a spy for them."

His father sighed. Red rimmed his eyes, but he said nothing more.

"And if you believe she was a spy, and if she came from the Theln lands, it stands to reason she was a Scribe—or whatever they call them in their lands."

His father took a deep breath. "She claimed that she was a collector of sorts. She always enjoyed old books. She would have me going from shop to shop so she could look in, hoping to find something interesting. She had a collection."

Alec frowned. "And you never shared this with me?"

Such a collection would be potentially important, especially if it was the reason she was in the city. Maybe his mother had her own references, information that could be critical to help Alec understand what she was asked to do. Maybe there would be things in her records that wouldn't be found anywhere else. But then he stumbled with a realization.

"Did they burn in the fire?"

His father nodded. "It was unfortunate. Some of those works were incredibly old. Most of them weren't useful, not to anyone other than a physicker."

"If she was a Scribe, many of those books would have been useful to others," Alec said. A different thought came to him. "Is that how you knew about the canal eels?"

His father shook his head. "Not from the books. Your mother said she'd had some experience with them when she was younger."

Alec smiled to himself. "I imagine her experience came from her time in the Theln lands."

Alec's father nodded. "I didn't think so at the time, but after she was gone, I began to piece it together. She was the one who taught me they could be filleted, and that there were many uses to the eel."

"Such as?"

"You apparently have discovered the two types of venom they carry." Alec nodded. "And I imagine some at the university have taught you that the flesh has some healing properties."

"They don't want that to be well-known."

"Of course not. If that were known, the eels would be hunted, and they wouldn't want that, not since they have another purpose for them."

"I don't understand the purpose. I don't understand how the eels are able to keep the Thelns out of the city."

"It's not so much that they can keep them out of the city as it is they obfuscate things. They make the city difficult for anyone to find."

Alec frowned. That wasn't his impression, not from talking with the master physickers. There had to be something more to it. Then again, maybe his father didn't know. His father had been promoted to master physicker, and he might have potential to be a Scribe, but he wasn't either of those things.

"Did she say anything about how the eels could be used in creating easar paper?"

"No. I'm still not completely convinced easar paper is tied to the eel venom."

"Master Helen seems to think it is."

"If anyone would know, it would be Helen. She is one of the brightest minds at the university, so I would recommend that you continue your studies with her."

"Do you think they will let me return after my trip with Sam?"

His father set down the pot he'd been cleaning and turned back to him. "Do you need to go? Your friend is capable, and there is no reason for you to go. You could stay at the university. Everything I hear—and everything I've seen from you—tells me you are not far from promotion to master physicker."

"Not far, as in years."

His father shrugged. "What is years when your promotion would grant you the ability to influence so many? Think about it, Alec. Once you reach that level, you can have a say in the running of the university. You can help influence what is charged, and how many people without money are helped. You can be the reason so many others are given an opportunity that few have been."

It all sounded right. And it all sounded like something that he wanted—or at least, that he once wanted. Was that what he wanted now? He didn't know, but he wasn't convinced that the way he would influence others most effectively was through serving as a master physicker. How could he, when he had seen that —were he to have a greater access to easar paper—he would be able to do even more? With the paper, he could heal the most obscure illnesses. People wouldn't have to suffer. All he needed was a way to create the paper.

And if his father didn't know, and if Alec wasn't able to discover it on his own, then he would have to go to the Theln lands to find that answer.

If nothing else, his father was giving him even more reason to go with Sam. Learning that his mother had apparently come from there and discovering that there was a family secret he didn't know—and his father didn't know—were reason enough for him to go.

"I will think on it."

"Was there another reason you came here?"

Alec nodded. "I thought perhaps you had discovered something about the eel venom, and that you might be able to come up with some method of creating easar paper."

His father frowned. "I imagine you have tried applying the venom to the paper directly?" Alec nodded. "And you have tried different papers?"

Alec nodded. "I have tried that. The only thing left to try would be to use the venom in the manufacturing of the paper."

"Something like that would be vastly more efficient."

"That was my thought, as well. It makes more sense for the Thelns to manufacture paper in that manner than to have them going page by page, adding various drops of poison to it."

His father turned back to the pot and began to scrub.

"I can think on this more, but I suspect you've come up with the most obvious answers."

Alec grunted. It was strange for him to realize that his father might not be able to help him. All these years, his father had been the one he had gone to for answers. And now... Now maybe he wasn't able to help. Maybe the strange happenings that Alec was encountering were beyond his father's capacity to understand and help. Maybe Alec's own experiences had surpassed those of his father in this regard.

It wasn't that his father wasn't useful. That wasn't the case at all. It was more that Alec had learned as much as he could from him. He had taught him everything he knew, from mixing medicines to making assessments to coming up with treatment plans, all of it had come from his father. Now he was at the university; he was learning other approaches; and he was moving beyond where his father could help him.

That, more than anything else, left him with a strange feeling.

He had enjoyed working with his father all these years. He had enjoyed the camaraderie, and the easy under-standing that had grown between them. Those were good memories. Happy memories. Those were the memories he needed to hang on to, not the memories tied to things his father had concealed from him.

And maybe his father had done so for a good reason. He had wanted Alec to believe that he was altruistic, and that everything he did was for the greater good. How could Alec feel otherwise?

"Thank you, Father."

"I'm afraid I didn't offer you much help."

"No. This time, you didn't. And I know it must've been difficult for you to share with me about Mother, but... I think I needed to know that, as well."

"Please, Alec," he started, turning back to him and grabbing for Alec's hands. "Don't risk yourself. I know there is temptation for you to go with her and learn more about yourself, but even if you go to the Theln lands, there's no guarantee you will find anyone who knew her. If she came here as a spy, they likely wouldn't speak of it. If she came here for another reason..."

"What other reason would she have come?" Alec hadn't given that much thought. As soon as his father had suggested that she had come from outside the city, and likely from the Theln lands, Alec had assumed she was a spy.

"What if she came here for refuge?"

Alec breathed out. If that was the reason she had come, then maybe he hadn't been an unintentional consequence. Maybe his mother truly had cared about his father. Maybe everything he had thought about her, even without knowing her, had not been a lie.

"If she came for refuge, there might be others. There might be family. There might be—"

"And if there are? How many do you think you can help?"

Alec swallowed. "I don't know. All I know is that Sam is going after Tray so she can have answers, and now it seems I have answers that I need too."

His father grasped his arm and pulled him close, forcing him into a hug. Alec stiffened for a moment before hugging him back.

"If you go, be careful."

"If I go," Alec started, not wanting to tell his father it was incredibly likely that he would, "I will go with others who can make sure I'm safe. Sam isn't without capability."

"It's not Sam I worry about. It's what happens to you. It's what happens to Scribes who go to the Theln lands."

"What is it that happens?" That was what he hadn't been able to discover.

His father shook his head. "I don't know. All I know is that there have long been rumors about Scribes who disappear. It's taken me years to learn where they've gone, and why they have disappeared. I still don't understand what changes, what temptation there is for them when they reach the Theln lands, but there is something. And it's enough that even the strongest Scribe is tempted. So, all I ask is that you be careful."

Alec sighed and hugged his father once more before turning away. He looked around the shop as he left, feeling a sense of loss. But was it loss? Maybe he wasn't losing anything, but rather gaining. He now had understanding about his family that he hadn't before. He now realized that his mother was something more, and that something more was an opportunity for him to learn about and discover.

With one last look around the shop, he stepped out into the street and took a deep breath, inhaling the familiar smells of his section. He glanced across the street and saw Mrs. Rubbles' sign and decided to visit. She had been so giving of her time and paper, and if he did plan to leave, he wanted to at least have the chance to say goodbye. If something went awry during his travels, he would hate to not have taken the opportunity to thank her for everything she had done for him over the years.

When he stepped into her shop, a small bell tinkled, much the same way his father's did. Mrs. Rubbles stepped to the front of her shop, and she smiled when she saw him. She was a thin woman with gray hair and a sharp jaw. Her eyes were bright, despite her age. As always, she was neatly dressed, with a long brown dress.

"Alec?"

"Mrs. Rubbles. I just wanted to stop in while I was visiting my father. I thought I would say hello."

"How is that paper working for you?"

"Well…"

"Apparently, it is not working quite as well as you had hoped."

"The paper is fine," Alec said, looking around the shop. There were rows of tables. On each table were various types of paper. It was her way of showing off her stationery. A cabinet along the back wall held the various inks she offered. Most were relatively inexpensive. Even in this section of the city, people didn't have nearly as much money as those who lived more centrally. She did keep some more expensive and exotic inks, but those were held in the back of the shop, along with some of the higher-end paper. Alec had always thought the shop had a particular odor to it, but that seemed to come from the ink, rather than from the paper. Most of the ink she mixed herself, though some of it she imported. "It's just that for my purpose, I suspect I will have to manufacture the paper myself."

Mrs. Rubbles frowned at him. "Why would you need to do that?"

"There are particular properties to the paper I need to explore," Alec said. Mrs. Rubbles had seen easar paper, but she viewed it as little more than some way to send hidden messages, rather than a way to perform great magical feats. And again, why would she think that paper could do anything more than leave messages? Before he had ever found the easar paper, Alec would never have thought it possible. Even knowing what it could do still surprised him.

"Making paper is something of an art form, Alec. There are many people who spend years attempting to manufacture it, and they never manage to make anything of much quality. It ends up too pulpy." She went to one of the tables and held up a sheet, handing it over to Alec. "Take this, for example. This is one of the least expensive types of paper that I have in my shop. I hate to carry it, but some people simply don't care about quality and only care about cost. I can acquire this for less than a copper, and people will pay a copper per page, but it's nothing quite like this," she said, going to another stack of paper. When she handed him that paper, it was thick, and the surface was smooth. Alec could tell that it would be easy for his pen to slide across, and easy for him to write upon. "So, if you think to manufacture your own paper, you will need to find someone who has experience with it."

Alec shook his head. "I guess I hadn't thought much about it."

"Paper is much more than what it seems. There is so much that goes into the manufacturing of high-quality paper, and…" Mrs. Rubbles shook her head. "And I can see you aren't quite as interested in this as I am."

Alec smiled. "That's not it at all. I'm pleased that there are people like you, people that love what they do so much that they can be passionate about it."

"You're not passionate about studying at the university?"

"I am passionate about that. It's just that I feel there is something else I need to do. My father wants me to stay, and he wants me to continue to work at getting promoted, thinking I can influence more people that way."

"I suspect that is because your father no longer spends his days at the university. He thinks you have potential he does not."

Alec had a hard time believing that. His father was incredibly intelligent, and had he remained at the university, he would have been not only a master physicker, but he likely would have risen to lead within the university. That he had chosen to depart and had chosen to come to Arrend and set up his apothecary shop seemed almost a way of settling.

"You need to go where your heart takes you," she said.

Alec smiled. Mrs. Rubbles had often offered him advice, and usually it went along those lines. She was a passionate woman, and she cared deeply. She cared about the people in their section, and she cared about making sure everyone was well cared for, and she cared about Alec and his father. She had always watched out for them.

"What if my heart takes me farther away than what might be safe?"

"Then that is where you must go," Mrs. Rubbles said. "And if your heart takes you to manufacturing paper"—she arched a brow at him, telling him what she thought of that possibility for him—"then at least search for a higher-quality wood. So many people find the cheapest wood to use and… Well, let's just say that it is not nearly as

pleasant as someone who takes the time to harvest something that can produce better results."

"Thank you, Mrs. Rubbles."

"Have you seen your father?"

"I was just there."

She sighed. "Good. He tells me that you were disappointed with something he did. He wouldn't explain what
that was, but I imagine it must've been something significant for the two of you to have a disagreement. You are so
alike, and I can't stomach the idea of you not getting
on well."

"I think we've worked through it," Alec said.

"What was it about?"

Alec tried to think of what he could say that wouldn't
disparage his father. Mrs. Rubbles didn't need to know
about his father's side business, and she didn't need to
know about where he managed to get his money, though
she was a businesswoman and would've had to question
how he managed, wouldn't she? Alec should have questioned, though he had simply thought the donations from
those he healed had been enough. Maybe that was his
mistake. Then again, maybe Mrs. Rubbles thought
the same.

"It was probably nothing," Alec said. "I think I was
being foolish."

"At least you're willing to admit that. It's not often a
young man your age is willing to admit mistakes."

"And it's not often someone my father's age is willing
to admit mistakes."

She chuckled. "No, men generally are terrible at
admitting when they're wrong. Then again, they have a
hard time believing that women are always right." She

winked at him. "Is there anything you need before you return to the university?"

"Well... I suppose anything you might have that would help me understand how to manufacture paper."

"Ah. I might have something for you there." She made her way to the back of the shop, disappearing behind the counter for a while.

Alec wandered along the rows of tables, looking down at the paper. All of it was of reasonable quality. Mrs. Rubbles wouldn't keep anything that was not, other than the single style she had shown him that was overly pulpy. None of the paper was nearly as nice as the easar paper. Maybe that was the answer. Easar paper was of such high quality that someone who manufactured it would have to be highly skilled. Could he find someone like that in the city? Would he have to leave in order to understand how it was manufactured?

But for him to fully understand it, he had to go to the Theln lands. For him to understand himself, he would have to go to the Theln lands. Alec wanted to go, and he wanted to learn more about where his mother came from, and he wanted to find what was so tempting to Scribes that they remained—or were drawn—when they went to these lands.

Mrs. Rubbles returned from the back of her shop carrying three books. Alec had stopped in front of the cabinet containing the inks, his gaze searching along them. All of them had a familiarity to them, as he had used most of Mrs. Rubbles' inks over the years, required by his father to document and take notes.

"I think I have something for you," she said. "And

surprisingly, one of these is something your father once gave me."

She handed them over to him. Alec looked at the covers and could tell that each of them would detail the process involved in making paper. One of them was older than the others, and the style of writing was different, so that when he flipped it open, he wasn't surprised to see that he didn't even recognize the language.

"Which one did my father give you?" he asked.

"The one you're looking at. He said it had to do with papermaking, but all he was able to understand were the pictures depicting the process. He couldn't translate the text."

"Do you know what language it's in?"

"Not at all. I'm not much of a scholar, and your father likely traded for it at one of the shoreline sections, thinking he could make a better trade with me." She smiled as she handed the books over. "Aelus never really understood that he didn't need to try to negotiate with me. I was always happy to make a trade with him, especially when it served us both. I think of how many times your father has helped me over the years. I wasn't willing to charge him anything more than what was needed to keep my doors open."

Alec flipped through the pages. He wondered whether his father really had managed to find this book at one of the shoreline sections, or if this may have been one of his mother's books.

If it was hers, the book might be truly valuable. Not only to him, and not only for sentimental reasons, but because if it was hers, maybe there was something to it that would help him understand how the Thelns used paper, or at least, how they made paper.

"May I borrow these?"

"Borrow? No, Alec. You may have them. I don't need them. They simply take up space. I'm getting old enough that it's time for me to begin getting rid of things I don't need. Without a child of my own to pass the shop on to, eventually, I won't need any of them."

"Thank you," he said.

"Alec, you know that your father is incredibly proud of you and how you were promoted so quickly. I don't know that I've ever heard of someone making full physicker after such a short time, though I'm not surprised it would be you. With your experience, and with your knowledge, you *should* be a full physicker. For that matter, your father should practically be a master physicker."

Alec suppressed a smile. "I'm sure he would appreciate hearing that from you."

"Maybe I'll tell him. Or maybe not. Sometimes, he tends to get a little… arrogant… with things." She smiled. "Maybe I hold that from him."

Alec gave Mrs. Rubbles a quick hug. "Thank you. For everything."

When he stepped back, she flushed. "Of course, Alec. You and your father are like family to me."

When Alec left the stationery store, he couldn't help but look up at the sign, wanting to remember it before leaving the city with Sam—and facing the risk of not returning.

3

SEARCHING THE SWAMP

The swamp carried with it an awful odor. Sam stared out over the water, the darkness making it difficult for her to see clearly, but she was determined to better understand what else might be out there. According to Elaine—her mother—she could cross the swamp using only her canal staff. She'd been practicing going out into the swamp day after day, trying to build up her stamina.

She perched on the top of her staff, no longer struggling to maintain her balance, not swaying quite as much as she once had. The staff had a slight bend to it, and she used that to push off, giving some extra spring as she flipped forward.

It was time for her to return to the city, but she was determined to figure out exactly how far she could go. She had managed to travel the entire day without becoming too fatigued, though her legs now trembled slightly. She was able to rest, remaining perched as she was on the staff, and that rest allowed her to maintain her position longer than she would have previously.

"You can come onto the barge if you want," Bastan said.

Sam looked over at him. It was a narrow barge, little more than a small vessel, but it was enough for him to trail her into the swamp. Bastan had been unwilling to allow her to go by herself, wanting to travel with her, afraid that something might happen to her if she were to venture too deep into the swamp.

"That's not the point of this, Bastan," Sam said.

"I'm afraid I don't understand the point," he said. He stood in the center of the barge, staying balanced, gripping a long, slender pole that he used to steer the boat through the swamp. He had been unwilling to hire anyone to come with them, preferring to make this journey himself.

"The point," Sam said, flipping forward until she could land near him but still be in the swamp, "is that I need to be able to move as quickly as I can without an augmentation."

"But if you have Alec with you, you can have whatever augmentation you need."

Sam surveyed the swamp. In this section, there were strange, twisted trees that grew out of the water. She suspected the water wasn't nearly as deep where they grew, though there weren't any islands nearby, nothing solid enough for her to spend any time on. Elaine claimed there would be islands here, places where she could rest, but so far, Sam hadn't found any. Short of stealing a map from Elaine—if she even had one—there wouldn't be any way for her to know how to make the crossing and have a place to rest.

"I can't continue to depend on Alec. Having Alec

means I need to have easar paper. There has to be another way. Besides, I need to continue to master forcing augmentations on myself."

So far, every attempt to do so had been less effective than what she liked. She was able to add an augmentation, but it wasn't anything quite like what happened when Alec placed them. Maybe she could get better if she spent more time training with Alec, but time spent working with Alec meant that she wasn't able to work on her own and continue to discover what she was able to do.

"So independent." Bastan push forward with the pole. "Haven't you seen that you need to have others to help you?"

"I'm not disagreeing with the fact that I need others to help. But I need to be able to understand these abilities. If I continue to depend on Alec, I won't know how—or when—I can rely on my own abilities, not the way I need to."

"I'm just saying that you have always been so fiercely independent."

"Because I had to," she said, glaring at him.

Bastan looked up at her. "You have never been nearly as isolated as you have wanted to believe yourself. You have always had someone with you, watching over you."

"Yes. It seems Marin has been watching over me much more than what she has let on."

Bastan grunted. "I wasn't talking about Marin, but then again, you knew that. Why is it you feel the need to torment me?"

"I'm not trying to torment you. I'm just trying to…"

Bastan shook his head, pushing forward with the barge. "Maybe it doesn't matter. You continue to develop your abilities. When you do, I think that will help us as much as anything."

"Us?"

"I have already told you, Samara, I have no intention of allowing you to venture into the Theln lands on your own."

"You have no intention? Bastan, I don't know how you intend to prevent me from doing anything."

"I am not without my own abilities."

Sam sniffed and pushed off, flipping forward into the swamp. She landed near a trio of trees that seemed to surround a hidden flat section of land. When she landed, she slid slightly down the pole, looking at the ground. All around in the rest of the swamp, thick reeds popped up through the water. In this spot, there were these series of trees, and they grew near enough to each other that their root systems seem to be intertwined.

When Bastan approached, she glanced back at him. "And I'm not without my abilities."

Bastan chuckled. In the darkness and stink of the swamp, the sound was strange. "I am well aware of that."

Sam crawled from the end of her staff and onto one of the tree branches. The bark was rough, and there seemed to be brambles that snagged at her cloak, but she plucked them free, careful not to let them cut into her clothing. She had to be sure they didn't pierce the skin of her hands or her thighs as she rested on the branch. Were she augmented, she would think about adding a thickness to her skin, some way of preventing the brambles from piercing her.

"What are you doing up there?"

"Resting."

"You could rest on the barge," Bastan said. "I brought food, and there's plenty of water, and—"

"And there is you. If you help, it means I'm not doing it myself. And that's what I need to do."

"Prove that you can rest, and then come down to the barge."

Sam shook her head. "I need to prove that this method works. If it doesn't, then I need to find another way to cross the swamp."

"I'm quite certain we have another way for you to cross the swamp." Bastan poled his way around the trees, making a small circle. He kept a watch out into the night, and she doubted he saw anything that she couldn't, but it was Bastan, and he was determined to prove she needed his help.

"If this is what having a father is like, I'm not sure I want it."

Bastan glared at her. "And if this is what having a rebellious daughter is like…"

Sam laughed. As much as she didn't want to tell him, having Bastan with her did provide a certain reassurance. She enjoyed his company. The swamp would otherwise be boring, and if something happened, no one would know. Having him with her gave her reassurance were she to slip and fall or were any number of other possible dangerous outcomes to befall her. She had fallen in the swamp before. And she had seen the way the canal eels swarmed, wanting nothing more than to devour the first thing that appeared. The eels seemed to follow her, clamping onto her staff, as though they were trying to unsettle her, waiting for her to fall into the swamp.

"Do you want anything to eat?" Bastan asked.

"Fine. I'll take…" Movement out in the water drew her attention.

Bastan looked up at her, but he knew enough not to break the silence. There was something he had taught her. "What is it?" he mouthed.

Sam shifted within the branches, trying to get a better view. The thick, strangely waxy leaves of the tree blocked her view. She thought to part the branches so she could get a better angle, but doing so would cause movement and draw attention. One of the first lessons Bastan had taught her about sneaking and thieving had been to avoid attention. The best way to do that was to avoid rapid movements. The eye was drawn to them.

What was it that she had seen?

She wasn't sure. No one moved through the swamp. No one other than the two of them, that is.

Could it be some animal?

The canal eels were not the only things that made the swamp their home. There were other creatures, though she didn't know most of them. There had been an occasional mournful sound, that which she suspected came from a bird, but she had never seen it. There would likely be other fish, but Sam didn't dare get into the water to search for them.

Whatever she had seen had been large enough to draw her attention.

Maybe someone else came through here.

What if it was one of the other Kavers? They kept mostly to themselves, but all served in the palace and all served the royals. Sam thought she would have known had one of the other Kavers been sent on another mission, but since she'd captured Marin, she hadn't spent as much time at the palace, struggling with exactly what response she should have.

Sam dropped down from the branch and into the barge. She leaned into Bastan. "There was something out there," she whispered.

"Samara—we are the better part of a day out into the swamp. Even the captains won't come out this deep."

"Which is why I'm concerned."

"What if it is one of your kind?"

If it was one of hers, then she needed to know.

The reason she was pushing herself as hard as she had been was so she could train and build up her strength so that when she finally made the journey to the Theln lands after Tray, she wouldn't be weakened by the time she reached them. Even if she did make that journey, she wouldn't be going alone. Marin would come with her. Bastan had already expressed his interest in coming with her. And Alec... Well, Sam wasn't sure she wanted Alec to come, regardless of the fact that he wanted to. The Theln lands carried some threat to Scribes, a temptation that might prove too much for him.

"I'm going after it," she said.

"You're going to draw attention to yourself."

"The barge would draw attention. It's too large and too unnatural. At least with the staff, I can balance on it and look something like one of the trees."

Bastan arched a brow at her. "One of the trees? Do you really think I should believe you can hide as a tree?"

"The barge is far more noticeable. Just stay here—"

"I'm not staying here."

"Then stay far enough back that you don't draw attention to yourself, Bastan."

He studied her for a moment before nodding.

Sam flipped forward. As she did, she tried to think of an augmentation, wanting her vision to be enhanced. The way that it worked for her was focusing on the sensation she had when the augmentation was written on easar paper. She focused on the words, and on the intent, as well as what Alec might do in order to grant her an augmentation. Somehow, that combination was important. She still wasn't certain why, but she had managed to add enhancements to herself using this technique.

Vision.

That was what she wanted. If she could enhance her eyesight, and find a way to see through the darkness, she would be better equipped for whoever—or whatever—she might be facing.

Slowly, the sense of the augmentation washed over her. It came as a cold chill, and it started deep within her and washed up through her legs and into her stomach before going into her head. With it came a shifting of the light, a change from darkness of night to something that was almost daylight, though more like a cloudy sky than anything else.

Sam perched on the staff, scanning the swamp. There was no sign of movement, but she was sure she had seen something. Whatever it was would be out there, and maybe it was nothing more than an animal, but she would see that too.

It had come from deeper into the swamp.

She jumped, pushing off with her staff, and flipped forward. It might only be her imagination, but she felt like her strength had improved recently, almost so that she no longer needed the same level of enhancement to throw herself as far forward. When she landed, she balanced on the staff and tried to remain as motionless as possible.

The flip to reach this portion of the swamp was enough movement to draw attention.

"Have you seen anything?"

She looked down as Bastan pushed up behind her.

"I thought I said stay behind me."

"I am behind you, Samara."

"You're going to draw more attention than me," she said.

"I'm not sure that I am. I think your jumps will draw enough on their own."

It was possible, but Sam was hopeful that the way she flipped—pushing up so that she arced high over the swamp—wouldn't attract as much notice. Then again, someone who knew what to look for would be able to see her and would likely know a Kaver traveled through the swamp.

She turned her attention back to surveying the swamp, and when she did, there was a flicker of movement in the far distance.

This time, she was sure she had seen it.

Sam pushed off, flipping forward. When she landed, she didn't pause, flipping forward again. One after another she went, chasing where she had seen movement.

And then, she paused. The movement had been from here.

This part of the swamp seemed even darker than others. There were thick clusters of trees that created hiding places. The reeds weren't nearly as prominent, but a cloud had shifted over the thin moon, giving off even less light in the night. Her augmented eyesight remained, but everything had a grayness to it. Eventually, the augmentation would fade.

What had she seen?

Once more, she focused on augmented sight, wanting to increase it even more. Now it was more about enhancing her eyesight, not just improving her night vision.

The augmentation came on slowly, washing through her.

Sam blinked, able to make out everything with much more clarity.

Staring into the distance, she finally saw the movement.

It was rapid and speeding away from her, away from the city, and moving more quickly than she would be able to catch up to without an augmentation.

Kavers.

There were at least three, and they were skilled, streaking through the swamp, flipping forward great distances as they launched from one landing point to another.

She might be able to catch them, but if she did, what would she do? What would she say?

More troubling was the question about where they were going.

They were heading toward the Theln lands, and that alone was unusual, especially as the Kavers rarely traveled there by themselves, let alone in trios. Either they were going for information, or they were going to complete a mission.

And Sam wouldn't put it past Lyasanna to finish what she had once asked Marin to start.

Bastan reached her, and she looked down at him for a moment before dropping onto the deck of the barge. "Did you see anything?"

She nodded. "We need to get back, and quickly."

"Why?"

"I think it's time for us to finish our training. And I think it's time to go after Tray."

4

ADVICE

Daylight sent swirls of color around the palace, the sun barely creeping over the top of it as Sam arrived back to this section. She was tired—well, really more exhausted—and she only came here because she needed to question Elaine. Had she not that need, she probably wouldn't have come.

Even at this time of the morning, there were the sounds of people training in the courtyard. It would be Kavers, most likely. The palace guards trained somewhere else and didn't seem to care for the fact that the Kavers spent as much time as they did here, training with staffs.

Sam entered the palace and hurried along the corridor as she made her way to Elaine's rooms. She no longer paid much attention to all of the signs of wealth in the palace. It was more than she once could have believed, but then again, *she* was more than she once would have believed.

When she reached Elaine's room, she pounded on the door.

It took a moment, but Elaine pulled the door open.

She was the same size as Sam, though the wrinkles around her eyes spoke of many more years, and the slight sheen of gray to her hair was different from Sam's dark hair. She was already dressed and had her canal staff separated into sections and hanging from a belt beneath her cloak.

"Samara. You have been away from the palace for a while. I wasn't sure that you were interested in training any longer."

"I'm plenty interested in training. What do you think I have been doing?"

Elaine studied her. She took a deep breath, smelling Sam. "The swamp. You remain fixated on the swamp?"

"You're the one who told me I needed to practice," Sam said.

"And by practice, I meant that you should continue to work with other Kavers, those like myself or some of the others who are even more skilled."

"Other than Marin, you're not the most skilled?"

Elaine was paired to Lyasanna, whatever that might mean. Marin had already proven herself to be a more skilled Kaver than Elaine, able to teach Sam things Elaine could not.

"I serve the princess, but that does not mean I am any more skilled than others. My connection to her has given me access I would not otherwise have, but…"

"But Marin is better than you."

It was blunt, but it needed to be said, especially if Elaine was to continue attempting to train her.

"I have never claimed to be anything more than I am," Elaine said.

"You haven't claimed to be anything."

Elaine stared at her. "Did you come here to disparage me, or have you come for another reason?"

"Why were Kavers crossing the swamp?"

Elaine frowned. "What do you mean?"

"What I mean is that I saw three Kavers crossing the swamp. Why?"

Elaine looked past her before grabbing Sam and pulling her into her room. "Where did you see them?"

"I told you, in the swamp."

"Where in the swamp? Were you close to the shore?"

Sam shook her head. "I was probably a day out," she said. Maybe admitting that was more than what she should do, but she needed to know why the Kavers traveled across the swamp. If they were going into Theln lands and going in numbers that were more than about ensuring safety, she wanted to know if there was anything she needed to be worried about.

Besides, it still didn't change what she had planned. But she was hopeful she could find out more, and if she could, then she could be better prepared.

"A day? You *have* improved."

"I told you."

"Are you still determined to go after… your brother?"

"Tray is my brother. I don't care that we might not be blood relatives. He is my brother. And if the princess means him any harm, I intend to protect him."

"Even if it means going against the Kavers?"

Sam licked her lips. "I don't want to. All I want is to help Tray. Why does it have to be one or the other?"

"I will not go against my princess."

"You mean you won't go against your Scribe."

"Are they so different?"

"They are."

Elaine took a deep breath and let it out slowly. "Perhaps if I were to have the same ability as Marin, and if I were able to apply augmentations without my Scribe, it would be different. Such an ability is unusual, even among Kavers."

Should Sam admit that she was able to do that? It wasn't consistent, and it didn't happen with nearly the same strength as when the augmentation was applied through easar paper, but she could do what Marin had taught her. And maybe there was more to it. Maybe if she were to spend more time studying with Marin, she might be able to do even more than what she had.

"Have you asked her?"

"Asked her what?"

"Whether what Marin said was true."

"What good would come of that?"

"The good would be the truth. You might discover that the person you have served so faithfully all these years has been deceiving you. The good would be that you would understand that she might not be worthy of your service."

"Worthy? Samara, we serve the Anders family. That is the way it has been, and the way it will always be. You are a Kaver, which means you are tasked with such service."

"No."

"No?"

"No. Just because I have this ability doesn't mean I have to blindly follow. I can do what I think is right. And right now, what I think is right is to see what Lyasanna intends to do with Tray. If there is nothing to it, then…" Sam hadn't given much thought to what she would do if

Lyasanna didn't intend to harm Tray, but if she did, she would have to help him, wouldn't she?

What if it meant siding with the Thelns?

That was something she didn't want to consider, but she knew she needed to. With Ralun as his father, and now with Tray spending time with him, getting to know him, how much would Tray have changed? Probably even more than she had changed.

"You can't go after him on your own."

"What makes you think I will?"

"You might think I don't know you, but I've paid attention. I know what you think to do. And you can't take your Scribe. You said it yourself, you can't cross using your staff if he goes with you."

"There are other ways to cross the swamp than using the staff," Sam said.

"Sam, we've discussed this already. There have been plenty who have tried to cross the swamp using barges, but eventually, they fail. Either they turn back, or…"

"Or what?"

"Or they are lost. There have been plenty of captains who have thought to venture into the swamp, and most of them never return. They think they can go after riches, but what they find is nothing more than their own destruction."

Sam looked around Elaine's room. It was sparsely decorated, the sign of a woman who either wasn't in her own room very often, or intended to not be there for long. It was nothing like the way Alec had settled into the university rooms he was given.

"If you want to try and deter me, you don't need to scare me into changing my mind. Telling me something more specific would be helpful. Otherwise, I'm simply going to risk it."

"I have little doubt you will risk yourself, regardless, Samara."

"And you don't intend to stop me?"

"Why should I?"

Sam frowned. "I thought you didn't want me to attempt reaching the Theln lands."

"I don't, but short of holding you captive, I don't know that I can prevent you from doing anything," she said.

"You would hold me captive?"

"I said *short* of holding you captive."

Sam studied Elaine for a moment. "What happened to Marin's Scribe?"

"He is being questioned. Until we figure out where she might have gone, he will remain in prison."

Sam shivered. She had spent only a few hours within the prison, not nearly as long as Tray, but her experience there was enough to make her not ever want to revisit there again.

"He is inaccessible, even to you," Elaine said.

"I have no intention of going after him."

"Not even to determine where Marin might have run off to?"

Sam still had not shared with Elaine that she knew exactly where Marin had gone, mostly because the moment she did was the moment she placed herself in opposition to the rest of the Kavers. Even holding her as long as she had—well as long as *Bastan* had—she had placed herself against the Kavers.

"The only reason I want to find Marin is to understand what else she might have lied about," Sam said.

Elaine studied her, and Sam wondered how much Elaine already knew. Could she have discovered that Sam had captured Marin? Would Bastan have sent word to her? That seemed less likely, especially since Bastan would only do what he thought would protect Sam, and he didn't think turning Sam into Elaine would protect her—he couldn't.

"That woman is dangerous. Whatever else you think about her, know that she is the reason you were taken from me."

"And if what she said was true, she is the reason that Tray still lives," Sam said softly. "If nothing else, that has value."

Elaine sighed. "What if Tray—the Theln you call your brother—decides to identify with the Thelns? What if he decides to take after his father and rule?"

"Then I would tell him that he has every right to it," she said.

"Even if that means that you are pitted against him?"

"Why would I be pitted against Tray?"

"Not against Tray. Against the Thelns. What will you do if you are forced to fight the Thelns which mean you fight against Tray?"

Sam stared at Elaine. She started pacing, trying to clear her mind. Movement helped, which was why spending time in the swamp, regardless of how disgusting it smelled, helped her think. "I won't harm Tray."

"You might find that you don't have a choice."

"What if I make a different choice?"

Elaine glowered at her. "You would go against the Kavers? You would go against me?"

Sam didn't like the idea of going against Elaine, but it

had less to do with the fact that she was her mother and more to do with the fact that the city was the only place she had known.

"I will do what I think is right."

"You will do what is your duty," Elaine said.

Sam stopped her pacing and turned back to Elaine. "My duty?"

"Yes, Samara. Your duty. You are a Kaver, which means that you have an obligation to help protect this city. You may not care for that responsibility, and you may not think you need to, but those beliefs are because of what Marin did to you, the way she used you. If you had your memories, you would not feel the same way."

Sam wondered. Wouldn't she? Even without her memories, she had always felt that doing what was possible to help her brother was the most important thing for her. And now, she felt that way about Bastan, recognizing that he was family. Alec too.

But the city?

What had the city ever done for her? What had it done other than put her in a position that made her feel she was somehow less than those who lived in the center portions of the city? What had it done other than show her that some people were more important—and therefore, more valuable—than others?

Did she have a responsibility to protect that?

"Is that all?" Sam asked.

"You came to me, so I suppose if you have said all you need, you may depart."

Sam breathed out. "If you learn more about those Kavers, will you tell me?"

"If I learn more, and if it's relevant to you, I will tell you."

Sam supposed that would have to be enough.

She turned away, and headed out of the palace, possibly for the last time.

5

WORKING IN THE WARD

The hospital ward carried a certain stink to it today. Alec had the books in his pocket, and he stuffed his hand inside it, running his fingers along the covers. He almost didn't want to stop here, but he knew he needed to. He had been gone long enough, and it would be unusual for him not to stop in the hospital ward. All he wanted to do was return to his room, sit down, and study the books. He wasn't sure if he'd be able to learn anything from the one he was increasingly convinced was his mother's, but he suspected there would be some way for him to work through it, trying to decipher the language so he could understand.

The ward was busier than it had been in quite some time. Alec liked to think he had something to do with that. He had continued to encourage the master physickers to relax the requirements for admission to the hospital, convincing them the students would learn more if they had more patients to study. Admitting more people didn't mean they charged anything less. No. In fact, the master physickers continued to charge just the same, not showing any willingness to reduce their fees. Maybe that didn't matter. All that mattered was that they had been willing to treat people they otherwise would not have.

He searched for anyone he might know. There were no master physickers making rounds this morning, so there were no students, either. There were a few junior physickers weaving through, stopping at each cot, and making a few notes in the patient's records.

Alec stayed away from them. He had the feeling that most of the junior physickers were frustrated with him. Mostly that came from the fact that he had been promoted straight to full physicker. Many of the junior physickers toiled for years at this level, and testing to be promoted from junior physicker to full physicker would be difficult, and some would never reach that level. It wasn't a guarantee a junior physicker was promoted.

As he stopped at one of the cots, this one holding a middle-aged man with long, flowing brown hair, one of the junior physickers approached. "Physicker Stross. I haven't seen you today. We thought perhaps you might not come."

Alec took a deep breath. This was the reason he had needed to come. There was now a certain expectation that he would visit daily. It was his own fault. He had started it by coming as often as he did to the hospital ward. But now, he had other things he needed to investigate, things that would make it difficult to keep up his daily visits.

"Has anything interesting come in today?"

"We have it covered," the junior physicker said.

Alec looked over at Darren. He was a weaselly-looking man, with eyes set too close together, and a peaked hairline. He kept his hair short, which only accentuated the sharp hairline.

"I'm sure that you have it covered, junior physicker," Alec said. He made a point of emphasizing the title. If they were going to push back on his promotion, he would use the only thing he had at his disposal, and that was his seniority. "I'm only asking if anything interesting has come in today."

Then again, asking what was interesting would be variable. What was interesting to Alec might not be interesting to the junior physickers. One of the many things he had learned in his time at the university was that the level of knowledge of the junior physickers was lacking compared to what Alec had once assumed. It wasn't the case with the master physickers. They were incredibly bright, and they were quite talented, but even they had limitations.

Alec wasn't sure why he would have once thought otherwise. Why should the master physickers be any more talented than his father? They might have access to resources his father didn't, but his father had a great analytical mind, and that was what he had tried to instill in Alec. It was the recognition of patterns and putting them together so he could make a diagnosis. Once he had that diagnosis, then it was understanding the treatments, but even that—at least at the university—wasn't quite as important, especially since the librarians could search through the various records and help come up with previous diagnoses that had worked.

"There have been a few things that have come in," Darren said. He wrinkled his nose and pointed to the man in front of Alec. "This one. He came in this morning. He smelled *awful*. We had several of the senior students clean him up."

Darren seemed particularly pleased with himself about that, though Alec couldn't blame him. There were times when patients did smell terrible when they arrived. He had cleaned many patients for his father, though his father had never shied away from doing the work himself, either. It wasn't that he avoided it. Not the way Darren seemed to.

"There are times when you can learn more about the patient by doing such things yourself," Alec said.

"And there are times when I can better use my expertise helping patients who need it," Darren replied.

"And what has your expertise told you about this patient?"

"He was dropped off at the university. We wouldn't have taken him in, normally, but…"

Alec looked over at him. "But what?"

"But the master physickers have been encouraging us to take on more hopeless cases. The masters know there isn't anything that can be done for most of them. Gods, most of the time, we don't even know what's wrong with them. How can we, especially with someone like this, who comes to the university unable to speak?"

There had been others who had come recently come unable to speak. One of them had been his father. What would have happened had some junior physicker abandoned his father? What would've happened to Cara, or even to Beckah, had no one been willing to work with them?

"Just because they can't speak doesn't mean there isn't

anything they can tell you," Alec said as he began his assessment.

It happened naturally. He started by looking over the man, surveying to see if there was anything that was obviously wrong. Often times, a simple survey would tell him all he needed. He knew the man had come in filthy and stinking, which meant he likely came from one of the outer sections. A lowborn. It pleased Alec to have lowborns coming here, especially now, and especially since Sam was so adamant that they devote time to working with them.

The survey didn't reveal anything. Maybe it would have were he to have seen the man before he was cleaned up, but now, there wasn't anything easily identifiable.

Alec rolled him, looking at his back, searching for any signs of injury. There was no bruising, and there was no evidence of a rash. He looked much like his father had looked when he had come in.

Could someone have been exposed to eel venom again?

Alec didn't think it was likely, though maybe it was. Maybe his father had been involved in spreading more of the eel venom than he had realized.

There was nothing external he was able to easily ascertain. He leaned down and listened to the man's heart rate. It was fast, much more rapid than he would've expected. He listened for long moments, trying to determine if there was any irregularity to it. There was none. It was nothing more than a fast heartbeat.

He shifted, listening to his lungs. The breathing was regular, though somewhat raspy. When he listened to the man's belly, he didn't hear anything unusual there.

"See? There's nothing you can determine."

Alec ignored him and pulled open the man's eyelids. Everything seemed normal there. He moved on, prying open his mouth to look inside. When he did, he resisted the urge to point. "What do you see, junior physicker?"

The other man blinked. "In his mouth? There's nothing there."

"There is. Take a look at his palate."

The junior physicker leaned in. Alec kept the man's chin pried down, holding his mouth open. The lighting in the hospital ward was generally good, but it would be difficult to see easily into his mouth, without shoving his face down as the junior physicker did. He needed some reflected light. Alec decided to help him and grabbed a silver reflector and placed it in front of the patient's mouth.

"Oh."

Alec nodded. "You didn't see that before?"

"I didn't."

"Then you weren't looking. A thorough examination— especially when someone comes in like this, dirty and unable to speak, with a heart rate twice normal—would easily identify the bluish blush on the palate that would indicate harbom mushrooms."

Alec had seen it before, though it was fairly infrequent. Mushrooms like that could be intoxicating, an effect that would eventually wear off, though there was a counter for it. "Are you familiar with this intoxication?"

The junior physicker shook his head.

"The mushrooms grow in only certain places, typically muddy places, likely along the edge of the swamp." Which explained why the man had come in filthy and stinking.

"And taking them can lead to several side effects. One is that, in specific concentrations, people can become obtunded. The effect will wear off, but it's possible he would stop breathing. That alone is reason to counter the effect."

"What is used to counter it?"

"Chollin seeds."

The junior physicker nodded quickly. "I will administer them immediately. What is the necessary dose?"

"Do you need me to look that up for you?" Alec asked.

He could have simply told the man. He had it memorized, his father making certain he knew the adequate dose, but he decided this man needed a little bit of humility.

"No. Of course not. I'm sure the library would have records of it."

"I'm sure they do. I have seen it there myself."

Darren nodded his head quickly. He hurried off and left Alec standing by himself. He hated that it had come to that, but he hated almost as much the fact there were junior physickers who thought he was promoted and didn't deserve it.

"You didn't need to be quite so harsh with him."

Alec turned and saw Master Harrison standing behind him. He was a thin man and had a scruff of a beard growing today. He had four students behind him, each watching Alec with wide eyes. They were all junior-level students, most of who had probably only recently gained entry to the university.

Alec flushed. "I was only trying to make a point."

"And it was a necessary one." Master Harrison turned back to the students. "What you have just seen Physicker

Stross demonstrate is that even patients who cannot speak often have a story to tell. If you don't take your time and perform a thorough evaluation, you might miss that story. You might miss your opportunity to help them. Now, in the case of this patient, if it is harbom mushrooms, then the effect will wear off naturally. It will take time, and since he's at the university already, it's unlikely he will suffer any long-term consequences, especially as the treatment is fairly straightforward. But there are other illnesses that you might encounter that a cursory evaluation would overlook, and could produce dire consequences. That is what you must focus on."

Master Harrison winked at him as he walked past.

Alec shook his head. "You could show them the blush. It's not something they will often see, but once they do, it will be impossible to overlook in the future."

"An excellent point, Physicker Stross."

Master Harrison stopped next to the man and pulled down his chin. He held the reflective mirror in place, and one by one, each student leaned down to see it. It was a distinctive bluish discoloration of the palate, one that none of these students would overlook in the future.

And maybe Alec had been too hard on Darren. It was possible that he had never seen the blush of the mushroom intoxication. It wasn't so common it could be easily identified, especially if all of their training came at the university. How many people with money—the kind who typically came here—would have been exposed to mushrooms like that? Such intoxication was more common in the outer sections, and more common where his father might have seen it.

It was even more reason for patients to be allowed entry to the university, regardless of their ability to pay.

"Harbom mushrooms are sought-after in some of the outer sections," Alec started while the students continued to examine the patient. "They are thought to have many benefits. Sometimes, they can be desired for their intoxication, but in low doses, many people believe they can make a person more appealing."

One of the students, a younger woman with mousy brown hair, screwed her nose up. "More appealing? Why would the lowborns think something like that?"

Alec had made a point of not using the term lowborn, but his reference to the outer sections had been enough. "There are many people who believe many different things. If you take the time to understand them, you can help them. It's best not to judge a person before you get to know them."

Master Harrison watched Alec. After moment, he nodded. "Excellent diagnosis, Physicker Stross." He guided the students off, leaving Alec with the patient.

If nothing else, he had done some good. He had helped this man. There was no question that the man would have recovered on his own, but without Alec here, he might not have recovered quite as quickly. And, regardless of what Master Harrison said, it was possible he could asphyxiate. It was not unusual for someone who was intoxicated, even with mushrooms, to asphyxiate. Considering the size of the university, and the number of junior physickers who were here, it wouldn't be typical for that to happen, but it wouldn't be unheard of for someone to die while under the direct supervision of the physickers.

Maybe his father was right. Maybe there was more for

him to do here than what he could do if he were to go with Sam. He didn't like the idea of letting her go into the Theln lands on her own, but if he wasn't here, would everyone be as motivated as Alec to help? Would all of the work that he had put in, attempting to coax the master physickers to help more people than they were inclined to, be lost?

Maybe he needed to focus his attention here a little longer.

He looked around the hospital ward. Not only did he need to focus his attention here a little longer, but he needed to take his own advice. He needed to continue to listen rather than to judge.

When Darren returned, Alec greeted him with a smile. "Junior physicker, I might have been a bit harsh with you. It has occurred to me that you might not have seen this intoxication before. May I show you the findings?"

Darren watched him for a long moment before nodding. "I would like that, Physicker Stross."

6

A MOTHER'S GIFT

Alec sat at his desk, the book flipped open in front of him. So far, he had not discovered any way of translating it. There were diagrams within the book, and that was what he suspected his father had used to help him ascertain that this was a book on papermaking, but the language was nothing familiar to him. His attempts to find a reference to that language in the library had been unsuccessful. Either the library kept it restricted in the masters' section, or there simply wasn't anything.

It made him feel even more confident this was a book from the Theln lands. If that was the case, and if it was a book on Theln papermaking, Alec was even more interested in knowing what secrets might be held within it.

There was a knock at his door, and he looked up. "Come in."

The door opened, and Beckah poked her head in. Alec didn't see her nearly as often as he once had. Ever since his promotion, it had been difficult for the two of them to spend as much time together. He suspected Sam would be pleased by that, especially given that she had a strange sort of jealousy about Beckah, but Alec missed his friend.

"You *are* here," she said, stepping inside and closing the door behind her. She took a seat on the edge of his bed and looked over at him. "I haven't been able to find you. I thought I could catch you in the ward, but you haven't been coming at the same time as you used to."

There was a hint of accusation in her tone. "I've been a little distracted. I've been trying to understand the easar paper and seeing if there's any way that I can re-create it, but I haven't been able to determine anything."

"Even with the eel venom?"

"Even with the eel venom," Alec said. "Master Helen and I have tried various techniques to apply the venom to paper, but nothing has been particularly successful."

"Then maybe it doesn't have anything to do with the eel venom," Beckah said.

"I don't know. It's possible, but I've begun to wonder if it has to do with the way the eel venom is integrated into the papermaking process."

She started to smile and looked down at the book he had flipped open. She stood and looked over his shoulder, studying the page. "So now you've decided to become a paper maker?"

"I've not decided anything," Alec said, laughing. He considered telling her about his mother but decided against it. He wasn't sure what he thought about it, not yet, and since he couldn't interpret the writing in the book, he wasn't even certain that this *was* a Theln book. Maybe he was wrong about it. "I just want to understand everything I can about what they might have done to create the paper."

"If anyone is able to figure it out, it will be you."

She took a seat and began to fidget with her hands. Alec turned and looked at her. "What is it?"

"It's... I've been put up for promotion to junior physicker."

Alec turned his attention away from the book and smiled at her. "That's wonderful."

"Is it? I know you're planning on doing something. You don't have to tell me, and I understand that for some reason, you don't think you can tell me everything, but if you leave, who will help ensure I'm promoted?"

Alec laughed. "I'm pretty sure I'm not the person you want involved in that discussion. Most of the junior physickers seem offended by the fact that I am a full physicker. The other full physickers seem to feel like I took a shortcut. And the master physickers..."

"You wouldn't have been promoted without the master physickers."

That was true, but it didn't change their opinion of him, for better or worse.

"Why do I get the sense you're nervous?"

"It's not that I'm nervous. I just... I just don't know what to expect."

"I can tell you about my testing," he said.

"That's just it. The way you were tested is different from how I will be tested. You went in and demanded testing," she said.

"It's not so much that I demanded testing..." Alec said. He had twisted in his chair so that he could sit closer to her. "And you know the reason I did it. We needed to find Jessup." Then again, that was before they knew that Jessup was the one who was Marin's Scribe. Even now that they had found him, and he had been captured, Alec wasn't sure why Master Jessup had remained hidden in the university. Why would he have stayed here?

Then again, where else would he have gone? Marin had remained in the city, and she had some other way of using her abilities, some way that Sam still didn't entirely know. It was different from the way Sam used her abilities.

"I understand why you did it, and I understand it was necessary at the time. I'm just saying I wish there was a better way for me to know what I'm going to be tested on."

"You could always speak with one of the junior physickers."

"I don't think they would tell. They like to make jokes about what's involved in the testing, so few have truly been open about it. All I know is that it's intense."

"The questioning I was put through was intense, but it wasn't anything that you wouldn't have been able to handle."

"I don't think that's quite true," Beckah said. "I don't make any claims to have the same depth of knowledge as you."

"You're one of the smartest senior students. I'm not surprised they have put you up for promotion."

"It's not about what I know. There is a big difference between what I can learn studying in the library and what you have learned through your time with your father. There is only so much I can do when working in the ward. I haven't had the same opportunity to test treatments on different patients the way you did."

"I can help with that," he said.

"But you said you didn't think that was a good idea."

"Then we do it secretly. If you have questions about the patients you're seeing, come to me and asked. I'm happy to offer whatever help I can."

She nodded, smiling. "I think I would like that." She fidgeted for another moment before looking up at him. "Can you tell me a little bit more about your testing?"

Alec chuckled. "My testing? I think Master Carl was trying to ensure I wouldn't pass. I doubt you're going to have quite the same experience. He tried to challenge me on every case they presented to me, questioning every diagnosis I offered, trying to ensure that I didn't get promoted, and if I had failed…"

"You would have been expelled."

"Yes. It's a good thing I didn't fail."

"I think Master Helen and Master Eckerd would've made sure you remained in the university."

"I'm not sure they have the authority to do something like that. It required all of the master physickers to come around." And Master Carl had come around in the time since Alec had been promoted. That was the most surprising of all. He had been standoffish before, and that hadn't changed—not really—but he at least gave Alec a grudging sort of respect. Then again, Alec continued to avoid him, which might have made that better.

"What sorts of questions do they ask?"

"Well, in your case, I suspect you won't have the full contingent of master physickers testing you."

"Why is that important?"

"It's important because the master physickers are going to question you based on what interests they have. If you can figure out which ones will be testing you, you might be able to get a sense of what you need to know, and what kinds of things they will ask you."

"Do you think they will tell me who's going to be there?"

They might not, but would they tell Alec? Even if they did, was that something he wanted to do? Did he want to put himself in that position, risking the possibility Beckah wouldn't succeed in promotion simply because he involved himself in her testing process?

No. It was better if he appeared neutral. If he attempted to get involved, it was possible one of those testing her would take it out on her, asking her questions that would be too difficult for her to answer.

"It might simply be better to prepare for all of the master physickers," Alec said.

She groaned. "I still think it would be better if you were involved."

"I can help you determine which master physicker has which interest, but I think you know as much as I do."

"You really can't spend time on the wards without figuring that out," she said. "And I've been here much longer than you, so it should be easier for me to do it, shouldn't it?"

"Yes. I can't imagine I have more insights to offer."

"Gods. I thought about how hard that must've been for you. You hadn't been here long enough to really know all of the master physickers and the different things they were interested in. It really *is* impressive you passed."

"Thanks, I guess."

"No. It's not like that. It's just that... It's truly impressive when one considers what you must've gone through to be promoted."

They fell silent. Alec looked around his room, realizing that if he did go into the Theln lands with Sam and whoever else she took along that he would be leaving the university. He would be leaving his rooms. Would there be a penalty for him in disappearing? Would he somehow be less likely to be promoted to master physicker if he went?

Maybe he needed to ask. Then again, if he asked, that would only draw attention to the fact that he intended to go.

"What is it?" she asked.

"I'm concerned about what will happen if I choose to go with Sam. I don't know whether I will be able to return to the university afterward."

"Plenty of physickers leave," she said.

"They do?"

"Well, not junior physickers. There is an expectation that once you reach junior-physicker level, you will staff the wards, as well as the intake rooms, but once you get promoted to full physicker, it is not uncommon for people to leave the university and see the rest of the city." She smiled. "Then again, most of the people who do that come from one of the inner sections, and they take the opportunity to go out and visit the outer sections of the city. They think it will make them better physickers."

"It will."

Alec hadn't realized the physickers even did that. That made him feel better about the fact that there was a certain breadth to the knowledge the physickers had. If they did leave the university section, then it was possible they would begin to see the needs of those in some of the lowborn sections.

"I'm not sure that you can do the same," Beckah said.

"Why not?"

"It's just you are so new to your promotion. And… Well, most people see you as nearly lowborn. It's your father, you know. An apothecary is viewed as a lowborn position, regardless of where in the city your section was located."

"There are plenty of children of merchants at the university."

"There are, but, well, you know how people view apothecaries, especially here."

It was something Alec had been dealing with since he first came. Apothecaries were viewed as less than physickers, and for the most part, they were. Then again, few apothecaries were like his father. Few were master physickers. Few were trained at the university.

"I might need to try, anyway."

"What would you say?"

"It might be more than what I say, but also who I say it to." If he told Master Helen he was leaving, she might know where he was going. She might know, regardless, but if he told her too soon, she might attempt to do something to dissuade him. If that happened, there might not be anything Alec could do to avoid it. It was possible Master Helen would find some way of preventing it. With her connections at the palace, and the fact that she was a high-ranking Scribe, whatever that meant, she might have much more influence than he realized.

Could he tell Master Eckerd?

He would be the same as Master Helen, in certain respects. He was also a Scribe, and also had a certain level of rank, but Alec didn't have the sense he had the same influence at the palace. Alec didn't know whether Master Eckerd had a Kaver that he was paired with, but it was likely he did. It was just that Master Eckerd never spoke of it. Then again, Master Eckerd rarely spoke to Alec, not anymore. Ever since Alec was promoted to full physicker, Master Eckerd had essentially abandoned him.

There was one master physicker he could tell. He could only imagine the excitement Master Carl would feel when he heard the news.

What sorts of rumors would he spread about him? That was the bigger concern. Not only about his absence, but when he returned, he was concerned about what Master Carl might have said in the time that he was away.

"It looks like both of us have something to prepare for," Beckah said.

"I can help you, if you help me."

"How can I help you?"

"See if there is anything codified for the full physickers and their ability to venture out of the city. We need to see if there's anything I can discover about what freedoms I have."

"How much time do you think you have?"

"I don't know. All I know is that Sam is preparing, and I need to be ready for when we depart. I need to be there with her, and for her."

"I wish I could go," she said in a whisper.

"If you went, you would be abandoning your position at the university. I will see if we can bring Tray back here. That way, you will have the opportunity to have your connection to your Kaver."

She sighed. "I wish there was more than that."

"But there might be someone I can ask." It hadn't

occurred to him, not before, but Marin might know. And now that she was captive, it was an answer he thought she could give and maybe she *would* give.

He turned his attention back to the book flipped open on his desk. "Before I go, I want to have a better handle on this whole papermaking process."

"You want to help with it?"

"I'd love your help, but I don't know that you should be spending your time making paper when you need to be studying for your testing."

"You can help me prepare while we're working on the paper."

Alec nodded. "That, I think, sounds like a good idea."

7

INTERROGATING THE PRISONER

S am jumped the canal between the palace and the university, hopping across the water. She cast a glance over at the university, debating whether she would stop and visit Alec, but she wasn't even certain he was there. It was possible he was where she was heading.

As she made her way through the city, Sam thought someone followed her.

It was a vague sense, but she had long ago learned to trust her instincts, and if she felt someone was following her, it was likely that they were.

The sun had risen above the buildings, and it was bright and warm. Despite that, she pulled her cloak around her. Sam always felt better having her cloak. She passed into the Uffen section and paused. This was a highborn section, and many of the homes here were incredibly ornate. Most had stretches of open space between them, something not common in the outer sections. There, the buildings were crammed close together, practically squeezed in so that everyone was falling over each other.

Sam drifted along the streets, knowing that she stood out compared to the well-dressed people making their way here. There were some merchants, those who were wealthy enough they could afford to make stops at each of the highborn houses, rather than waiting for the highborns to come to them for purchases. What must that wealth be like?

After jumping another canal, she bumped into one of the merchants. The man cast her a harsh glare. "Shouldn't you be back in your place?" the man said.

Sam spun. She tapped her canal staff on the ground, shaking water free. The man jerked back from the water that splattered, almost as though it might harm him. Sam resisted the urge to smirk at him. It would only anger him, and though she didn't care whether she did, she didn't want anything that might draw attention to her as she made her way to Caster.

"I'm sorry."

She turned, but the man grabbed her sleeve.

"That's it?" He leaned closer and sniffed. His nose wrinkled, and he took a step back. "A lowborn. I can see it in your face. I can *smell* it on you."

Sam jerked her arm free and swung her staff, sweeping it beneath his legs and dropping him to the ground. She leaned over, tapping the staff on his chest. "Don't. Call. Me. A. Lowborn."

With each word, she jabbed her staff into his chest, accentuating it.

The man screamed.

She heard the sound of footsteps racing toward her,

and Sam started off, shaking her head. She needed to be more careful. She knew better than to attack a merchant, especially in this section, but his words struck home and reminded her of everything she had ever been angered by in the city. She was tired of being called a lowborn. She was tired of feeling like a lowborn. And even though she had spent the last few months within the palace, she had never stopped thinking of herself that way.

When she reached the next canal, she jumped across.

On the other side, there were the sounds of pursuit. Kyza! Had she drawn the attention of the guards? Her presence in the palace and her connection to Elaine wouldn't protect her, not if she assaulted someone, and certainly not if she assaulted a wealthy merchant.

Sam hurried along the streets. Experience had taught her the way from section to section, and she made it quickly to the outer sections of the city, reaching Caster as the sun peaked in the sky.

When she reached Caster, she felt a sense of relief. Caster wasn't one of the nicer sections, but it was the one she knew best, and it was home. Many of the buildings had fallen to disrepair long ago. Without the wealth found in some of the inner sections, they were left that way. Sam hurried along the streets, weaving toward the center of the section where Bastan would be keeping Marin. She took a roundabout way, curious whether she had been followed.

As she went, it became increasingly clear that someone did follow her.

Maybe more than one person.

Sam jumped, flipping to the rooftop of a butcher. The smells that came from the shop were a mixture of smoke and rot, telling her all she needed to know about the quality of meats the butcher prepared, but it might prevent others from coming after her here.

Looking toward the ground, she scanned the street, waiting to see if there was anyone who followed.

It didn't take long.

A petite figure came down the street. It wasn't Elaine, but the person had a similar appearance to her.

A Kaver.

Why would a Kaver follow her?

She knew why. And she knew *who* would have sent them.

Had Elaine known that Sam knew more about Marin than she let on?

It was good Bastan kept her somewhere besides his tavern, and that he had enough control of the section that he could conceal his presence easily.

Sam waited for the Kaver to disappear down the street before hurrying onward. Now, she stuck to the rooftops. It was more dangerous for her up here, and a single wrong step could lead to her falling and crashing to the ground, but with her training, her footing was much more assured. She couldn't push off with her staff quite as easily as there wasn't a good place to plant it securely, but with the buildings as close together as they were, she could easily make the jump without it.

Sam ran quickly across the rooftops, jumping from building to building. When she reached an intersection, she would hesitate and search below to see if the Kaver still followed before anchoring her staff and flipping across the street, coming to land in a roll on the other side.

Even though she didn't think she was still being followed, she took a zigzagging approach as she continued deeper into the section. If someone did follow, she wouldn't be easy for them to track. That was something Bastan had taught her. If there was any concern that she was tracked, she knew enough to ensure that she stayed unpredictable. Predictability only meant that she would be caught, and that someone could head her off, or even meet her where she headed.

When she reached Bastan's area, she saw no sign of the Kaver, or of anyone who might be following her. Still, Sam paused, taking time as she looked around, not wanting to be caught unaware. If someone was here and watching, she needed to be careful. She didn't need to have Bastan's location discovered, not by the Kavers and not by Elaine, until she knew what information Marin might be able to share.

When she was content that no one was there, she jumped.

Sam landed and hurried forward, moving along the street before slipping down a darkened alleyway. There were four doors on this alley, and each of them led into Bastan's building, but only one of them was the one that would take her down, deep below this section, and into a hidden corridor. She couldn't imagine how long Bastan had toiled to construct this and couldn't imagine how much money had gone into the building of the network of tunnels. More than she could have imagined. The existence of these tunnels told her everything she needed to know about Bastan's priorities. He had always claimed he was most concerned about protecting Caster, and that he wanted to use his influence to protect those who were with him, but this proved it more than anything else.

Bastan could easily have used his money and influence to buy his way into a highborn section, and from there, he could have used his connections to gain greater control over even more of the city, yet he didn't. He had created a place where he could protect Caster.

Before heading down the alley, Sam paused and glanced into the shadows, but saw no movement. She looked up, knowing that the alley should be concealed, but wanting to ensure no one came this direction either, and finally knocked. There was a particular pattern Bastan expected when she knocked, and she made certain to do it in the correct rhythm.

The door opened, and a bald-headed man poked his face out. "Samara. You come alone?" He looked up and down the alley before turning his attention back to Sam.

Michael was a large man, muscular, but most of it was concealed under several layers of flab. He had a bushy beard that occasionally caught fragments of food, much as it did now. Yet, friendliness sparkled in his eyes. "Yes, I came alone, Michael. Would you move aside and let me in?"

He glanced up and down the alley one more time before backing up. When she was inside, he closed the door, sliding a thick bar across it. Michael took his place on the stool and picked up a book and began scanning the page again.

"I never would've figured you for a reader."

"I never would have before, but sitting here... Well, it gets boring."

"And Bastan doesn't care?"

"Bastan doesn't care so long as I pay attention. There's not a whole lot that can get through this door, not without drawing attention."

It *was* a stout door, but the massive bar that prevented access did most of the heavy work. "Is he down there?"

"Not yet. I thought he was with you?"

"He was, but we separated when we returned to the city."

"Then he's probably at the tavern. You know how Bastan is."

Sam huffed. "Yes, I know how Bastan is." She waved and headed down the hall, taking the stairs at the end. There was no light, but Sam knew her way well enough and had traveled along the stairs often enough that it wasn't difficult for her to reach the bottom in the dark. From there, a few lanterns provided light to allow her to see where she was heading. Two more doors were set on to either side of the wall, and only one of them would take her to Marin.

Sam tapped on that door and waited for it to open. Bastan kept layers of protection, so that anyone who might reach this place would have difficulty getting all the way inside. She suspected he had even more layers than she was aware of, something typical of Bastan.

The door opened, and another balding man with a thick beard poked his head out. Many of Bastan's men had a similar look to them, and she suspected they were related, though she had not questioned.

"Ricken."

"Samara. Bastan isn't with you?"

Had Bastan really shared so much detail with each of his men? Could they all know that they had been together? "No. Bastan isn't with me. He's probably at the tavern."

"Maybe he'll bring some food," Ricken said.

Sam patted his belly as she slipped past. "I'm not sure that you need any more food."

A hurt expression briefly crossed his face as he closed the door and slipped a massive bar over it. "There's nothing wrong with enjoying a little food."

"Nope. There is nothing wrong with you enjoying a little food."

He frowned at her. "Why do I get the sense that you're mocking me?"

"I'm not mocking you." She flashed a smile. "Has she tried anything?"

"Nothing more than the last time."

The last time, Marin had been restrained by two men, each the same size as Michael and Ricken, and both of them had nearly been thrown off. That was enough to tell Sam the extent of Marin's ability. She was incredibly talented, even without a Scribe to assist with her augmentations.

Ricken waved her past him. Sam headed toward the back of the room and still another door. This time, she didn't knock. She pulled it open, and a row of cells greeted her. She didn't know how long the cells had been here but suspected it was years. The metal was thick, almost as wide as her wrist, and spaced closely together. None of the other cells were occupied. Marin was the sole prisoner here.

The man sitting in front of Marin nodded at Sam.

"Can I have a moment with her, Timod?"

Timod was even fatter than Ricken and Michael but

was probably the strongest of all of them. Though he didn't bear much resemblance to the Thelns, he was solid and created an imposing appearance. "Be my guest. Just be prepared for her to try something stupid."

"What has she tried already?"

"More than she should have," he said.

He squeezed past her and stepped outside the door, closing it behind him.

Marin stood and approached the bars, gripping them. Her hands barely made it all the way around them. Sam couldn't believe she had managed to escape—twice.

"Samara. Have you come to taunt me again?"

Sam stood far enough away that Marin couldn't attempt to squeeze her arms through the bars to reach her. "Taunt? I came to see what else you might want to teach."

Marin grunted and attempted to shake the bars. Had she placed an augmentation on herself? Though there were times when it was obvious, Sam couldn't always tell. "Teach? You continue to hold me here. Why do you think I would teach you?"

"What else would you do? Bastan has made it clear that he intends to hold you here for… For a long time."

Marin grunted. "Maybe it would've been better if Lyasanna had captured me. At least then, the end would have been quick."

"Are you sure you deserve quick?"

"Are you sure I deserve this?"

"I haven't decided." Sam decided that she could be honest with Marin. She wasn't sure what she would do with the woman, just as she wasn't sure what she deserved. There was no debating that Marin had done evil

things to her, but there was the fact that Marin had done
so because of what she perceived as a good reason. And
without Marin having done what she had, Tray could
have died long ago.

And had that happened, Sam might never have had a
brother. Regardless of anything else, she was better for
having Tray in her life. She was better for him being her
brother.

"What is it that you would like to know this time?"

"I have been wondering why some of the augmentations I place upon myself aren't as strong as what Alec can
place on me."

Marin offered a half smile. "Some?"

"Fine. None. None of them are as strong as what Alec
can place on me."

"Because you are inexperienced, and likely because
you are trying to use them ineffectively."

"Ineffectively? I did manage to beat you."

"You beat me, but you still had your Scribe assisting
you. Without him, would you have managed to be quite as
effective?"

Both Sam and Marin knew she would not have been.
Without Alec adding to her, she would have failed, but
then, maybe what Bastan told her was valid. Maybe she
did need to stop trying to do things on her own. Maybe
she *did* need to have the help of her Scribe.

"Are there any ways that you can teach me to improve
the efficacy of my own augmentations?"

"That has to come from within you. You have to find
your own way of augmenting, and your own way of
making them effective." Marin released one of the bars

and started to turn away before pausing. "How do you manage it?"

"I do as you told me. I imagine the augmentation, and the effect that it has, and let it wash over me."

"That's not it. There has to be more."

"I also try to think about what Alec would have done," Sam admitted.

"That's why your augmentations are weaker."

"Why? Because I'm relying on what Alec would have done?"

"Because you are still depending on your Scribe. You need to focus on the power that comes from you, not on the power that comes from him."

"But the power that comes from him and from he does is what allows me to be augmented."

"In the way you achieve it. There are other Kavers who have a different technique. That is what you need to accomplish."

"Why can't you simply tell me?"

"Why can't you simply release me?"

"Because you want to hurt me."

"You? Had I wanted to hurt you, I would have done so years ago. I've never wanted anything but your help. It's because of you that Tray lives. The only person I want harmed is Lyasanna."

Sam shook her head. "Sometimes, I think I want the same thing."

"Only sometimes?"

Sam sighed and started to turn away. Marin wasn't going to tell her anything, certainly nothing of use. And her threats were doing nothing. How long would it be before Marin attempted to escape again? Sam would have to ensure that Marin never had the chance to run.

"I think she sent Kavers after Tray," Sam said.

Marin grabbed the bars and shoved her face between them, glaring at Sam. "How many?"

"I saw three."

"You saw them?"

"I was training in the swamp. I saw movement, and there were three Kavers making their way across the swamp."

Marin pounded her fist against the bars and turned away. "If you saw three, it means there were probably more."

"How many more Kavers could there be? I've only seen a few in my time at the palace."

"You've seen what she wanted you to see. You've seen what they *all* have wanted you to see. There aren't that many Kavers, so the fact that three were sent is enough to tell me she intends to finish what she had asked me to start."

That was Sam's concern, as well. "She didn't send Elaine."

"Because Elaine isn't nearly skilled enough. There are others, those who taught me, and they would be far more formidable for the Thelns. Most of them would not require a Scribe, but I suspect that given their joint training, they have access to enough knowledge."

"What sort of joint training?"

"Why do you think Lyasanna has been sneaking one of the master physickers into the palace?"

"I thought it was so that she could study without heading to the university." It wouldn't do for the princess to be seen at the university and studying. Master Helen had been going in and out of the palace, but Sam couldn't be sure it was because she had been working with Lyasanna.

"Is it so *she* can study, or is it because others needed to study?"

"What others?"

"The other Kavers. With enough knowledge, and armed with enough easar paper, the augmentations they are able to generate on their own, along with the assistance of their Scribes, would be quite formidable. Maybe unstoppable."

Unstoppable Kavers heading toward Theln lands. Tray there with his father, Ralun, and trying to understand who and what he was. And Lyasanna trying to cover up a mistake she made when she was younger.

All of it told Sam what Lyasanna intended.

"I can help you," Marin said.

"I can't trust you."

"You don't have to trust me. You have to trust that I want to help Tray. When have I ever done anything that would tell you otherwise?"

Sam let out a heavy sigh. Marin was right, and it was exactly what she had intended, thinking that she would need to trust and rely on Marin to tell the truth, but she couldn't get past the idea it would require releasing her, and if that happened, if Marin disappeared on her, any expertise and knowledge that Marin might be able to provide would be gone.

"If I do this, you need to share with me everything you know about the Thelns before we go."

"What do you think that will accomplish?"

"What it will accomplish is that if you try to run on me, I still have every chance at succeeding. I will keep Tray safe."

Marin stared at Sam for a moment before smacking the bars of the cell. Sam resisted the urge to jump back and held Marin's gaze. Finally, the woman nodded.

8

REACHING THELN LANDS

"Once you get past the swamp, then it becomes difficult," Marin said, sitting just inside the cell with a large piece of paper in front of her. She had a pen and used nothing more than regular ink. Sam made certain that no one else was with them in the row of cells, but Bastan had insisted on being present to listen.

"So you don't think getting across the swamp is difficult?" Bastan asked.

"No. Getting past the swamp is the easy part. If you prefer, you can head across the steam fields, but then you have to climb the mountains, and once there, you have to venture through the Farlesh Forest. That is where it becomes incredibly difficult."

Bastan grinned. "Getting through the forest? What is this, Marin? Are you trying to ensure you remain useful? I think you've already proven that to Samara." Bastan glanced over at Sam, and he shook his head. Sam knew he was not thrilled with what she intended—or the fact that she intended to leave as quickly as she could. Bastan had always been more in favor of meticulous planning. He claimed it was how he had maintained his control on his section for as long as he had.

"There are parts of the forest much more dangerous than others. Knowing the way through is tricky, and even if you know the way, you still can run into situations where you are in danger. So yes, I would say crossing the swamp is the easiest part. For a Kaver, she can simply use her canal staff. Sam has already demonstrated a talent with jumping, and I suspect she has discovered she can rest in the trees along the way. Even if she were to fall into the water, the eels wouldn't attack her immediately."

Sam laughed darkly. "You want to bet?"

Marin looked over at her. "The eels aren't that aggressive, Samara."

"What about the one that bit you?"

"That was because we were close to the shore. You drew it to me with all of your splashing around."

Sam shook her head but decided not to debate Marin on that. She wasn't convinced that the eels had only been drawn toward them because of their splashing around. The eels seemed to be drawn to her every time she was in the swamp. Almost as if they didn't want her to attempt the crossing. Maybe she should ask Elaine about that.

"Why is the forest so difficult?" Bastan asked.

Marin proceeded to dip the pen into the bottle of brown ink, and she started drawing out what she represented as the city and then the swamp. From there, she depicted the forest. It abutted both the mountainous access as well as the swamp, pointing out that they would be forced to navigate the forest either way. "Not all of the ground is trustworthy. There are areas of sinkholes, places where one misstep will cause you to disappear beneath the ground."

"Can you travel through the trees?" Bastan asked.

"You could, but you would need to know how to navigate through the trees, and even then, you run the risk of the chamyn."

"Am I to presume those are some creatures that live in the trees?" Bastan asked.

"Enormous cats. They prowl along the trees, preferring to prey there, as it is much safer to find their meals than on the ground. They are fast, and they can streak along the branches, with claws that hold them in place. Some have been known to walk upside down and drop down to attack."

Bastan started chuckling loudly. "It sounds to me like you are telling us children's tales, Marin."

"I'm telling you what I have seen and experienced."

"And if you have seen and experienced this, and if what you have told us about Tray is accurate, then you would have managed to navigate this forest with an infant. Either it's not nearly as difficult as you would have us believe, or there is another way."

"I'm just telling you what I know of the passing. Kavers over the years have made maps, and those maps allow safe crossing through the forest." Marin's gaze shifted to Sam. "There was a time when I had access to those maps, but…"

Sam frowned. "Did you have something in your room that help you make this crossing?"

"Not in my room. What I had there was nothing more than a few references. I made my own notes, but that was from memory, and not from the Kaver guide."

"You're suggesting I need to find this guide?"

Marin shrugged. "We can certainly try to go by memory. If you have access to my records, I did make notes that should provide help, but it may not be enough. We may still end up falling into one of the sinkholes or end up in one of the chamyn dens."

"Even if we don't end up in one of their dens, I thought you said they prowled through the trees?"

"Through most of the trees. It seems there are certain places they avoid."

Bastan chuckled again. "Of course, they do. Why wouldn't they avoid certain trees so that Kavers like yourself can guide us?"

Marin glared at him. "I don't need you to believe me, Bastan. I have done nothing other than tell the truth—"

"Have you?" Sam asked. "When did your truth telling begin?"

"When it no longer mattered. When you discovered that you were a Kaver, and when you discovered Elaine, lying to you no longer mattered."

"I'm not going to continue debating this with you, Marin. You have continued to lie to me, even when you told me you were telling the truth. It wasn't until recently that you shared with me that Lyasanna was Tray's son."

"Had I told you sooner, what would you have done?"

Sam bit her lip as she thought. "I don't know," Sam said.

Marin held her gaze for a moment before looking back down, and she began to draw something more on her makeshift map. "This is the Unseen Plain."

"I suppose that you will tell us the grasses here will try

to kill us," Bastan said. "Or that there is some dangerous creature hiding within the grasses."

Marin shook her head. "No. The only thing dangerous about this is how tall they grow. It's easy to lose your way. Some have wandered aimlessly for days, long enough that they get lost, never to be seen again."

"And I suppose you have some way of preventing that?" Bastan asked.

"Nothing that will help. If it's overcast, you will lose your way. If it's sunny…" She glanced from Sam to Bastan. "This is the least difficult part of the crossing."

"Not the swamp?"

"The swamp is only difficult for those who aren't Kavers. The plain is not physically taxing, but it is challenging, and without the right preparations, it is possible that you will fail when you try to cross it."

"And your guide?" Bastan asked. There was a smile, almost a look of incredulity, on his face. "Will this help us somehow pass through the plain?"

"Unlikely," Marin said. "The only thing you need to know is that you must head straight west. From there, you will cross into easier places to access. There will be villages leading to cities leading to the Theln capital. Once you cross through the plain, though, you are in Theln lands. They are nearly inaccessible, difficult even for a skilled Kaver, so know that the moment you reach their lands, you will be in danger."

Bastan stared at Marin for a long moment. "I don't know whether you're lying or if I should be impressed that you survived this with Tray when you claim to have escaped."

"If you are determined to come with Samara, you will see for yourself."

"Oh, I am determined to accompany Samara. I don't have any interest in allowing you to be the one to guide her, especially if that means that she will be thrust into danger that relies on your ability to get her free."

Sam stared at the paper. If what Marin told her was true, maybe she never would have been able to reach the Theln lands on her own. She thought she could cross the swamp—at least, she thought she could learn enough where she could eventually cross the swamp, even if she had so far not managed it—but finding a way through this forest? There might not be an easy way through without having access to the map the Kavers had developed.

"If we find your records?" Sam asked.

"If you find them, it is only a partial reference. You might need more in order for you to safely cross the forest." Marin held her gaze. "I can see that is what concerns you the most, as it should. I'm being honest when I tell you that my records are incomplete. But, if you had the Kaver guide…"

It meant that Sam would have to somehow find it.

Bastan tapped her arm and guided her away. "Samara. I don't think it's wise for you to allow Marin to convince you to break into the palace and steal a Kaver guide."

Sam cast a glance over at Marin. If she augmented her hearing, she could hear what they were saying, though why would it even matter? Marin likely knew the debate they were having even without attempting to listen in. "I don't have to break into the palace. I have access."

"You might have access, but you told me about how

they followed you. You told me you weren't certain that your mother was interested in you going after Tray."

"She wasn't interested. She actually warned me against it."

"So, for you to gain access to this guide, you would need to break in. All I am saying is that I'm not sure that is the best idea."

"Then what is?" Sam turned her attention back to Bastan. "If we believe her, and I think that we should, what other option do we have?"

"You could ask your mother."

"My mother. The woman who has made it abundantly clear that we shouldn't go after Tray."

"The woman who is happy to have you returned to her. The woman who would have searched for you for a decade, angered about what Marin had done. The woman who—"

Sam shook her head. "The woman who has continued concealing things from me, even now that I have returned to her."

Bastan huffed a frustrated sigh. "I can see I'm not going to change your mind."

"Do you want to?"

"I want to ensure that nothing happens to you. I want to help you if I can, but mostly, I want to make sure you don't do anything too stupid."

"Thanks, Bastan."

"Don't thank me. Not yet."

"And what if I can't find the guide?" she asked him.

"If you don't find the guide, then we have to rely on Marin. Even if you do find it, we probably have to rely on her. I'm just saying that I don't care for that. I would rather that we not need someone like Marin, someone who is just as likely to betray us the moment we reach Theln lands as not. She has her own agenda, Samara, and you shouldn't ever forget that."

"I am aware that she will have her own agenda. Just as long as it coincides with mine, I think we will get along fine."

Bastan grunted. "And if it doesn't?"

Sam smiled slightly. "If it doesn't, maybe we leave her in the forest."

Bastan considered her for a moment. "Now who's being the bastard?"

9

MAKING EASAR PAPER

Alec stood over the pot in the classroom. It stank. There was simply something awful about the combination of ingredients. If he was following the recipe correctly, mixing these ingredients together would allow him to create paper, though he struggled with how. Then again, he had enough experience with mixing various concoctions to know the outcome of mixtures often had little to do with what they looked like when mixed together.

All he wanted was to do a test run. If he could successfully create paper, he could vary the recipe to determine which combination of ingredients yielded the best quality paper.

Where was Master Helen?

He had expected her by now, thinking she would have come to work with him, wanting to know more about the overall process. This wasn't something he intended to keep from her, not needing to conceal his methods.

Rather, he would prefer to have someone assisting him, especially someone as bright as Master Helen.

How long would he be able to keep this room concealed? The odor had to be noticeable out in the hallway. Then again, the classrooms were used for purposes like this all the time. Maybe people simply didn't notice it. Or maybe Alec was only attuned to it because he had his nose stuffed over the pot while trying to work through this process.

It was tedious. Mixing the wood pulp took a long time, and he wasn't entirely certain he was doing it correctly. It might've been far easier—and better—for him to find someone in the city who actually had experience with this. Maybe then he could simplify the steps, shortening the amount of time required for him to experiment.

Better yet, he would find someone able to translate the book. If he could do that, then he wouldn't have to worry about whether he was making paper according to the Theln manner. That, he suspected, was the most important part.

Alec looked at the book. He'd come to a realization that he hadn't needed to recognize every word in the book. He could integrate the information he read about the process in the other two books with the things that he understood from the Theln book. At least that was what he was calling it. It may not be a Theln book, but for now, it was how he saw it.

Within the book, he had discovered a few lines of words he recognized. They were similar enough to words he used, names of woods and various leaves and even a few oils, likely of medicinal property. Nothing he found would make sense in a healing concoction, so he suspected that rather than a healing treatment—or poison, though he hadn't ruled that out—it had to do with the process of papermaking. He wasn't sure, but it seemed more likely than anything else, especially considering the pictures in the book.

Most of the items he had been able to readily find. The only thing he hadn't was something called svethwuud. He suspected that was the pulp used in the papermaking process, but what tree was used? It would be something found in Theln lands, but as he had no way of knowing what would be found in Theln lands, Alec had no idea what type of tree to try first. So, he decided it was necessary to try many different trees.

Surprisingly, there was nothing about the eels required for the process.

That was unexpected. After what Master Helen had said, Alec had expected the eel venom would be incorporated at some point, but she wasn't from Theln lands herself, so she could have been mistaken.

There came a quick knock and the door opened. Alec looked over as Master Helen stepped inside. She wore a long gray jacket, the marker of a master physicker, but in this case it had another purpose. She had begun wearing it for protection ever since they'd started experimenting with eel venom, and even now chose to where it to protect her skin from any splatter from their various concoctions.

"You sent word?"

"I did. I thought you might want to be here as we try this," he said.

"What are you trying?"

"I'm trying to mix the paper."

"I thought you didn't know anything about making paper."

"I found a few books, once of which might be Theln, and discovered something that might help us," he said. He decided not to tell Master Helen about his mother.

"Theln? We haven't found anything that would be Theln."

"Maybe it's not Theln. It's written in a different language—"

Master Helen shook her head. "Then it could be anything. We do have ships that travel extensively, Physicker Stross."

"Then I'm simply experimenting," he said. "I don't know whether it will make a difference or not, but if I can understand the process for paper, maybe we can see what the eel venom will do."

"Where is your recipe?"

"I have it memorized," he said. It was better that way. He also thought it best to keep the books hidden in his room, than to have Master Helen ask questions about where he might have come into possession of such books.

"What is the recipe?"

"There are several necessary components," Alec said. He started listing them, beginning with the first few that he had discovered, matching them with what he identified from the books he could read. When he reached the svethwuud, he hesitated. "Have you ever heard of anything called svethwuud?"

Her mouth pinched in a frown. "What is it?"

"I suspect it is the name of the tree used in this. The wood pulp is what forms the paper, but it's not any tree that I know of."

"Then we should just choose any tree."

"I'm not sure any tree is the right solution. If we're trying to match the Theln recipe, we need to use what they would use."

"And what makes you think that this svethwuud is part of the Theln recipe? I thought you said the book was simply written in another language?"

Alec sighed. What would it hurt to tell Master Helen? His father respected her, and Alec should trust her with this, especially if it could help them. "My father told me about my mother."

"What about your mother?"

"He told me she wasn't from the city. He told me that she was a collector of various items. I managed to find a book I think was hers."

"And you believe that your mother was from Theln?"

"I don't know if she was or not, but it seems as likely as anything else."

"I knew your mother, Physicker Stross. She could not have been from the Theln lands."

"How do you know? Weren't you the one to tell me that we've had Scribes go to Theln lands and disappear? What if she was a Scribe from their lands?"

"She would not have come back here. We've lost our Scribes, but they have never come the other direction."

"Why?"

"Without risking ourselves going over there, I don't know if I can say with any certainty."

"What do they do to the Scribes?"

"We don't know," Master Helen said.

"Do they still live?" She nodded. "How can you know?"

"Because Kavers have detected them. That's how we know."

Alec sighed. That made sense. If he were to perform an augmentation now, Sam would notice, and she would be influenced by it. If some of the Scribes left the city and went to the Theln lands, and remained there, they might perform augmentations that would remain. If they had access to easar paper—possibly unlimited access—there would be many things they could do. The only limitation would be the access to the Kaver blood.

"I don't know whether she was from the Theln lands or not," Alec said. "All I know is what my father said about her. If she was, then it makes sense we might be able to use something she had to help us make easar paper."

"And this recipe, you are certain it's the accurate one?"

"I can't read the language in the book, Master Helen. What I have done is correlate what I was able to determine from the book, words that did make sense to me, with what I was able to tell from the other books. Combining them together has allowed me to come up with what appears to be a workable recipe."

He leaned toward the pot and took a deep breath of it. "Only it smells terrible."

"From what I understand, papermaking has a horrible odor."

"Do you have some experience with it?" If she did, then they could work together with it. Maybe Master Helen would be a better help with the entire process than he had realized.

"I don't, but my family does."

"Your family?"

She came up to his side of the table and leaned in,

taking a deep breath of the pulpy mixture. "My family has tried many things over the years. Not all were successful."

"I don't really understand why anyone would try making paper. From what I understand from those who sell it, paper isn't necessarily all that profitable, not unless you have perfected the technique over a period of years."

"That would be quite true. If you are right, and if you manage to create easar paper, you will have done what no master physicker—and no Scribe—has done before."

"And I'm not even sure how necessary it is," Alec said.

"Not sure? How else can you place an augmentation on your Kaver?"

"Sam has come up with some way of augmenting herself even without needing easar paper. The only benefit I see for the easar paper would be to help others."

"Or to harm others," Master Helen said.

Alec looked over to her. "I don't think that it makes sense to create another Book of Maladies. I think the one volume—that which the Thelns possess—is enough."

"Are you certain that is the only one?"

"I don't know anything about the Thelns and what they do with their Book of Maladies. It's possible there are others." All he knew was that when Ralun had come to the city, he had possessed a volume, and it had been used on Lyasanna, to poison her. Sam was convinced that she could find the Book and come up with some way to use it to reverse the effects of her amnesia. There had to be something that could be done, though in order to do so, it would involve finding the page that Marin had used to wipe Sam's memories. Marin might reveal that, but then again, she might not.

Though, how would Marin have used it?

Alec hadn't given it much thought, and perhaps now wasn't the time, but Marin wasn't a Scribe. Could Jessup have used it?

The Kavers held him at the palace and questioned him. Maybe Alec should suggest to Sam that she go question Jessup too. If there was anything that he might be able to reveal about what happened to her, Alec knew she would be thrilled to discover it. She was tired of not knowing, though he didn't know whether it would make a difference if she discovered the truth or not.

"I still believe eel venom is necessary to create the easar paper," Master Helen said.

"There was nothing about eel venom in the recipe," Alec said. "Maybe it's not the venom that grants the power to the easar paper. Maybe it's the svethwuud."

Master Helen leaned over the pot, stirring slowly. "Interesting."

Each time she swirled it, the stench seemed to waft up to him even more. The solution suddenly splashed, and Master Helen released the spoon, dropping it in with another splash. She stepped away and wiped her hands on her jacket.

Master Helen patted him on the shoulder. "You are really quite clever, physicker Stross. Let me know what you come up with."

She strode from the room, leaving Alec alone.

He tried to suppress his disappointment. He had hoped that Master Helen would stay longer and help him with this, but maybe she felt much like the junior physickers did with the dirty patients. Maybe this was something she believed was beneath her, requiring him to work on it by himself, so that when he was finished, she could swoop in and see the end result, not needing to endure those intermediary steps.

But had Alec not done this, he wouldn't have known everything that was involved. He didn't know whether it mattered and didn't know whether this concoction would even create paper, but he had a feeling he was on the right path. Especially since the recipe seemed to mirror what he found in some of the books he could read.

He continued to stare. The odor burned his nostrils. It hadn't done that before, but maybe he it had to do with the duration of exposure to the mixture.

He went to the door, needing to ventilate the room.

He opened it and took a deep breath.

His head began to swim.

Was it too much exposure to the stink of the pulp mixture? Or was there something else? Was there something about the creation of the easar paper that was harmful? He took another breath. His eyes continued to burn. His throat felt like it was closing.

Something had happened.

Easar paper. He needed to get some easar paper and try to reverse the effects. He knew everything he had put into the mixture and thought he could counter it, but the effect would be delayed.

He staggered forward, practically stumbling along the hallway until he reached the staircase. He had to drag himself up, weakness beginning to overwhelm his body.

What had happened? What had he done?

Could he reach the easar paper in his room?

He needed to be strong. He needed to get there, and then... then he could write down the necessary combination that would be required to counter what was happening to him.

Alec fell.

He tried standing, and tried dragging himself up, but he wasn't strong enough.

No. He willed himself along. He needed to get to the easar paper.

He collapsed again. This time, he couldn't get himself back up. He tried calling out, but his voice didn't seem to work. His throat had closed up.

Worse, not only had he poisoned himself, but if anyone else happened upon that mixture, they would be poisoned as he was.

He had been a fool, and now others would suffer because of it.

10

A VISIT

How long had it been since she had been to Marin's home? Sam tried to think about when she had last come here and couldn't come up with the timing. It had been months, probably longer, and much had changed for her in that time.

The home was nicer than most in the Caster section, and rose several stories high, made of stone and decorated with an ornate style not found on many of the more centrally located buildings. Caster was older than most of the city, something she suspected was important but still had not determined the reason why, and Marin had claimed one of the more impressive buildings within the section.

She tested the door and found it locked. That didn't surprise her, and it didn't present much of a barrier to her. One of the earliest skills she had learned from Bastan was how to break into locked doors. Once again, she was thankful for his tutelage.

Sam grabbed a few slender metal rods she had in her

pocket and stood with her side to the door, working them in the lock. She tried to look as nonchalant as she could, not wanting to draw any attention to herself, but knowing anyone on the street might be watching her. Marin once had her own network, and though it may have been disrupted, there was still the possibility someone remained under her employ.

The door popped open. Sam pushed it open wider and slipped inside and then hurried up the stairs. She was careful not to let the steps creak too much. She didn't think anyone was here, but she didn't want to alert anyone if they were. It was better to come upon them rather than be surprised.

When she reached Marin's door, Sam jiggled the lock before using her lock pick to break into it. This took a little bit more work than the last one, and when the door popped open, she hesitated before stepping inside.

It wouldn't surprise her to discover Marin had placed some sort of trap here. Sam would be prepared for that.

Nothing happened.

She stepped inside and looked around. A layer of dust covered everything, telling her it had been a long time since Marin had come here. She looked for evidence of footsteps in the dust, or traces of places where it might have been disturbed, but there were none. Marin had not been here. Nor had anyone else.

It was much like she remembered from her last visit. There were a few shelves, each filled with books, though fewer than the last time. Alec had taken some of them, and Marin had likely removed some herself. There was the bed with the lockbox at the end, and she popped open the top, but found nothing inside.

As she scanned the room, she noticed a cloak hanging behind the door.

Sam grabbed it. This cloak was much like the one she wore, possessing the ability to shed light, to somehow obfuscate someone's eyesight, practically as if it carried its own enhancements.

She heard the sound of footsteps below her.

Sam tensed. She went to the door, checking to make sure she had locked it behind her. Anyone who would come here would likely have followed her.

Had she revealed the location of Marin's home? She didn't think Elaine knew of it before, especially as Sam hadn't shared it with her, but that didn't mean she couldn't have discovered it in the meantime. More likely, Elaine had sent someone to follow her, and Sam had been too careless with making her way from Bastan's prison over to Marin's old home.

She should have known better. She knew she had been followed earlier in the city, and knew she needed to be more cautious. Normally, such a thing wouldn't be an issue for her. Had she gotten so out of practice? Then again, it had been quite a while since she had worked in Caster—or the neighboring sections—in a way that required her to remain that vigilant.

Sam hurried over to the shelf. That was what she had come for. If she could discover what Marin kept here, and maybe grab her personal record, they would have some way of discerning what they might need to know as they traveled through the forest.

There were too many books for her to take all of them. Not only would they be heavy, but it would slow her down. She glanced over at the window, realizing she might need to go out that way once again.

She crouched in front of one of the nearest shelves and began to search the titles. There was nothing obvious about them. Many of them were books that would likely have been of more interest to Alec, books that described the workings of the body, and some that appeared to be a history of the city. Sam grabbed that one and stuffed it into her pocket. Others were personal journals, so she grabbed all of those and stuffed them into her pocket. She would have to look through them later when she had more time.

She went to the other shelf, and it was much the same.

The sound of footsteps on the stairs was unmistakable, but not loud.

It was a soft sound, and it was clear that whoever was coming attempted to conceal their presence.

As soft as they were, it was strange that Sam could hear them so clearly, or maybe it wasn't. Maybe Marin had chosen this building as her home because the old construction and creaking stairs ensured she could know whether someone was coming.

Sam scanned the titles, deciding to stuff all of them into her cloak.

When she was done, she looked over at the door. Was that someone trying to twist the handle?

She wasn't sure she could go out the door. There was no way of really telling if someone was out there, not without unlocking and opening the door. That meant either she would have to risk it—or she would go out the window.

It wasn't that she feared going out the window. She

had gone that way enough times that she didn't worry about climbing down, but when she had before she'd had rope. Now she was equipped only with her canal staff.

The doorknob turned.

Sam was certain of it this time.

She raced over to the window. When she reached it, she pushed it open and glanced down at the street, looking to see if there was anyone else out there. She saw no sign of anyone. That didn't completely reassure her. Any good thief would be able to hide in the shadows, especially at a time like this with a moonless night overhead, but once she was down on the street, she would be able to disappear more easily.

She crawled out onto the ledge, focusing on an augmentation. She wanted strength, but she also wanted to lighten her body. If she did so, landing wouldn't be quite as jarring, even if she used her canal staff.

Holding herself steady on the ledge, she focused on the intent of the augmentation and then on the feeling she would have if it took effect. Even if she was only partially successful, she would be able to jump down safely.

As the augmentation washed over her slowly, she heard the door open behind her.

Sam jumped.

She arced out and away from the building, moving much farther than she had anticipated, strength coming from the augmentation and the distance coming from the fact that she had made herself lighter than normal. Sam sailed across the street, landing quite a ways away from Marin's building.

When she came down, she turned and looked up at the window.

Someone looked out, but it was not anyone she recognized.

Sam wrapped her cloak around herself, hoping it obscured her as it usually did. She waited for a few moments until the person standing in Marin's window disappeared. Then she spun, turning away and heading back along the street.

Her pockets were heavy, practically the only weight she had, and she sailed over canal after canal as she crossed through the city. When she reached the university section, she snuck in the side entrance Alec had shown her and hurried through the hallways until she reached his room. At this hour, she was hopeful he would be there, and if he wasn't, she would sit and wait for him. She needed his help to determine what Marin had written in her books and to quickly help her assess whether there was anything more she might have before she took them over to Marin.

There was no answer at his door, but she let herself in. The room was in disarray, much more chaotic than was typical for Alec. He usually was much neater, quite organized, so this chaos within his room surprised her. There was a stack of books on the table at the center of the room, one of them lying flipped open in the middle of the table. A bottle of ink rested on the corner of the table, with a piece of paper set in front of it, notes made by Alec in his tight script set right near the book.

Sam started pulling the books out of her pocket, setting them on the floor next to his table. She would wait, but how long would it be before Alec returned?

While waiting, she started to look around his room. It was strange to see it as messy as it was. Maybe he had just been preoccupied, but even that didn't fully explain it. Alec was always so organized.

She found a jar of liquid underneath the desk, when she pulled it out and opened the top, she gasped.

The pale yellow liquid was unmistakable. She had seen it often enough and had seen the effects from it.

Eel venom.

What would Alec be doing with eel venom in his room?

It was dangerous—possibly fatal—and he knew that.

That's still didn't explain the state of his room.

She began to look more carefully at everything that was scattered about the room. She found another jar and pulled it open. She recognized the milky white liquid as the other venom he'd extracted from the eels. Mixed together, they were relatively benign, but individually, they had potentially dangerous effects.

She had known that Alec still had the venom but hadn't really known he had so much. And why keep that in his room? That seemed the most surprising to her, especially as he was usually so careful. Anyone could come in here—at least, anyone willing like herself to break into his room. She knew Alec didn't have many people who were fond of him at the university. Many were angry about the fact that he had been promoted as quickly as he had, moving on to the rank of full physicker. She doubted that it would be long before he became master physicker, though Alec believed it would take several years, or even longer.

She took a seat at his desk and began to skim over the notes.

As she did, understanding swept through her.

She looked down at the eel venom with a renewed understanding. But if he had figured out a way—or, at least tried to figure out a way—of making easar paper, where was it?

If he uncovered the secret of making easar paper, they would be much less restricted than they were now. Currently, the supply of the paper was a limiting factor when it came to augmentations. It was a limiting factor when it came to everything Alec could do for others at the university.

Could there be any paper here?

Sam began to search for paper. She could tell from Alec's notes he had attempted to use standard paper and add various concoctions to it, all mixtures of eel venom, ways he thought he could prepare the paper so it would carry the same benefit as easar paper. From his notes, none of them had been successful. That didn't change Sam's curiosity, nor did it change her interest in seeing his trials. Maybe there was something she could offer, though she doubted it.

She wasn't the brains behind their partnership—that was definitely Alec—but that didn't mean she didn't have helpful input. She had a more practical type of knowledge than Alec that came from her years on the street.

She saw no sign of the trials. There was nothing other than the mess in the room.

The door to Alec's room opened, and she looked up expecting to see him.

Instead, Sam frowned.

"Beckah? What are you doing here?"

"Oh. I didn't know Alec had asked you to come."

"He didn't ask me to come. I came to see him. I didn't realize I needed an appointment to do so."

Beckah shook her head. "You don't. He's a full physicker, and he is allowed to have visitors anytime he wants." Beckah licked her lips. "What are you doing here?"

"I needed his help, but it appears he's working on making easar paper."

Beckah's eyes widened. "You knew?"

"I can tell from his notes. Alec documents far too well for that to be difficult to determine."

"That *is* what he's trying to do. I'm not sure how far along he is. He doesn't share that with me, mostly because he tells me I need to stay focused on my studies."

Sam chuckled. The irritation in Beckah's voice was obvious. Sam even understood the source of it. There had been a time when Beckah and Alec had been a similar level and had come up through the university together. Now, Alec was a full physicker while Beckah remained a student, senior-level student or not. That formed a division between them, one that was necessary, but that didn't mean Beckah had to like it. And from the look on her face, Sam didn't think Beckah cared for it at all.

"What are you doing here?"

"I…" Beckah glanced over her shoulder before stepping into the room and pulling the door closed. "I came to talk to Alec about a patient."

"And that's something you need to whisper about?"

Beckah shook her head. "It's not that I need to whisper about it, it's just… Not all of the physickers are thrilled with Alec. If they know I've come to him, that will cause some consternation."

"For you?"

Beckah nodded. "I wouldn't care, but I've been put up for promotion, and he and I agreed that it was best to eliminate any possible problems until then." She flopped into a chair. "Once I'm a junior physicker, there won't be quite as much of a distinction between our levels, and he can work more openly with me on my studies."

As it often did when Sam heard Beckah discuss her relationship with Alec, she couldn't help but feel a surge of jealousy. There was no reason for it, especially as Alec had made it somewhat clear that he had no interest in Beckah other than as a colleague, but it didn't change the fact that she felt it.

"Congratulations, I suppose," Sam said.

"Thanks. But if he's not here, I really should be going. Besides, I don't want to get in the way of the two of you."

Sam almost told her *too late* but decided not to. "I can tell him you stopped—"

The door opened, and this time, Alec did come in. He glanced from Beckah over to Sam, a smile spreading across his face. As he stepped into the room, he staggered and fell forward unconscious.

11

HEALING THE HEALER

S am raced over to Alec and quickly rolled him onto his back. He had a faint sheen of sweat on his face, but there was none anywhere else. She noticed a small marking on his cheeks, but nothing else.

"Can you help?" she asked.

But Beckah was already crouching next to Alec and had her arms on either side of him, assessing him. Sam recognized a similar technique to the one Alec used when he was detecting injuries. It was methodical, and she noticed the way Beckah ran her hands along Alec's arms and his legs, then listened to his heart before leaning back on her heels.

"I don't know what's wrong with him. We need to get them to the hospital ward."

Sam looked around the room. "What we need is easar paper."

"That's just it. It doesn't work unless you know what you're targeting. Even if we had a supply of easar paper, it wouldn't make a difference."

Sam frowned. Why did it have to be so difficult? She could use easar paper to augment herself and had used it on herself. But then, she remembered Alec saying he hadn't been able to use it when attempting to heal his father because he didn't know what to target, just as Beckah had said.

"I can carry him," she said.

"*You* can carry him?"

Sam glared at her. "I'm stronger than I look." Especially when she placed an augmentation. She focused, needing to do it right now for Alec, thinking about strength only and focusing on what it would feel like as the augmentation took hold. It washed over her, and as it did, she felt the flush of strength fill her.

Sam stood, holding Alec in her arms.

Beckah stared at her, as though she couldn't believe that Sam was able to do it without augmentations, before she shook herself and headed out the door, waiting for Sam to follow. When she did, she hurried down the hallway. She knew her way to the university hospital, having gone that way enough times now that she recognized the path, but never before had she had such urgent need to reach the hospital.

Her mind raced. What could Alec have been exposed to? What could have happened to him?

"Do you know what he has been working on?" Sam asked as she caught up to Beckah.

Beckah glanced over at her. "I know that he has been trying to find out how to make paper."

"Why would he want to make his own paper?"

"Because he's convinced that's the only way to make easar paper. I know he and Master Helen have tried using eel venom to add to already existing paper, but it wasn't successful."

Sam looked around the hall, thankful that it was empty. They really needed to be more careful as they spoke about easar paper, especially out in the open like this. "Master Helen has been working with him?" She should have remained closer to Alec, but she'd been focused on trying to understand her own training, so that she could be ready for her trip out of the city. But maybe that had been a mistake.

"Master Helen thought she might have some key to helping him with the paper."

"I'm not sure that was the best idea," Sam said.

"Why is that?"

"Because Master Helen has been in the palace."

Beckah frowned at her.

"It doesn't matter," Sam said. "All that matters now is that we get Alec the help he needs."

"Without knowing what he's been doing…"

"You can't do an assessment without knowing?"

"You can, but that's part of the challenge. If there is nothing we can find physically wrong with him, and without being able to question him about where he's been and what he's been doing, it becomes difficult to know what we need to counter."

They made their way down a set of stairs and reached the hospital ward. It was a set of wide doors that led into a room with dozens of cots and dozens of people who needed help. Beckah pushed the doors open and when she stepped inside, one of the people wearing a long gray jacket hurried over to her.

"Senior students are not allowed to bring patients into the ward. You have to have permission of—"

Beckah shook her head. "This is Physicker Stross. I don't know what happened to him, but he needs help."

The man looked down at Alec, briefly glancing to Sam, his eyes widening as he seemed to realize that she was carrying him by herself, before nodding. "Bring him in. Place him on a cot over here."

Sam followed the physicker and set Alec down. It was good timing as her augmentation was beginning to fade. She needed to practice maintaining her augmentations for longer. If she could, then she wouldn't have to worry about her strength fading at an inopportune time. That was a consideration for later.

The physicker began to assess Alec, repeating many of the same steps that Beckah had done. He ran his hands along Alec's skin, removing his jacket and then shirt, exposing his chest and arms. After that, he pulled down his pants, leaving him in his small clothes, surveying his skin.

"What are you doing? Why do you need to get him undressed?" Sam asked. She could only imagine how irritated Alec would be at learning he had been exposed like that. He was much more modest than that.

"I need to assess the patient completely," the physicker said. "Without him being able to speak, I must inspect his body for any insights it might offer."

Beckah was watching the physicker strangely.

The man continued to work on Alec, listening to his heart and then his lungs and then his stomach. He checked his neck, before pulling open his mouth and examining it thoroughly. He rolled Alec to the side, looking at his back.

"You've been working with him, haven't you?" Beckah asked.

The physicker looked up. "Physicker Stross has been teaching me."

"Why do you ask that?" Sam asked.

"Because Darren has never been this thorough with his assessments before," Beckah said.

The physicker frowned at her before shaking his head. "Physicker Stross has helped me see that performing a complete assessment helps ensure nothing is overlooked."

That sounded like Alec. It impressed Sam that he had already had such an impact. It shouldn't. Alec had always wanted to impart his knowledge, and he hadn't been shy about sharing it, going so far as to even share what he knew with Sam, but Beckah seemed surprised by it for some reason.

"I don't know what it is," the physicker said. "Perhaps one of the master physickers can be as of assistance?"

Beckah glanced over at Sam. "I will see if I can find anyone."

Darren nodded. "I'll stay with him."

Sam glanced from Beckah to Darren. She wanted to stay with Alec, and she probably needed to, but she couldn't rely on these two knowing enough—or caring enough—to offer him the necessary attention. There was one person she could go to, but she wasn't sure whether his father would be willing to help.

Sam slipped out and quickly screwed together the ends of her canal staff. All of her thoughts were on getting help for Alec, but if he didn't get the help he needed, what did that mean for her? If something happened—if Alec died— she would lose her Scribe. Would she ever be paired again?

She didn't know how the Kaver and Scribe relationship worked, other than the fact that she was dependent on Alec. It wasn't the same dependence it once had been. Discovering that she had her own means of accessing augmentations had shown her that there was another way, but it wasn't only that Alec was her Scribe.

She cared about him. She would *not* lose him.

When she reached the canal, she jumped.

Enough of the strength augmentation remained, and she soared over the canal. When she landed, she went racing off. While running, she focused, trying to summon another augmentation. Fear and urgency helped make her strong, and she felt the speed augmentation wash through her.

For Alec. She would move quickly for him.

It didn't take long for her to reach his section. She raced along the street, finding his father's shop as it always was, with the light glowing in the window. She checked the lock and was surprised that it was locked.

Kyza!

Though anxious, she knew she didn't want to damage his father's door by breaking through it. She slipped her lock pick out and went to work on it, quickly getting it to *snick* open. As she entered, she reached for the bell she knew was above the door, silencing it.

Sam closed the door quietly and turned her attention to the front of the shop. Rows of shelves greeted her, all of them containing the apothecary medicines. The smells that assaulted her were overwhelming. She'd felt that way from the very first time she'd entered the old apothecary, and nothing had changed in the interim. Alec must have been exposed to it so often to have muted his reaction to it, but Sam had not.

Where was his father?

With the light on, she suspected he was here, but if he was, why would the door be locked?

She saw shadows moving near the other end of the shop.

Sam hesitated. What would Alec's father think about her intruding?

It was for his son. She knew how he would react. It would be the same way she would react were someone to come to her with word of Alec suffering.

Yet a small voice in the back of her mind warned her to be careful. Sam moved cautiously, and as she approached the back of the shop, she decided to sneak in between a pair of shelves.

She moved around them, getting close enough that she could listen and look out.

"This is a simple job. I thought you would be more excited about it."

The voice was rough and carried with it the same tone Sam had heard from so many others who lived and worked in the underground.

"It's not a simple job. What you have asked of me is highly complex." This came from Alec's father. Sam recognized his voice, and he sounded irritated. "And what you have offered is not nearly enough."

"Not nearly enough? This is five gold coins!"

This came from yet another man.

"And I have told you that it is not enough."

"It's always been enough before."

"That was before."

There was a silence.

Silence like that always made Sam uncomfortable. There were different types of silences that she had experienced in her time on the streets. There was the silence of the night, which she was careful not to disturb, especially when she was sneaking through the streets and working a job. There was the silence of sleep. That was a comforting sort of thing, especially when she could have dreamless sleeps, something that didn't happen nearly as often as she wished it did. There was this kind of silence. One she was all too familiar with, especially from her time in Caster.

This was the silence that preceded violence.

Sam crept forward.

She peeked out between the row of shelves. Alec's father sat in a chair, and two men stood on either side of him. He was in a position of weakness where he was, yet he still resisted. That impressed her. Perhaps Alec's father was stronger than she had known, though that shouldn't be surprising, especially with the strength that Alec had demonstrated.

One of the men slipped out a knife, and he jammed it into the table. He was a large man, with a thick beard and closely shorn head that reminded him of Michael, though Bastan's employee was far kinder and would never have made a threatening gesture like this to Alec's father. Well, not unless Bastan had instructed him to. The other man was thinner but seemed all muscle. Neither was familiar to her, but both had the appearance of men who understood violence.

"You already accepted the job," the man with the knife said.

"And I've already told you that the details of the job needed to change," Alec's father said.

"The details don't change."

"Then find someone else to do your task," Alec's father said. "You can't. That's why you came to me. There's no one else in the city who can do this job, and certainly not for what I am demanding now."

The two men glanced at each other.

Sam felt a prickle along the skin of her neck. It was a tingling sort of nervousness that told her something was about to go awry.

She steadied her breathing and focused on augmentations: strength and speed.

Would it work? She'd already called on augmentations twice in short succession, but she didn't know what her limitations were. She hoped she wasn't limited, certainly not such that she would be restricted from helping Alec's father.

It came slowly. There was the washing cold that started in her feet and worked its way upward, before settling in her head.

With the augmentation set, Sam lurched forward.

She needed every bit of the speed augmentation.

The man with the knife jerked it out of the table and brought it up toward Aelus's neck. If she didn't reach it in time, the knife would slice through his throat and there would be nothing Sam could to do to help him.

She smacked with her staff, sending his knife arm flying out. There was a satisfying crack as his arm shattered with the impact of her staff. She flipped it around, and caught him on the head, dropping him.

The other man reacted quickly, seemingly taking in the threat Sam posed, and unsheathed two belt knives before she could react.

He jammed one of them into Aelus's shoulder, and started to bring the other one around, but Sam struck, catching him with the staff in the center of his chest. With her augmented strength, he went flying and smashed into the wall. She stabbed again with the staff, crunching his sternum.

Alec's father glanced over his shoulder and gingerly removed the knife, placing pressure on his shoulder with his good hand. "I should thank you, but I fear your arrival will only lead to greater complications for me."

"Really? I think if I hadn't arrived, you would be dead." She nodded to the knife that lay on the other side of the shop. "He nearly took your head off with that."

He glanced over at the wall. "I suppose you are right." He stood and made his way over to the larger of the two injured men, crouching down and assessing his injuries. He shook his head as he stood and made his way to the other. Within a moment, he stood once more, still shaking his head. "I presume that you have an augmentation?"

Sam nodded. "Why?"

"Because neither of these two men will survive this attack. Is Alec with you?"

"No."

"Then how do you have an augmentation?"

"That doesn't matter. I need you to come with me."

"Why?"

"Because something happened to Alec. He's at the university."

"I know he's at the university, and I hope that you will find it within you to let him stay there. I know you have intentions of heading across the swamp—I've seen it myself—but I think Alec needs to remain at his studies. He can do so much more good as a master physicker than he can as a Scribe."

Sam frowned at him. She couldn't deny the fact that Alec could do more good as a master physicker. That was the truth. As much as she needed Alec, as much as she wanted to have Alec with her, there was much more value in his connection to the physickers, especially as she began to recognize her own ability to augment herself.

"He's not going to be doing anything in his current state. Something happened. That's why I need you to come with me."

Aelus's eyes widened, and he glanced over at the two fallen men before turning his attention back to Sam. "Of course. For Alec, I'll do anything."

BACK TO THE UNIVERSITY

S am kept an eye on Aelus as she led him toward the hospital ward. She had been forced to sneak him across the bridge, especially at this late hour, and the bridge was closed to anyone coming to the university for healing. She didn't want to wait until morning.

When they reached the doors to the ward, Aelus paused.

"What is it?"

"The last time I was here, I was nearly dead."

"This time, you're not. This time, it's your son who needs you."

"When I left," Aelus said, closing his eyes, "I never thought I would return and certainly not like this. I wanted nothing more than to get away from here."

"It seems you went quite a ways away from here, especially if you have become a poisoner."

"Alec told you?"

"He did. Can't say that I'm all that bothered by it. I've seen plenty of poisoners who do good work. There are bad people in the world. And there are good people who live in bad places." She shrugged. "I don't see the world quite as black and white as Alec does."

"No. I suppose your time in Caster has shown you a lot more gray than my son has known."

"He's begun to see the gray, but..." Sam shook her head. "There are times when I think it's too bad. His innocence can't be returned to him."

She remembered Alec as she first had met him, the healer who had been so focused on that singular task. Now, he was something different. There was no disputing that he was something more, but he had changed, and much of his change was because of her. She wasn't convinced she had done him a favor by forcing him to work with her and helping her understand what it meant for her to be a Kaver. He was a Scribe, but what would he have been had he never learned that? Would he have missed out on anything? Or would he have been better off? There were times when she suspected Alec might have been better off, especially now, knowing it might have kept him from this state, and she had a suspicion that whatever had happened to him now was because of her.

"Maybe," Aelus said. "Or maybe it's that he needed to see it. I've tried to protect him from so much, not wanting him to be exposed to the darkness that exists in the world, wanting him only to know healing, but maybe I have protected him too much. Maybe he needed to be exposed to that darkness, so he could understand light when he sees it."

He took a deep breath and pushed into the room.

Sam followed him, and she saw Beckah waiting near the cot where they had left Alec. She looked distraught, and the physicker who leaned over Alec was working frantically.

"What?"

Aelus ran across the room, with Sam right on his heels.

"What do we know?" Aelus asked.

"He's unresponsive. His temperature has been rising, and his heartbeat has been quite erratic, and…" The physicker stopped as he looked up and saw Aelus. "Who are you?"

"This is his father," Sam said.

The physicker's eyes widened. "The apothecary?"

"He was a physicker once," Beckah said. "Alec said he could have been a master physicker."

"Not could have been," Sam said. "Was."

The other physicker looked at Aelus, his eyes wide.

"Alec always did see the best in me," Aelus said.

He began to evaluate Alec, and his examination was much more thorough than what either Beckah or the physicker had done. As he worked, he spoke. "Are there no master physickers available?"

"I went to see if I could find anyone to help, but the masters' quarters are empty."

"Just because the communal hall is empty doesn't mean that you can't check within each individual room. Who is responsible for the wards today?"

"I am," Darren said.

Aelus glanced up. "A junior physicker? What happened to the days when a full physicker was responsible for the wards?"

"Full physicker? The junior physickers run the wards."

Aelus snorted. "Perhaps now, but that wasn't always the case. I need hashel leaves and a tincture of sirand."

"Why?" the physicker asked.

"Because I intend to settle his heart, which will help with his breathing, which can ultimately stabilize him. Then we can take a few moments to determine what exactly he was exposed to."

"You think he was exposed to something?" Beckah asked.

Aelus glanced up at her and seemed to survey her coat. "You are a friend of Alec's."

"I am. We were working together, he's been trying to understand the…"

"Yes. I am well aware of what he has been trying to understand. I'm not sure he should have been."

"He gets to choose what he does," Sam said.

"Do not lecture me," Aelus said.

The physicker hurried back with two small jars on a metal tray. Aelus tapped out some of the leaves onto the tray and then mixed a few drops of liquid into them. He stirred them with his finger, and then picked up a pinch of it and stuck it inside Alec's cheek, holding it there for a few moments.

"It doesn't take much. It's possible to under do it, but you certainly can't overdo it, not with this concoction. It's basic, but it's quick-acting, and when you're dealing with something like this, quick-acting is often the most important feature."

He pulled his finger out and wiped it on his pants. Aelus leaned forward and rested his head on Alec's chest, listening. He stayed there, his eyes closed and his finger tapping on the side of the cot. She presumed the tapping represented Alec's heartbeat. It tapped rapidly at first, and then far more gradually than what Sam thought was acceptable, it began to slow.

When it did, Aelus stood and quickly looked around the room.

"He should be stable, for now. I need to see where he's been working."

"He has been working in his room," Sam said.

"Not completely," Beckah said.

"But his room is a mess."

"That might be my fault," Beckah said. "We have been studying together, and…"

Sam clenched her jaw. She tried not to let that get to her, knowing that it shouldn't, and knowing that Alec would tell her that it shouldn't, but the familiar surge of irritation bubbled within her. She didn't want to hate Beckah, but it was so easy to do.

"Where else would he have been working?" Aelus asked.

"He did say he's been working with Master Helen," Sam offered.

"If that's the case, then I suspect there would be a classroom where they would have experimented."

Aelus waved for them to lead him. Beckah guided them off, and before they went, Aelus glanced over at the physicker. "Use more of this combination if his heart rate increases."

The physicker nodded. "I will stay with him."

Aelus stared at him for a moment before nodding.

"Where is Master Helen?" Aelus asked Beckah.

"I don't know. I went looking for her, but I couldn't find her."

"Where do you think Master Helen would go?"

"Probably to the palace," Sam said.

Aelus stopped short and looked over to her. "The palace? Why would you say that?"

"Because I've seen her there," Sam said.

He frowned and then hurried forward, following Beckah to Alec's room.

When they reached the room, he hurried inside and looked around. There was something to the set of his chin and the way he looked at everything that reminded Sam of Alec. Much like Alec, Aelus seemed to take in everything with a single glance. Much like Alec, he had a certain wrinkle to his brow, and his jaw tilted just so to the side. The only difference was that Alec would tap his hand at his side as he thought whereas Aelus seemed to tap it on his cheek.

"What were you working on here?" he asked Beckah.

"We've been working on the easar paper," she said.

"He said he wasn't able to find the right combination."

"That's right. He's been trying something else."

"If he's been trying something else, it's not been here." His gaze drifted around the room before it stopped at the table. "Where did he get this?" He leaned over the table, his gaze skimming across the book. Sam came up behind him and looked over his shoulder.

She didn't recognize the writing. It wasn't the script that made it difficult. It was that the words were not familiar to her.

"I don't know. He had these too."

"These?"

Beckah pulled a few other books out from beneath the stack and handed them over to Aelus.

He thumbed through them quickly. "Marcella. What have you done?"

"Who is Marcella?"

"Marcella Rubbles. That must be where Alec obtained these books."

"And why is that a problem?" Sam asked.

"Because these—this one in particular," he said, tapping the book that still rested open on Alec's table, "will describe papermaking. This one is likely one of his mother's."

"His mother's?"

Aelus nodded. "Maybe I made a mistake telling him about her. I hadn't expected him to go looking for things she might have collected. I thought he might have known better than that."

"What is it about his mother?"

Aelus glanced over to Sam. "It doesn't matter."

Sam thought that it might, but she didn't press, not in this. There was no point, especially since there didn't seem to be anything Aelus was saying that would change their situation now.

"Beckah, do you know where he might have been working with Master Helen?"

Beckah shook herself. "If it's a classroom, then it would likely be one that wasn't used very often. Otherwise, they would have been noticed, which would have only raised questions."

"Why would there be questions raised?" Sam asked Beckah.

"Because Master Helen doesn't work with people very often," Aelus offered. "She is independent, almost fiercely so. It would attract attention." "And Master

Helen, of all people, would not want to attract unnecessary attention."

"Why do you say that?"

"It doesn't matter."

Beckah guided them out of Alec's room, and they closed the door, locking it quickly behind them. She raced down the hall and to another level of the university where Sam hadn't been before. Doors lined the hallway. Most were simple doors, though on each side of the door, there was a marking. It took a moment for her to realize that it was room numbers.

"These are the classrooms?"

"I haven't been here in…" Aelus shook his head. "It has been a long time."

"I don't know which one they would have been using."

"Which ones are typically used by the master physickers?" Aelus asked.

Beckah pointed. "Most of these front rooms are the ones used. They are little bit larger, and they have boards that can be easily written on. The ones toward the end of the hallway are rarely used."

"That's where they would have been," Aelus said.

They made their way down the hallway and stopped at each door where Aelus popped his head in, scanning the room before withdrawing and looking back around. Each time he did, he shook his head, and Sam sensed a growing irritation within him.

Her heart was racing, and it wasn't just because she had been hurrying with Aelus. Something was wrong with Alec, and she felt helpless, unable to help them, despite the fact that everything in her being told her that she needed to find a way to help him.

If she wasn't able to do so, what would happen to him?

Maybe nothing. But maybe he would never come around. Maybe the poisoning he was exposed to was similar to what had happened to Aelus.

"You think it could be eel venom?" Sam asked.

"If it were eel venom, he wouldn't have had the irregular heartbeat." Aelus sighed and squeezed his hands into fists. "Were it only so simple. At least with that, you have already proven that you know the antidote."

"I don't know that we've proven anything. I think we were just lucky."

"There was nothing lucky about it. Alec used his analytical skills to determine what was needed. I wish he were alert enough to assist us with that now."

"He often wished for your help when he was trying to work on you," Sam said.

"He always underestimated himself. He has earned every bit of his promotion within the university. He talks about years to be promoted to master physicker, but I suspect it will happen much sooner than that, at least if they can get over themselves and the fact that they weren't the ones to train him. I suspect there is some pride in them that prevents them from promoting him to master physicker, they would like to believe he doesn't have the necessary experience, but in many ways, Alec has much more experience than most of the physickers here."

They reached another door, and Aelus pushed it open. When he stepped inside, he froze. "This is it."

Sam followed him in with Beckah behind her. The room was surprisingly clean. There was a long table at one end of the room. Several other tables had been pushed off to the side, and now lined each of the walls.

Chairs were pushed up underneath them. On the long table at the front of the room was an enormous pot that emanated a stench. How had they not smelled it from the hallway?

"What is it?"

"He was attempting to make paper," Aelus said.

"In a pot?" Sam wasn't sure what it took to make paper, but she didn't think that it could be mixed like some concoction. Maybe she was wrong. Maybe Alec had discovered some magical way to make paper. Maybe easar paper required something very different. She had no idea what went into making paper.

"He was mixing the pulp. Pressed and dried, it would form sheets. This would be crude, but he's already starting to gain some skill." He fingered something in his pocket, and Sam suspected it was the book that he had claimed from Alec's room. "What was he doing? What was he getting himself into that would make it so challenging to restore him?"

Aelus stepped up to the pot and stuffed his head inside. He took a deep breath, closing his eyes. Sam resisted the urge to grab him and jerk him back. What was he thinking exposing himself to the fumes? They'd already seen how whatever Alec had been exposed to was enough to poison. Was Aelus willing to poison himself simply to discover what Alec had done?

"I don't detect anything obvious." He turned to Sam. "Do you have access to the eel venom?"

She shook her head. "Alec kept it." She blinked. "But it was in his room. I saw it there earlier. Both kinds. Why is it important?"

"I suspect what happened to him *is* related to the eel

venom, but not in the same way as I was afflicted. I think Alec, in his attempt to create easar paper, managed to poison himself in a different way."

"Can you reverse it?"

"Possibly. I need that eel venom. We don't have much time."

They raced back to Alec's room, and when they stopped there, the door was cracked open. Had it been that way when they left?

Sam didn't think so. She was certain that she had closed the door and sealed it tight.

Someone else had come.

She stepped in front of Aelus and Beckah and screwed the two ends of her canal staff together. Aelus watched her, eyes wide, and Beckah stared at her.

"That shouldn't be necessary, not here."

"It shouldn't be, but look at his room. Someone has been here."

And if someone had been here, there would be only one reason for them to have come.

When she stepped inside, she saw the room was empty. It was more of a mess than it had been before, and when she hurried over to the table, and looked down to the floor, she saw what she had feared.

The eel venom was gone.

13

FINDING HELP

The mess all around them left Sam uncomfortable. "What now?" Sam asked Aelus.

"You said Master Helen was working with Alec?" he asked Beckah.

"She was. But when I went looking for her, I couldn't find her…"

He closed his eyes. "Alec must've figured something out. He must've determine some way of mixing paper, though I'm not sure how he would have, especially since he shouldn't have been able to read what was written in that book."

"What if he didn't have to read everything in that book?" Sam asked.

Aelus frowned. "Why wouldn't he need to?"

"Well, shouldn't he only need to read the essential parts?" She glanced from Aelus to Beckah. "If this is all about making paper, and if that book," she said, pointing to the book in his pocket, "has some sort of recipe in it, then wouldn't he only need to find the recipe and repeat it?"

Aelus's eyes widened. "Samara, you are much brighter than I have given you credit for."

"Uh, I'm not sure I should be thankful for that. That seems almost like you're insulting my intelligence."

"Not an insult at all. I understand why Alec would be drawn to you. You have a quick intellect. Perhaps not the same studious knowledge he has, but there is something to be said about street smarts."

Sam grunted and shook her head. "All I want is some way to help Alec."

Aelus set the book down on Alec's table, flipped it open, and began thumbing through the pages. He moved quickly until he reached a middle section of the book where he began to slow, he turned one page back and forth, before settling on it and running his finger along the text.

"We need eel flesh," Aelus said.

"Eel flesh?" Beckah asked. "First the venom and now the flesh?"

"It has healing properties," Sam said. "Of course."

"I don't know that it will completely counter it, but if what I am reading here is accurate, then it should be able to. Or at least bring him around enough that he should be able to speak to us." Aelus looked up at Sam. "Do you happen to know if you have eel flesh?"

"I don't, and if Alec didn't have any in his room, then he doesn't, but I think I might know someone who will."

But could she reach Bastan in time?

"How long do you think I have? Wait… Why can't we use easar paper if we know what might help him?"

"Because I suspect the paper is what is causing his difficulty."

"Kyza!"

"I will try to keep him stable. I suspect Beckah will assist me," he said, glancing at Beckah. She nodded quickly. "You go, see if your crime lord friend can help us."

"I'd be careful who I'm calling a crime lord, poisoner."

Aelus's eyes narrowed. "Fine. Do what you can to help my son."

Sam wanted to like Alec's father, but he made it difficult. There was something almost arrogant about him. His thank-you for her saving his life had been half-hearted at best. She hadn't bothered checking his wound since dragging him to the university, but it must not be life-threatening, not if he managed to continue moving around as easily as he did. Every so often, he had touched his hand to his shoulder, and she suspected that he would need the assistance of a physicker, but who would Aelus trust?

Only Alec.

Sam raced from the building, once more drawing on her own augmentation, seeking strength, speed, and adding a lightness to herself, trying to find a way for her to move even faster. When she jumped across the canal, she soared, clearing it and going racing along the street. She moved faster than she ever had before, reaching Caster more quickly than she ever had.

When she found Bastan's building, she hammered on the door and was quickly let in, pushing past Michael and then past Ricken, before finally getting to the lower level where Bastan waited.

"Eel flesh."

Bastan looked up. He sat in a chair, a book flipped open on his lap. From where Sam stood, she could tell it was something relating to artwork.

"Can you put your damn book away? I need eel flesh. Do you have any?"

"Now tell me, Samara, why would I have eel flesh?"

"Because I am sure you've been harvesting them."

Bastan frowned. "And why do you need them?"

"Because Alec has been poisoned, and it's the only thing that might be able to help him."

Bastan sighed and went to the door, pulling it open and whispering something softly. He nodded to Sam when he was done, motioning for her to sit. She didn't want to sit. She wanted to pace. She wanted to think. She wanted to find some way—*anyway*—to help save Alec.

"It won't get here any faster by you pacing," Bastan said.

"I can't help it, Bastan. All I can think about is trying to find some way to get help for Alec."

"I know you care about him. All I'm trying to say is that you need to take a deep breath and wait. While we're waiting, you can tell me what happened. Tell me how he was injured."

"I don't really know. All I know is that he was working on making the paper and something happened during the process that left him sick. It… It's almost as if he was subjected to something with the easar paper, but…"

"What do you mean subjected to the easar paper?"

Sam looked around Bastan's small room. It was an outer area before it led into the cell where he held Marin. She wasn't surprised that she had found him here but was surprised that he seemed to stay here more often than not, especially lately. Was he finding out anything from Marin? Or was this mostly his way of keeping an eye on her and making sure that she didn't hurt anyone else he cared about?

"There is something the Thelns have, something that uses the easar paper. They call it the Book of Maladies."

Bastan started laughing, watching Sam. "That's quite the formal name."

"Maybe, but that's what they call it. They use the easar paper, and they have people who have placed a particular pattern on the easar paper which leads to power, and this power can be used to poison others."

Bastan frowned. "Poison?"

Sam took a deep breath, nodding slowly.

"This is what the business with the princess was all about?"

She nodded again. "She was caught up in it. Bastan, it's bigger than just the princess. It's bigger than Marin. It's—"

Sam didn't have a chance to finish. The door opened and Ricken entered, carrying a bundle wrapped in wax paper. He crinkled his nose as he held it out from him, lile he didn't want to have it in his hands.

Bastan quickly grabbed it from him and shook his head. "It's not going to hurt you."

"I heard what these damn things did to other people."

"These things? The creature is not living, and you aren't anywhere near the poison it carries. I think you're perfectly safe."

Ricken shivered. "That doesn't change the fact that I'm happy to have you hold it."

Bastan grunted. "Watch the door," he said.

He opened the wrapping and a stench wafted toward Sam. The eel flesh was gray and spongy and looked nothing like the deadly creature that she had seen in the canals.

"What does this have to do with helping your friend?"

"Because the eel flesh has healing properties," Sam said.

Bastan arched a brow. "Interesting. And the university knows this?"

"Some at the university do. Most of them don't. Those who do have chosen to keep it secret."

"Of course they have. Why share something that might be of benefit to countless others?"

"Because alive, the eels are of benefit of countless others," Sam said. "The eels protect the city, keeping the Thelns out. I'm not sure I understand how, but they have a purpose. If people knew the eel meat was curative, think of how they would hunt them."

Bastan grunted. "Fine. What's your plan with this?"

"I intend to see if it works with Alec."

He cast a glance over to the cell. "I will go with you."

"You don't have to do that, Bastan."

"I don't have to, but I want to. Your friend Alec is now my family too."

Sam would have argued, but she understood what family meant to Bastan. It was surprising the way he felt, especially considering what he was, but he felt very strongly about the people that worked with him, and firmly believed he needed to care for them, to provide for them, which was why he had done as much as he had for Sam.

They headed out, and with Bastan coming with her,

she had expected the journey to take longer, but Bastan had contacts at each of the bridges, not slowing them at all. He also knew the city incredibly well and guided her quickly from the Caster section to the university, taking the most direct path. Sam might have been able to go faster by jumping over the canals, but it wouldn't have been *much* faster.

When they reached the university, she took him around to one of the side entrances, not wanting to come in through the main door. Going that way would have delayed her unnecessarily, and she wanted speed.

"You know your way around here quite well," Bastan said.

"I've been here often enough," Sam said.

"At least you haven't been here as a patient," Bastan said.

Sam chuckled. She hadn't, but people that she cared about had been.

"It will be okay, Samara," Bastan said. He grabbed her wrist and turned her toward him. "I can tell you are nervous, and I know you worry about him."

"Of course I worry about him. We have a connection."

"It's more than this shared bond that the two of you have. I understand he is your Scribe, whatever that means for the two of you, but he is something else to you. You have someone you care for. I also know it's difficult for you to care."

"You've gotten sappy on me these days, Bastan."

"Not sappy. I just recognize there are things we need to not take for granted. People you care for are top on the list."

She stared at him for a moment before swallowing. "I

don't want to lose him. With everything that we can do, I…"

Bastan pulled her toward him and wrapped his arms around her, hugging her. "I will do everything in my power to help make sure that you don't lose him."

He said it with such a ferocity that Sam almost laughed, but coming from Bastan… He did have considerable power, so there was probably quite a bit he could do. But in this case, she didn't think his power could help, no matter how much he hoped it could.

They reached the hospital ward and Sam hurried in, scanning quickly to see if there was any sign of Aelus or Beckah. She found Aelus near Alec, and he was ministering to him, wiping something across his brow and stuffing something into his cheek.

"You brought the apothecary," Bastan said as they walked over.

"I went for him. The master physickers weren't available."

Bastan shot her a hard look. "You are at the university. How were the master physickers not available?"

Sam shook her head. "How am I to know? They weren't here."

Bastan practically growled. "I am growing tired of this division between highborns and lowborns. If it consumes one of their own, I think…"

Sam sighed. "You and Alec both."

"Why?"

"Because Alec is incredibly frustrated by the idea of a separation between highborns and lowborns too. He is frustrated by the idea that highborns are able to afford treatment while the lowborns are not. He thinks everyone should be able to be treated."

They reached Alec, and Aelus looked up, his eyes wide as he looked from Sam to Bastan.

"Did you get it?"

"We have it," Sam said.

"Let me see it."

Sam handed the bundle of eel meat over to Aelus. He took it, unfolding it, and cut off a section, quickly slicing it into thin fragments. When that was done, he began chopping it even more finely, swishing it into something that resembled a paste. He mixed that with a few drops of what appeared to be in the oil, and then stuffed that into Alec's mouth, shoving it all the way down into the back of his throat.

"Is that really necessary?" Sam asked.

"It doesn't look pretty, but it's the only way to ensure that the medicine gets as far down as possible— as quickly as possible."

"How much do you need to give him?" Sam asked.

"All of it," Aelus said.

Sam looked at the eel meet. "All of it?"

He nodded again. "I don't know what the proper amount is. I'm determined to give him every chance that I can. So, I will stuff as much of this I can down into him."

"And then what?" Sam asked, looking around the hospital ward before settling her gaze back on Alec. She couldn't tell if his breathing had changed. His skin looked pale, and she understood why Aelus was wiping his brow. Sweat beaded on it.

"Then we wait."

14

UNDERSTANDING AN ILLNESS

S omewhere, Sam had found a stool.

She sat crouched on the stool, looking over Alec, resting her elbows on the cot. Was he breathing more easily, or was it only her imagination? She'd lost track, not able to tell, and not certain whether she could trust her observations, anyway. Alec was the one who typically made observations, especially when it came to healing, not her. He would have laughed had he known she was trying to determine whether a patient was improving or not.

She wasn't the only one sitting at his bedside. Aelus had taken a stool and rested his head on his hands as he leaned forward. He murmured softly, speaking to himself. Sam had given up trying to understand what he was saying.

Bastan stood behind her, and his hands rested on her shoulders. Every so often, he would pat her shoulder, as if trying to reassure her, but it really didn't do much.

Beckah had stopped in a few times, but she continued

to search for the master physickers. So far, none had come in here.

"What is this?" a booming voice said.

Aelus jerked his head up and stood with a start. He looked toward the voice and frowned. "Carl."

The other man sneered at Aelus. He was enormous, with a huge belly that stuck out, and he strode forward with his hands clasped behind his back, marching through the ward like a man heading off to war. Sam knew from the name who he was. And she knew the master physicker had always had it out for Alec. "Aelus. Just because your son is a physicker doesn't mean that you have any right to be here."

"I can be here as a visitor," Aelus said.

"There are particular hours when you are allowed."

"It is between dawn and dusk," Aelus said.

"Not any longer," the physicker said.

Sam remembered what Alec had told her of this man. They didn't always get along, but he respected Carl's mind. Alec had claimed he was brilliant, and for Alec to make such a claim, she suspected he truly was.

"Alec was exposed to something," Sam said.

Master Carl frowned at her. "And who are you?"

Bastan stepped forward. "She is my daughter. And she is his… friend."

Master Carl took a look at Bastan and blinked. Bastan had that effect on many people, and even someone as massive and blustery as this Master Carl took a moment to reconsider when faced with the reality of Bastan.

"When student physicker Reynolds came to me with the report that one of our physickers was injured, I didn't realize it was Physicker Stross. What happened?"

Sam was pleased that he addressed Aelus, asking him what he knew. He lifted the binder at the end of the cot and began flipping through it. His brow furrowed as he read what was on the page. Would he be angry that Aelus had been the one to make documentation? Would he even know?

"It's all right there, Carl."

"This is you?" the physicker asked without looking up.

"I still recall how to document appropriately," Aelus said.

"I'm only asking because you have been gone from the university for so long," Master Carl said.

"Just because I've been gone doesn't mean I have forgotten everything that I learned when I trained here. In fact, from what my son has told me, there are many things I remember that others don't."

"Is this necessary?" Sam asked, stepping forward. "Is this helping Alec, any of it?"

Aelus shook his head. "You're right."

Master Carl looked at Sam, and he frowned for a long moment before glancing at Aelus and then back down to Alec. "What happened to him?"

"As Sam said, he was exposed to something," Aelus said. "He was attempting a mixture, and it is likely that there was something toxic in it."

Master Carl glanced back down at the binder and scanned the page. "None of these items are toxic."

"That was my thought, as well."

"Then what do you think?"

"Well, nothing that he's suffering from seems to be a typical symptom of any of the individual components, and even when mixed in combination, I don't think they would cause this level of impairment."

Master Carl took a deep breath, and then he nodded. "Agreed."

"Which makes me suspect there was something else added to it."

"Your son is nothing if not a diligent recorder of what he does. What do his notes say?"

Aelus shook his head. "His notes record only what I've shown you there."

"There has to be something else, and you must have missed it. It wouldn't be the first time you've made a mistake, Aelus."

Aelus took a step forward, and his jaw clenched.

Sam glanced over at Bastan. "I didn't realize physickers were as stupid as men from Caster."

Bastan chuckled. "Men are stupid regardless of where they come from, especially when they have a grudge against each other."

"How do you know they have a grudge?"

"Look at them," Bastan said. "Something happened between them."

Sam decided to ignore the two men arguing and looked down at Alec. This time, she was sure it wasn't her imagination. She was sure he was breathing differently. Color seemed to have returned to his cheeks, much more than had been there before. "Aelus?"

The two men continued their seething argument.

Sam gritted her teeth. "Idiots."

The two men looked over.

"I think you should look at your patient. Is it just me, or is Alec…"

Aelus hurried over and began to perform an assessment. Master Carl joined him, and together, they worked Alec over. As they did, she could tell that Alec was breathing more regularly. Every so often, his eyelids would flutter, and his fingers twitched.

"What did you treat him with?"

Aelus glanced up, appraising Master Carl as if debating whether to answer. "There are only a few compounds that provide the necessary healing effect when the treatment is unknown."

Master Carl's breath caught. "You know that's forbidden. You know the consequences if you attempt that. What would make you even think to try it?"

"Because this is my son," Aelus said. "Do you have a son, Carl?"

Master Carl frowned. "That has nothing to do with what the university has forbidden over the years. You know the price we all pay if that safety is compromised."

"I know much more than even the university."

Master Carl glared at Aelus. "I suppose you had a supply of this?"

Aelus shook his head. "He did," he said, motioning to Bastan.

When Carl looked up at Bastan, Bastan only tipped his head, as if shrugging. There was a hard edge to his eyes, and it was enough that Sam would have laughed, had the situation not been so dire.

"Alec?" she asked, taking his hand.

His eyes continued to flutter, and finally, they opened. "Sam? What are you doing…" He blinked. "Father."

Aelus leaned forward. "What were you doing? Where did you get that book?"

"That's your first question for me?"

"It shouldn't be the first, but I think it's the most important."

"If it was mother's…"

"If it was your mother's, then it would be even more dangerous for you to work through," Aelus said, glancing up at Master Carl.

"What is this?" he asked.

"It's nothing," Aelus said.

"It's more than nothing. And it likely has to do with you and now your son—a physicker at the university who hasn't been here long enough to understand exactly what it is he should and shouldn't do, especially when it comes to something like this."

"My son has been involved in far more than you understand," Aelus said. "And my son has been far more essential to—"

"I am well aware of what your son has done," Master Carl said. "He shares your arrogance."

"Arrogance? Alec?" Sam said.

Alec squeezed her hand, seeming to try to distract her.

Sam shook her head, getting annoyed. "I'm sorry, I don't know you," Sam said, stepping up to Master Carl. He was probably a foot taller than she was, and easily outweighed her by two hundred pounds, but she summoned all of the strength she had at her disposal, even going so far as to force an augmentation through her, drawing on strength she didn't necessarily feel. "We haven't met. My name is Samara Elseth."

"Is that supposed to mean something to me?"

"I don't know. How much time do you spend in the palace? If you would like to learn more about me, I would suggest you go to Princess Lyasanna. She would be happy to tell you all about me."

Master Carl paled. It was the necessary—and desired—effect. Sam remembered what Alec had said about Master Carl, and his political ambitions that had long ago failed. Throwing out the princess's name, whether or not she would vouch for Sam, seemed to be the most effective way she would get his attention. Even if Lyasanna didn't vouch for her, she would admit to knowing her.

"And if you would like to speak with someone at the university to reassure you that I am telling the truth, you can speak with Master Helen. I have spent some time with her in the palace, as well."

Master Carl stared at her for a moment before taking a deep breath and straightening his back. All it did was serve to jut his stomach out even more. It would have been comical if the situation wasn't so serious. "Fine. Now that it seems your… friend… is well, I will leave the two of you."

He turned and started away, casting a glance back at Aelus every so often before heading toward the double doors leading out of the hospital ward.

Alec let out a deep sigh. "What did you do to him?"

"I didn't do anything," Sam said. "It was mostly an empty threat."

"Not you," Alec said, trying to sit up. He was weak, and despite that, he managed to get up on his elbows, propping himself up so he could look around. "And your threat wasn't empty. If he goes to Princess Lyasanna, she at least has to admit she knows you. And if she doesn't, Elaine will." He looked over to Aelus. "What did *you* do to Master Carl?"

"It's a long story," he said. "And I'm just glad that you are here. I'm glad that we were able to get you out of it."

Alec looked around, seeming to realize for the first time that Bastan was there. He nodded to him, almost a sign of respect. That surprised Sam. She didn't know that Alec and Bastan had reached that point of connection. She wasn't surprised that Bastan would attempt to form that connection, especially since he saw himself as something of her father, but she was surprised that Alec had taken the time to work with Bastan.

"I don't understand what happened. I was following the instructions in Mother's book. It matched up with the other books, from what I was able to tell. Both Mother's book and the others described the process for making paper. I thought I would use that and see if it made the easar paper," he said. His voice was hoarse, but he was seeming to grow stronger the longer he talked. He looked at Sam more often than he looked at his father, seeming to avoid making eye contact with him. Hadn't they worked things out? Aelus had come, barely hesitating when Sam told him Alec needed him, so she had assumed that they had, but maybe the two of them still hadn't worked through the issues that had divided them.

"I don't think any of the ingredients you were mixing should have caused these symptoms, individually or in combination," Aelus said.

He held out the record and handed it over to Alec when he reached for it. Alec looked at the record of his own illness, scanning the page and nodding. "Nothing should have. I tested them individually, just to make sure, and even when I started mixing them, there was nothing more than the strange odor."

"There was more than a strange odor," Aelus said.

"You found it?"

Aelus nodded. "Your friend Beckah took us to the classroom. She was the one who helped us find where you and Master Helen were working on this project."

"Well, it had been me and Master Helen, but mostly it was me. Master Helen hadn't spent as much time working as I did. I think she was hoping to come in at the end and have the easar paper ready for her to use."

"This Master Helen, she is the same one I have met?" Bastan asked.

Aelus looked over at him. "How is it that you know her?"

"Possibly the same way that you know the Shuver."

Aelus paled.

Sam glanced from Bastan to Aelus. "Who is the Shuver?"

When Aelus didn't answer, she grabbed his shoulder, the one where he'd been stabbed. "Is the Shuver the same one who had something to do with this?"

Alec seemed to notice the injury to his father's shoulder for the first time. "What happened?"

"I went looking for your father, and I came upon two men who thought to attack him."

"They wanted to change the terms of the agreement," Aelus said.

"That is the Shuver," Bastan said. "Why were you doing business with him?"

"Who is the Shuver?" Sam asked.

Bastan snorted. "He is someone like me, and yet not like me. He works primarily in the eastern sections of the city and has a reasonable amount of power."

"Then like Ryn."

"Not like Ryn. He doesn't seek to expand his influence, not beyond what he already has. If he did, I would have eliminated him long before now." Bastan said it so matter-of-factly that Sam couldn't help but feel somewhat uncomfortable. "He serves his purpose. He is able to maintain stability in some of the more violent sections. And because of that, he allows trade to move through, the kind of trade the palace doesn't always allow to come into the city. With his access to the sea, that is meaningful to me."

It surprised Sam to hear Bastan talking so freely about his business ventures, especially here in the university, but then, Bastan had begun to speak more freely about them in general.

"He wanted a certain concoction," Aelus said.

"He wanted a poison," Bastan said. "And I have little doubt where he would use it."

"I didn't give it to him."

"Good. But if he comes to you again, I would suggest that you offer him an alternative."

"He's not going to come again," Sam said.

Bastan glanced over at her. "Just because you eliminated a few of his operatives doesn't mean others won't make their way to him. Do you think removing a few of mine would remove the threat of me?"

"Why do I get the sense that you're not concerned about him?" Sam asked.

"Because I'm not. We have worked together, so there's no reason for me to fear the Shuver. Besides, he knows that if he were to make a move on me, I would have him eliminated."

"If they come, they will likely try to kill me," Aelus said.

"Possibly, which is why you should simply offer them an alternative."

"What alternative?" Aelus asked.

"Offer him a poison, but make sure it's one that is not fatal. If you do this, I will be in your debt."

Sam cleared her throat. "If we're done with our underworld dealings, we need to get back to the matter at hand. We need to get back to figuring out what happened with Alec."

"I need to get back to the classroom," Alec said. He tried to step off the cot and put weight on his legs, wobbling slightly. Sam remembered how she had felt when she had been seriously injured, and how it had been difficult for her to get back on her feet and feel as if she could do anything. Then again, when she had been injured, she had broken her spine, and this was not quite as severe, though maybe it was more severe than she realized.

"Let me help you," she said, slipping Alec's arm around her shoulders. Bastan grinned at her as she did. She wanted to elbow him, or maybe kick him, but she did neither. "It would be helpful if the two of you gentlemen would lead us," Sam said.

"I know the way," Aelus said.

"Good, because you're going to have to be the one to guide Bastan." They made their way from the hospital ward, and Sam paused before deciding to grab Alec's record of treatment. She didn't know whether she should have left it behind, but if the combination of things that he had used to create the pulp was dangerous in any way, she didn't want to leave any documentation of it for others to find. And if it wasn't dangerous, but really did help create easar paper, she definitely needed to keep it out of the hands of others.

They made their way up the stairs and down the hallway. When they reached the end of the hall, the odor drifted from the room. It was stronger than it had been before.

"You are working on this?" Bastan asked, glancing back at Alec.

"It wasn't quite this awful."

"How were you able to stand it?" Bastan asked.

"As I said, it wasn't that bad, not until Master Helen came in and helped stir."

Bastan grabbed his arm, holding on to him. "What was that?"

Alec shrugged. "Only that the combination of things didn't smell quite as foul until Master Helen came in and began to help. I don't know if it was the timing, or if she had some different technique was stirring."

Bastan glanced from Aelus to Alec before looking down the hallway.

"I think we need to find another place to try this mixture."

"Why?" Alec asked.

"This Master Helen. You trust her?"

"I always have trusted her," Alec said.

"She is one of the brightest minds at the university," Aelus said.

"What is it, Bastan?" Sam asked. "I've seen that look on your face before."

"Just a hunch. And you know what I've told you about trusting your hunches."

Sam looked down the hallway. She had learned from Bastan that she needed to trust those hunches, and it had saved her more times than she could count. If Bastan had a hunch, she would trust his. He had been at it a whole lot longer than she had.

15

THE APOTHECARY

A lec tried not to look at the bloodstain on the floor of his father's apothecary. He tried not to think about what it meant that Sam had been the one to kill those two men Bastan had dragged out of the back door of the shop, depositing them on the street behind. He tried not to think of how Bastan intended to take care of the problem as he had said. He wasn't naïve. He had worked with Sam long enough and often enough to know that she had worked in the underworld, and Bastan had connections—and a distinct lack of scruples—but seeing it firsthand was quite a bit different.

"Why are we here?" Alec said. "We could have stayed at the university."

"At the university, we run the risk of someone coming in on us," Bastan said. "And this is all part of my hunch."

"Someone has already come here," Alec said. He couldn't take his eyes off the bloodstain. He seemed drawn to it, though maybe that was still his tiredness. He felt sick, not nearly completely restored, not the way that he thought he should, especially if he had been administered eel flesh. It was a curative, at least from what everyone said, which meant he shouldn't still feel quite as rundown as he did. And yet, he felt exhausted.

Aelus set the book down on the table and folded open the page. "Can you re-create this?" he asked.

Alec looked at the page. "I don't need the book to know what it says. I did memorize it."

"Of course you did. I just thought you might want the reference…"

Alec took a deep breath and began to mix the various ingredients of the concoction required to make the paper. When he was finished, he took it over to the hearth in the far corner of the shop. "This will smell," he said.

"What did you use for the svethwuud?" his father asked.

"I didn't know what that represented. I suspected it was some sort of tree, so that was the part I was going to try to work through, trialing various woods to see what might be the most effective."

"What did you start with?" Aelus asked. "I think we should re-create exactly what you had done, just as Bastan said."

"It was nothing more than maple." Maple was easy enough for him to acquire, and the wood had been listed in the back of one of the other books as a kind that would be helpful in papermaking.

"I think I have…" Aelus disappeared for a little while before returning with a hunk of wood. Alec cut it down, adding it to the pulp mix, and then placed it over the flame to boil. Every so often, he would pull the mixture off and stir it. It stank, but it wasn't anything like what he had smelled when he'd returned to the classroom.

"This isn't the same," Bastan said.

"It might just take longer," Alec said.

They waited, and the longer they waited, the more it became clear that nothing was going to change.

Maybe it was the combination he'd used. Could he have done it in a different ratio? If that were the case, it might throw off how effective the whole process was.

"I don't know what I did differently," Alec said. "If I had my notes…"

"I thought you said you had this memorized," Bastan asked.

"I did."

"Then you don't need your notes," Bastan said. "Besides, you have proven my suspicions," he said.

"And what suspicions are those?" Aelus asked.

"Only that something changed when Master Helen came." He looked from Alec to Aelus. "How well do you know her?"

"Well enough to know that she wouldn't do anything like that, and certainly not to Alec," Aelus said.

"No? And I believe Samara thought the same thing about Marin for a number of years. Most of the time, you don't know people nearly as well as you think you do. Most people allow themselves to have a public face and then there is the private face." He looked over to Sam, smiling widely. "Tell me, Samara, do you have a private face?"

She unfastened her canal staff and poked Bastan with one of the ends. "I'm going to smack you in your face if you keep up with this. What are you trying to get at?"

"Only that I think we need to see what else Master Helen might've added to that mixture."

"It's unsafe," Aelus said. "Until we know whether it was how Alec was poisoned, we really shouldn't go there."

"Someone has to," Sam said.

"Why?" Alec asked.

"Because we need to make sure no one else gets exposed to it. I can go."

Alec shook his head. "I've already fallen to it. I'm not even feeling back to normal. I don't want you to subject yourself to it."

"I don't have to, not entirely. I can use augmentations and find a way to seal myself up."

"Augmentations don't work like that, Sam."

"They do if you document the right way," she said.

Alec sighed and licked his lips. They were dry, and he worried that they would be cracking. Maybe there was something in the combination that was an irritant. Then there was the sickly way that he felt. His energy continued to drain away from him. That was most likely a result of the poisoning and his subsequent recovery, but if there was anything else to it, he would need to investigate further.

"I don't know that it's safe for me to assist you with an augmentation, Sam. I'm just recovering…"

Maybe that would be enough to keep her from attempting to go back to the university and risk herself.

"I don't need to have you help me with the augmentation."

Bastan arched a brow. "I thought the two of you needed to come together, and you needed the use of the paper."

"And you know Marin has been sharing a few secrets with me," she said.

"I've heard the sorts of things she has told you. Nothing that would be of much use in this case."

"They were more useful than I realized," Sam said. "And I was able to at least understand some of what she was trying to teach me. Part of it is how to add an augmentation on my own. That's why Marin has been so difficult for us to contain."

Alec licked his lips again. If Sam was able to place augmentations on her own, she didn't need him, not anymore. That left him feeling strange. Then again, if she didn't need his assistance for augmentations, maybe it meant that he could remain at the university and continue his studies.

But that disappointed him, as well. He wanted to head out, and he wanted to reach the Theln lands, if only to learn what was so tempting to the other Scribes. There had to be something there that drew them, that encouraged them to give up their connection to the city and to their Kavers.

"I don't like the idea of you doing this," Alec said.

"Neither do I," Bastan said. "Maybe we should send one of my men."

"Who?" Sam asked. "Who would you trust to do this, and who would you trust not to get hurt in the process? I can do this. Besides, if I don't do this, it's possible others will be hurt." She looked at Alec, meeting his gaze. She always knew exactly what to say to convince him to help. She knew exactly what would be the most meaningful to him.

"I don't know that you should go alone," Alec said. "I

can go with you."

"You said you were weak."

His father approached, and he pressed his fingers to Alec's neck. "You were given eel meat. You shouldn't still be sick."

"I don't know what I should or shouldn't be, all I know is the way I feel," Alec said.

"Tell me," his father said.

There was something in his tone that reminded Alec of when he reported on other people's illnesses. This time, he would be forced to report on his own. "It's a sort of nausea. It sits in the pit of my stomach, a nagging sort of discomfort. That combined with the overall sense of malaise, feels like my energy continues to drain from me, makes it feel like I just need to sleep. I feel like I could lie down and rest for hours. Days even. And then there is the weakness."

"What weakness?" his father asked.

"I don't know how to describe it. It's my arms and legs. I feel generally weakened."

His father frowned, tapping the side of his cheek. He did that when he was thinking, and Alec wondered what his father might be thinking about now. What was it that Alec had told him that troubled him, because the expression on his face was definitely a troubled expression.

"Father?"

"The eel meat should have restored you," his father said. "It's not only a curative, but it also adds something of an energy boost. It's not well understood, but typically, it lasts for several days, often longer. That's the reason the university has forbidden its use. If others were to gain access to the eel meat, they would use it, likely stay awake for days on end, and eventually, the supply of eels would be destroyed."

"Maybe you didn't give him enough," Sam said.

"He was given an entire eel. That is much more than most have been given. Seeing as how I didn't know exactly what he was suffering from, I thought that the most prudent. There is no harm in administering too much."

Alec looked at his father, trying to understand. "If this was a restorative, and it failed…"

"It is most unusual," his father agreed.

"There is only one other instance of me coming into contact with something that failed to respond to treatment," Alec said.

"But you weren't exposed to the Book," Sam said.

He wasn't, but he had been exposed to the same substances, hadn't he? He had been working with a combination of things that theoretically would create easar paper. What if he had done something—and what if the poisoning did something—that had caused him to fall ill?

"I know that I wasn't exposed to the Book, but…" He looked over to Bastan. Maybe Bastan was right to think there was more to what happened to him. Maybe Master Helen was responsible for much more than he realized.

If that was the case, then he needed to get back there with Sam. The two of them needed to make sure no one else was harmed.

"I see that look on your face, Alec," Sam said.

"I need to be there. I need to be a part of going back."

Bastan glanced from Sam to Alec before shrugging. "It seems we are all going back."

CLOSING THE CLASSROOM

S am looked over at Alec as they headed up the stairs into the university. It was late, night having long since settled, and everything in the university had a sort of quiet about it, almost a stillness. The air had a pungent aroma, and it left her worried that perhaps the stink from whatever Alec had been mixing had now permeated the rest of the university. That shouldn't have been the case, especially since the stench had been contained in the classroom, at least it had been before they had left the university to go to Aelus's shop, but maybe it had.

Alec leaned on her as they walked.

It was becoming increasingly evident that something wasn't quite right with him. Whatever he'd been exposed to, consuming the eel meat had not restored him completely.

"We could try the easar paper," she whispered.

"I don't know that we can," he said. "If this is similar to the Book, there may not be anything that we can do."

"Don't speak like that, Alec."

"I'm being realistic," he said. "It's not that I want to give up hope. It's just that I understand there may not be anything that can be done."

"We will wait and see what we discover with your experiment," his father said.

Alec only stared straight ahead, saying nothing.

Sam didn't like the fact that Alec seemed to have given up. It had happened far more easily than what she was expecting. He was always the one to keep her motivated, the one who tried to encourage her. So now that he needed her, she would be the one to lift him up.

"I'm not going to let anything happen to you," she said.

"I don't know that you can decide that," he said.

"No one gets to tell me what I get to decide," Sam said with a smile.

She had hoped that it would draw out a reaction from him, but it didn't.

He kept a serious expression on his face as they reached the upper level, and they headed toward the classroom. The smell as they neared was almost over-whelming.

"They shouldn't have been able to hold classes here," Alec said.

"There have been no classes," a voice said behind them.

Sam spun, readying to grab for her canal staff, when she saw an older-looking man. He had gray hair and was medium build.

Alec smiled at him. "Master Eckerd?"

"Are you responsible for this?" he asked.

"I'm not responsible. I was trying to—"

"You were trying to make easar paper."

Alec swallowed. He glanced over at Sam who nodded

at him. "I was trying to make paper. And if it happened to be easar paper, then so be it."

"Carl spoke with me. He said your father had returned to the university. I didn't believe it, as he hasn't been back here in years, but now I see him with my own eyes." He turned his attention to Aelus. "Is this your doing? Are you the reason that he risked so much attempting to create easar paper?"

"I would never have asked him to do that."

"But you did treat him with eel meat in an attempt to restore him."

"There was no choice."

"I had already harvested the eels," Bastan said.

Master Eckerd seemed much less impressed with Bastan than Master Carl had been, and he shot Bastan a withering look. To Bastan's credit, he didn't shrink away from it. Sam didn't think Bastan shrank away from anything.

"Did Carl go to you?" Aelus asked.

He turned his attention to Master Eckerd and seemed to glare at him. Sam was surprised. It seemed most of the masters were irritated by Alec's father. Was it all because he had abandoned his opportunity to be a master physicker? Or was there more to it?

"Carl did tell me that he had made a mistake with thinking to use the eels. I didn't realize that you would have been involved with it."

"I don't disagree that harvesting the eels randomly is inappropriate, but I do think there are times when the eels can be useful."

"Such as when someone you care about is suffering?" Master Eckerd asked.

"Such as when there is an unknown poisoner involved," Aelus said.

"And you think you should be the only poisoner, is that it?"

"It didn't work," Alec said, stepping between his father and Master Eckerd. "The eel flesh didn't make a difference. I'm better, but I'm not well."

"That shouldn't happen," Master Eckerd said. "We know the benefit of eel flesh. That's the reason that it's limited, restricted to—"

"I know what it's restricted to," Aelus said. "And it didn't work."

"It's possible that you didn't give him the right amount."

"I fed him an entire eel."

Master Eckerd's eyes widened. "Then I don't know what to say."

"That's why we're here," Aelus said. "I wanted to see whether there was anything here that would explain what happened to him. The paper Alec was attempting to make shouldn't have done this. There wouldn't have been anything in the pulp mixture that would be dangerous to him."

"We evacuated this level. The fumes were too irritating to most."

"That's good," Bastan said.

"And who are you?" Master Eckerd asked.

"I'm someone you don't need to worry about."

"You're in my university. I think I will worry about whoever I choose to worry about. Tell me what you are doing here."

"I have come with Physicker Stross and his Kaver friend."

Master Eckerd's breath caught. "Stross. You should have been more careful with who you share with."

Alec flushed, and Sam patted him on the arm. "It doesn't matter. Bastan isn't going to say anything about us."

"Bastan?" Master Eckerd asked, glancing from her to Bastan. "The Bastan?"

"You've heard of me. That is good. Then you know what I will do, and what I'm willing to do."

"I've heard of what you have done. I've heard of the people you hurt."

"Then you've only heard rumors," Bastan said.

Master Eckerd glared at him before shaking his head. "We can't get any closer. The room is dangerous, and with whatever fumes are there…"

Sam flashed a smile. "This is where I need to come in."

Alec turned to her. "I don't know that it's safe for you to do it," he said. "I think that if you try to get too close, you will end up like me."

"I won't end up like you. I just need to dispose of the liquid."

"Not all of it," Aelus said. "We need a sample so that we can test it. Most of it needs to be covered, or better yet, countered. I don't know that there's any good place to dispose of it."

"How can I counter it?" Sam asked.

"You will need some way of thickening the solution. If Alec was making paper, then it would be quite thick already, but you will need some way—"

"Flour," Bastan said. When they all looked at him, he

shrugged. "If you're looking to thicken a mixture, add flour. I imagine even the university has supplies of flour?"

Master Eckerd frowned and finally nodded.

"Good. We will need as much as you can give us. Samara, when you take it in there, you can dump it into the mixture," Bastan told her.

"I need something to put the sample in," she said.

"There should be a jar. It would be kind of like the one that we used to hold the eel venom, Alec said."

Master Eckerd stared at him. "Not just eel flesh, but you have harvested eel venom?"

"Had you been around, I would have shared that with you, but I haven't been able to talk to you about what I've been doing."

"Because I've been pulled…"

"Pulled where?"

"Pulled by the"—he glanced from Bastan to Aelus to Sam—"the palace. They have had assignments for me."

"A Scribe?" Aelus asked.

"Can we have this conversation later," Sam said. "I'd rather just get this over with so I can get away from the stench that's in the hallway. Then again, I'm not sure I'll be able to get away from that until Bastan leaves."

He glared at her, and she flashed a smile.

"One of us needs to go get flour," Sam said.

"I think Eckerd here knows the way," Bastan said. "I will go with him."

Master Eckerd's eyes widened, but he nodded to Bastan. They hurried off, leaving Sam, Alec, and Aelus alone in the hallway.

"Those two…" Alec started, but he took a deep breath, his strength fading.

Aelus glanced over at Alec. "I don't know how long we can wait. I don't have any more eel flesh, and until we figure out what has happened, there's no good way of keeping him well."

"I could go in and get a sample, and we could begin trying to understand what happened to it a little sooner."

Aelus glanced from Sam to Alec. "I think it might be necessary."

"No," Alec said, but his voice was weak.

She couldn't wait. Waiting any longer would end up with Alec back in the same condition he had been in before. And maybe that would happen regardless, but she wasn't willing to do nothing, not while Alec suffered.

She focused on an augmentation. This time, she focused on how she wanted to feel, letting the sense of the augmentation wash through her. She needed an ability to resist illness, and she needed an ability to move quickly, and she might need skin that was impervious, all things that she wasn't sure she could manage at one time. Had Alec the ability to augment her, maybe she could, but without him, and with him in this state, she didn't dare risk him getting weaker by trying to place an augmentation.

"Sam..."

"Alec just rest. I'm going to go in there and—"

Alec shook his head. "I don't know what the fumes might do. I didn't ingest anything, so it had to have been the fumes. You can't breathe when you're in there, and if there's any way of sealing yourself..."

Alec sank to the ground, and Aelus crouched next to him, quickly examining him.

"Is he..."

"He's alive. His heart is regular. I think he's simply exerted himself too much." He stood and looked over at Sam. "The eel meat should have been enough to have restored him. It troubles me that he is like this so quickly after consuming it."

"What does he mean by sealing myself off?"

Aelus sighed and ran a hand through his hair, scratching his head for a moment. "He's right. If there are fumes that are toxic, you don't want it reaching any of your inner tissues."

"Like my nostrils?"

Aelus nodded. "Your nose. Your mouth. Everything must be covered. You can't breathe, which means you need to move quickly. And…" He looked down the hallway, toward the classroom. "We're going to have to be somewhere else. As soon as you open that door, the fumes are going to escape. If they are dangerous and more than simply irritating, we need to make sure that we aren't nearby. I don't know how much more Alec can withstand."

"You take him. I will move as quickly as I can," Sam said.

Aelus lifted Alec, scooping him off the ground with a grunt. He started along the hallway, and when he reached the stairs, he veered off into a nearby room.

Hopefully, that would be enough.

It left her with no choice but to get moving.

She needed some way of covering her mouth. Her cloak would work, but not in this way. She pulled it off, twisted around, and arranged the hood so that it could be pulled up and tied around her mouth and nose, leaving only her eyes visible. She could breathe through it, though if Aelus was right, she didn't want to breathe at all.

And now she needed to hurry.

Sam ran toward the room. She focused on her augmentations, feeling them wash over her as she ran, and reached the door at the end of the hallway.

When she pulled it open, the smell nearly made her gag. That would have been a mistake, and she thankfully had enough presence of mind to keep from gagging. She hurried inside, closing the door behind her, trapping the fumes and with her. Where was the jar?

Alec claimed there would be one here, and she needed to find it.

She spotted it on the corner of the table.

Sam grabbed it and reached for the pot. It was boiling, and she realized that a flame still burned beneath the pot, continuing to cook whatever Alec had been working on. She turned the flame off, tamping down the oil, and then lifted the pot, her augmentations making that easier than it should have been, and poured a little bit into the jar.

She was running out of breath. Eventually, and much too soon, she would need to take a quick breath, but she didn't dare, not yet.

Was there some way she could cover the pot? Was there some way she could protect anyone else from getting exposed to this?

She needed something large enough to place over top of the pot.

But what?

The tabletop.

She set the pot on the ground and ripped the top of the table free. It came with the tearing of wood, and she grunted unintentionally, expelling almost the last of her breath, and kicked, splintering the wood. She slammed it on top of the pot, covering it and trapping the fumes inside.

Sam scooped up the jar and raced out.

17

SEARCHING FOR A MASTER

Alec rested on his bed, leaning against the wall. His gaze drifted around his room, settling first on his desk, and then on the people in the room with him. Fatigue overwhelmed him. He was tired and wanted nothing more than to go back to sleep, but he couldn't. Not while they still were trying to understand what had happened.

"We will find her," Sam said.

Alec was shaking his head. "Beckah shouldn't have been gone this long. She was looking for Master Helen..."

"We looked in the masters' section," Sam said. "We have looked everywhere. She's. not anywhere in the university."

Alec frowned. "She wouldn't have left. She would have been just as worried about me as anyone else."

He tried not to meet Sam's eyes when he said that.

"I know she would have," Sam said. "And we're doing all we can to find her."

But it wasn't all they could do. Sam wasn't looking for

Beckah herself, which he understood. She wanted to be with him, should he need her help. But it meant more really could be done. But Sam wasn't the one who should be doing it. It should be him, but he was too tired, too weak, and didn't feel he had the energy he needed to go after her.

When was last time he had seen her?

It was a while ago. Sam told him that Beckah had been there when he was sick, waiting by his bedside, but she had gone after Master Helen to find out what she might know, and then… Then she hadn't returned.

As much as his mind tried to refute the idea, he had a growing fear that Master Helen was somehow involved. How else could he explain the fact that the fumes had worsened after Master Helen had come in and stirred the mixture?

"What is it?" Sam asked.

Bastan looked over from the row of books he'd been looking through. All of them were notes that Alec had taken since coming to the university, all of them documenting illnesses he had treated, and people he had worked on, integrated with his notes from lectures. Nothing there was secretive, at least not so much that he cared whether Bastan looked at it.

"It's Master Helen," Alec said.

"You worry that she's involved," Bastan said.

Alec nodded.

"You should. It's the only thing that seems to make any sense. It's the only part that connects everything else. You said she had come in shortly before the fumes became unbearable. What you need to determine is what reason she would have to poison you."

"She shouldn't have any reason to poison me. She's a Scribe, and she works at the palace."

"That would be the reason," Sam said softly.

"What?"

Sam shrugged. "It's possible that she's working with Princess Lyasanna."

"Why would the princess want to harm me?"

"Because it would harm *me*," Sam said.

Alec shook his head. "That doesn't make any sense. The princess—"

"The princess has already proven she's willing to do things that others would disagree with," Sam said. "And maybe Lyasanna learned that we know what she'd done. Maybe she knows we captured Marin."

"There should be no way Helen would have known," Bastan said.

"If she did, then we need to go after her."

Alec wasn't sure there would be any way to find Master Helen. If she wasn't in the masters' section, and if she did have ties to the palace, how would they find her? All of this made his head swim, making it difficult for him to think what more he could do. He had no answers.

The door opened, and his father entered. He was disheveled, his face gaunt, and his eyes had that look about them that warned Alec something was wrong.

"What is it?"

"It's the poisoning," Aelus said.

"What about it?"

"I don't really understand it. There was something added, but I'm not able to isolate it."

Bastan stood and dusted his hands on his pants. "So now, it is my turn to try."

Master Eckerd had followed Aelus into the room, and a grin spread across his face. "You? You would have us believe that you are some sort of physicker as well? Have you been secretly training with Aelus?"

"No. Mine is about finding information. If this Master Helen is still in the city, I will find her."

Bastan turned and started from the room. Sam glanced over at Alec, tipping her head, before hurrying after him.

It left Alec alone with his father and Master Eckerd.

"You shouldn't have tried this, Physicker Stross," Master Eckerd said.

"I shouldn't have, but I—"

"Why shouldn't he have?" his father asked.

"He understands the danger of easar paper. If he understands that, and he understands attempting to make it has potential complications, then he should have involved—"

"Involved what? Who? He's already had Master Helen working with him, and somehow, she has disappeared. If she is involved in this, and if there is something more taking place because of Master Helen, we need to know and understand."

Master Eckerd took a deep breath and turned to Alec. "I shouldn't have avoided you. I should have trusted my own feelings," he said.

"Why did you stay away?" Alec asked.

"There were needs within the palace."

"What kind of needs?"

He glanced over at Aelus before turning his attention to Alec. "Things I can't talk about."

Aelus laughed. There was bitterness in his voice, a

tone Alec was not entirely familiar with. With a sudden moment of clarity, he wondered if something had changed in his father after his poisoning. When his father had been subjected to the eel venom, had he become different? Alec had thought he'd cured him, but maybe the curing had been incomplete. Alec wasn't entirely sure what it was, but his father seemed a different man. Maybe it was simply Alec who had changed. Maybe it was his interaction with his father that was different rather than his father having actually changed.

"My son is a Scribe. My son has fought the Thelns and helped push back the threat within the city multiple times. My son has—"

"I'm not talking about your son."

Aelus sighed. He tipped his head and flashed a tight smile at Master Eckerd. "Fine. I will give you a chance to speak to my son. Maybe you can reveal to him what he needs to know. Besides, maybe it's time for me to return to my shop."

"You could stay here," Alec said.

His father glanced over to Eckerd. "I think... I think after seeing what everything is like at the university, it's probably for the best I've stayed away."

He stepped from the room and pulled the door closed. Master Eckerd studied the door, a frown on his face as he turned to Alec, squeezing his hands together. He scanned the room before taking a seat in the chair behind Alec's table. "All of this is unfortunate, Alec."

"What? The fact that you have to share with me what you know about being a Scribe?"

"The fact that we have to have this conversation at all.

There was a time when all master physickers at the university were trained as Scribes." Alec turned his attention to the door, thinking of his father. "Yes, even him. He would have made a good Scribe, had he wanted to. He had the talent and the potential, and I suspect he still does, but there is more to it than that." Master Eckerd shrugged. "I can't really explain it. All I can say is that we once were more than what we are."

"What changed?"

"There is much that has changed. It has been decades since we were as strong as we once were. Oh, the university hasn't changed, not that much. Other than the fact that there are fewer and fewer who come to us with the appropriate skill set, but beyond that, we still train physickers, it's just that training anyone other than physickers is less and less common."

"What about Master Carl?"

"Carl… He is a unique case. He has the talent and the potential to do great things, but he has chosen a different path. It's not that he couldn't be a Scribe. He simply hasn't chosen to apply himself in such a way."

"It's more than simply applying oneself," Alec said.

"For the most part, it is. There is a certain level of choice that goes into it. And then, there is a certain level of experience that goes into it. There is exposure, and… We also only offer testing to those who have potential."

"How do you know?"

"The bloodlines are quite clear."

"What do you mean?"

"We have records, dating back centuries, about the bloodlines of people within the city who would have potential to be Scribes."

"And that's why most of the physickers come from the highborn sections?"

"That's…"

"There is something to it, Master Eckerd. How many lowborn physickers are there?"

"There are none."

"And is that because you haven't offered, or is it because they don't have the potential?"

"It's because we have lost track." He sighed and looked at the books on Alec's table. "It becomes more and more difficult to follow people when they move to the outer sections. Even tracking you when your father moved you to your section. The merchant sections are difficult for us to have much of a presence, and try as we might, we simply can't follow everyone."

"But you don't even try."

Master Eckerd sniffed. "You are one of the first people in a long time to care about such things. I think if you were to remain at the university, you might cause great change. I suspect that is why I have been tasked with keeping an eye on you."

"Tasked by who?"

"Tasked by those who sit even higher than me."

Alec tried to focus on the words. He didn't think the poisoning had gotten any worse, but he did think he was getting more tired again. He would have to rest soon, but when he did, he would not be able to offer any assistance in their searches. For Master Helen. For Beckah.

"Who sits even higher than you?"

"That… That is a difficult answer."

"Is it the king? Is it people in the palace? Is it—"

"The Anders family came to the city, settling here

centuries ago, solidifying their rule over the city," Master
Eckerd started. His voice took on the tone and inflection
of someone giving a lecture. "When they came to the city,
this place was little more than a collection of villages, set
on two distinct islands that were naturally occurring at
the time. They sought this place out, wanting it for its
isolation." Master Eckerd looked up and met Alec's eyes.
"Have you ever given much thought to why we are
isolated in the way we are? We have the swamp to the
north. We have the steam fields to the west. We have the
ocean to the east and south. All of it making us quite inaccessible. Oh, skilled merchants can sail here, but even they
have a difficult time making it through the harbor. It takes
knowledge, and it takes flat-bottomed boats to travel out
to them, to ferry in everything off those ships before
bringing them into the canals and through the rest of the
city. Barges like that are not meant for warfare, which
keeps the sea inaccessible."

"What are you getting at?"

"What I'm getting at is that the Anders family ran from
something centuries ago, Alec. Those of us with any sort
of power are descended from those who came here
long ago."

"I'm not descended from them." If anything, he might
be descended from Thelns.

"You are a Scribe. Because of that, you have abilities
others do not."

"What does this have to do with anything?"

"We had peace for a long time," Master Eckerd said.
"From what I can ascertain, and my ability to reach
records that old is limited, restricted the same as yours
would be, tells us that we came here to get away from

violence. That was the reason the Anders settled in a place that would be mostly inaccessible. They were safe. The people of these lands were welcoming, and as the Anders demonstrated abilities and magics the people here did not possess, they gradually took on more and more power, ultimately ruling. They shifted the center of power to the place where it now stands."

"The palace?"

Master Eckerd shook his head. "The university."

"What?"

"The first Scribes were the original rulers here. The Kavers protected them."

"I don't understand. I thought the Anders family ruled in the city."

"Over time, the family has changed, but for the most part, the university still sets policy within the city. The royal family is perceived as ruling, but only because it draws attention to them rather than to us."

"So, the Scribes—"

"There are only a few people who understand the true nature of the politics within the city. Even I don't understand, not entirely."

"And Master Helen?"

"Master Helen has sat on the ruling council for a long time."

"Then why would she have attempted to poison me?"

"I'm not certain that she did."

"It's the only thing that makes sense," Alec said. "The mixture I was working on was not enough to do this to me. We tested it at my father's apothecary shop."

"If she did, then there was a reason for it. Perhaps that

reason is she believed you threatened the safety of the city."

"It doesn't have anything to do with the fact that the princess attempted to murder her son?"

Master Eckerd frowned. "The princess has no children. She has chosen to continue her studies, wanting to develop as a Scribe. She has said that will be her focus, at least for now."

"Since you have shared so much with me, let me share something with you," Alec said. Master Eckerd leaned forward, resting his elbows on Alec's table as he listened. "The princess made a trip to the Theln lands."

Master Eckerd frowned and nodded. "That was many years ago. How is it you know of it?"

"When she was there, she met a Theln by the name of Ralun. He is some sort of royalty there. As far as I can tell, while she was there, she and Ralun had an intimate relationship. She had a child. That child would be half Anders and half Theln." Alec decided not to tell Master Eckerd that the child had been born half Kaver and half Theln. "And when she realized what she had done, she ordered the Kaver who served her to destroy the child. That Kaver refused, instead rescuing—I guess kidnapping—the child, bringing him here, and offering herself as his protection. But she didn't think that was enough. She decided she needed to ensure others with power didn't try to destroy this child if they ever discovered him. She needed a different sort of protection. And so she managed to convince another, the same age as this child, and together they grew up as brother and sister."

Master Eckerd stared at him, blinking. "Marin?"

"Marin. She was assigned to kill Princess Lyasanna's

son. She refused, and she escaped with that unborn child. She raised him but stayed distant enough that he didn't know anything. He believed he had lost his mother, but he lost his father, and knew only his sister."

Master Eckerd gasped. "Your Kaver. That's what you're trying to tell me, isn't it?"

Alec nodded.

Master Eckerd looked down at his hands. "I was on that trip," he said. "At least, in a way. The Kaver I serve was there, and she took a supply of our blood, prepared for any augmentation she might need. I felt several of them as they swept through me. I know something happened, and that when they returned, one of the greatest Kavers in the city was gone, dead."

"You still haven't answered my question," Alec said.

"The Thelns continued to offer peace. There had been no fighting with the Thelns for... a long time. As far as I know, it had been a decade since there had been any fighting with them. They were content to leave us alone in the city, content to not pressure us here, as we were too isolated. There was nothing for them to gain by coming here. Instead, we sent envoys every few years, and those envoys would always return to ensure peace remained. Occasionally, some would stay behind—"

"Scribes?"

Master Eckerd nodded. "Scribes would remain. Always Scribes. It got to the point where those who went no longer took Scribes along, knowing that it was possible those who did go would be corrupted, and coerced into staying behind."

"What happened then? Why have the Thelns begun to attack?"

"Princess Lyasanna went on that envoy. We always ensured that somebody with some rank would go. They had to be high enough ranking that it was believable. Typically, we sent Kavers, and since the Anders have always been Kavers, Princess Lyasanna was chosen."

"But she's a Scribe."

"It was a risk, but we thought… we thought she might have a different perspective. Having her back was a relief. It was dangerous for her to go, at least in hindsight. At the time, those who were with her said she was never in any danger."

"Did they talk about her relationship with Ralun?"

"Those who went didn't talk about anything, other reporting that the Thelns had refused the peace that was offered. They returned, claiming that peace talks had failed. It was the first time that had happened in many years."

"And then what happened?"

"And then we began to train. We began to prepare. And we began to lose those with abilities. It began slowly, but the numbers increased over the years."

Alec leaned his head back against the wall and closed his eyes, trying to think. What Master Eckerd was telling him was important, but he couldn't think straight. He couldn't think about why it was important and what he needed to do, if anything.

"We need to know what happened back then," he said to Master Eckerd.

"There is no way for us to know. Short of Princess Lyasanna sharing, and I suspect if what you've told me is true, she will do everything she can to protect herself and her secrets. We have no other source who could tell us what we need to know."

Alec breathed out heavily. He needed a way to find out what had happened decades ago. Strangely, that seemed to be pivotal now. And it might even help him help Sam. If they understood what had happened, they might be able to get to Tray more easily, even use that to convince Ralun and keep him from destroying them.

That was if Alec was allowed to go. He wasn't sure it was a journey he was fit enough to take, not anymore. As weak as he felt, he might have to remain in the city and let Sam go on her own.

That pained him.

"What is Master Helen's role?"

"Master Helen is a Scribe, you know that."

"And who is her Kaver?"

"I'm not supposed to say. That is reserved for only the inner circle of master physickers."

"I thought you were going to continue sharing."

Master Eckerd breathed out heavily. "Her Kaver is the king."

18

CHASE

Sam chased Bastan down the hallway, catching him as he neared the stairs that would lead down and back out of the university. Lanterns glowed softly on the walls. The halls were lined with smooth marble, polished and gleaming, giving the entire university an almost palatial feel. She wasn't sure why she had never noticed that before. The only place where it felt different was the hospital ward, the place where people from outside were sequestered.

"What are you doing, Samara?"

"I'm going to help you."

"This is something I have the capacity to do myself. I'm not sure you are able to help with this."

"You're going after information about where to find Master Helen."

"I am."

"And then I am going to go after information."

He glanced over. "I think Marin has shared with you about everything she can, at least everything she will."

"We haven't ever asked her specifically about Master Helen."

"Do you think that will matter?"

Sam shrugged. "I don't know if it will matter or not. All I know is that somehow, we have to get this resolved so that I can go after Tray." That still drove her. She needed to finish this task so she could move on to the next one. It felt like barriers were being continuously put in front of her, blocking her from what she needed to do. Alec's poisoning being the most disturbing event so far. She didn't mind staying in the city and continuing to parse through everything that cropped up, but eventually, she would need to go and reach her brother. She would need to know what danger he was in with the Thelns. She would need to stop them from damaging him and leading to greater damage in the city.

"I don't know what matters anymore. I thought that when I gained these powers, and when I began to understand everything I could do, I wouldn't feel quite so helpless. No matter how much strength I can augment, no matter how much my skills improve, I still feel like I'm not enough."

Bastan stopped her outside of the university on the lush, rolling lawn. Trees dotted the grounds, and flowers were planted in beds, giving a fragrance to the air. "You should never question whether you're enough. Everything that you have done has proven you are stronger than you let on. I know that you blame Marin for everything she did to you, but in a way, I think you should be thankful of what she allowed you to do and see. Were it not for Marin, you would never have realized the strength you possess. You never would have known the depths of abilities you have. And you never would have—"

"Yeah. I know. I never would have known my brother."

"I wasn't going to say that. I was going to say that you never would have known me."

He guided her to the bridge leading them off of the university section. Like all bridges in the central sections, the stonework was exquisite. As they neared the outer sections, the bridges were more dilapidated, stone crumbling in places, though still quite stout. Masons worked diligently to repair the stone as needed throughout the central portions of the city, but they were less likely to spend time in the outer sections. It was left to the citizens of those sections to take care of on their own. Often, they didn't have the same skill, which meant the repairs were done, but the results didn't retain the original beauty .

"I'm not unhappy that I know you, Bastan. The life I lead is… Well, it's the life I lead. I don't think anything could change, and even if I could go back and unlock those memories, I don't know…" She shook her head. Sam didn't know what she wanted. She still didn't even know how old she had been when Marin had taken her and didn't know what would happen if she were somehow able to restore those memories. What would she recall?

Maybe she was too young to recall anything. Maybe it didn't matter, and the only thing she had lost out on was a mother who was too cold to care what happened to her. If anything, Bastan was much warmer than the Elaine she knew now. Had she always been that way?

"I think," Bastan started and then looked around, his eyes darting from side to side as he took in their surroundings. Sam followed the direction of his gaze and wondered what it was he saw. "I think we should move more quickly."

"Bastan?"

"There are at least three following us," he said.

"Three what?" Sam asked.

"Since they each seem to be wielding a staff, I would venture a guess that they are like you."

"Kavers?"

Why would Kavers be following them?

"We can get away from here, but then one of us should go back and warn Alec. If they're after us, and have already made an attempt on him, he may be more danger than we know."

"One of us? He's at the university."

"We've already seen how that's not safe, especially when faced by someone in a position of power. If nothing else, we can alert him of what we've seen. Considering you have the abilities that you do, I would normally suggest it be you, but I think that in the university, you would be at a disadvantage. We need someone who can go in and can be less obtrusive."

They hurried along the street, and Sam pulled out the halves of her canal staff, readying to put them together. If there were Kavers coming after them, it was possible they would be augmented.

"What do you propose?"

"I don't know that it can be me, either, but I think…" Bastan looked around, then nodded to the next bridge. They hurried toward it, now running. If they were to separate, Sam could use her canal staff to clear the canals and could move more quickly, but it meant abandoning

Bastan. There was a time when that wouldn't have bothered her, but that was a time before she had said felt the same affection toward Bastan as he clearly felt toward her.

"Yes. There is someone I can contact. I will send help to Alec and get him out of the university if needed." He looked over at her. "I can't promise that it won't be violent."

"I don't care about violence. I care about Alec getting out safely." She looked around and saw one of the people following them. A man. It wasn't anyone she knew, and there was a stealthiness to him. Bastan had been right. He carried a canal staff openly. "Bastan, can you acquire more eel meat?"

He frowned but nodded. "You think to have him continue to take it until you find the solution?"

"I think we need to," Sam said. "Until we understand what happened, and what Master Helen did, Alec needs to take the one thing that might help him, even if it is forbidden by the university."

Bastan clapped her on the shoulder. "Move quickly, Samara. Get to Marin and see what she might be able to tell you. I will send someone to get Alec, and once I find the information about this Maser Helen, I will return to the cells."

Sam and Bastan separated, heading in different directions. She watched him go, feeling anxious for him. She didn't worry about herself, not much. Even though there was the potential of Kavers coming after them, that didn't worry her, though she wondered if perhaps it should. With her command of the canal staff, she thought she would be able to escape, at least stay ahead of them. But she worried about drawing them into Caster and gaining the wrong kind of notice.

Sam screwed the ends of her canal staff together and started off.

When she did, movement behind her surged.

She reached the canal and launched herself over, pushing off with the staff as she cleared the canal in a single jump. When she landed, she glanced over her shoulder and saw the two Kavers. One of them was the nondescript man she had seen out of the corner of her eye. The other was an older woman with dark brown hair and a weathered face. She'd never seen her before, either. How was it there were so many Kavers she didn't know?

Was it something that Elaine was keeping from her?

She had met a few other Kavers, but they had only participated in her training, and had done little else. As Sam ran, she continued to look over her shoulder, watching them as they followed. They were skilled, jumping with nearly the same ease as she did. It reminded her of when Marin chased her.

Which meant they either had their own augmentations, or they had Scribes working with them... Unless they were more like Marin and able to augment themselves without the help of Scribes.

Sam jumped to a rooftop, pushing off with her staff and flying where she could land in a quick roll. From here, she looked down and studied the Kavers as she took them on from a different angle.

There was something about them that was familiar. She *had* seen them before.

They were servants in the palace.

Maybe not servants, but they were people in the palace.

Kyza. There were plenty of others like them, which meant there would have to be plenty of other Kavers in the palace as well. How many more would be there, and how many more would be concealed, hidden from her so that she didn't know exactly how many she had to potentially deal with?

Sam raced along the rooftop. As she did, she focused on strength and speed. She needed an augmentation now, mostly so she could stay ahead of these two Kavers.

The next building required that she clear the street. She jumped, managing to reach the next rooftop.

The movement must have attracted their attention. One of the Kavers—the man—pushed off, launching himself into the air and after her, flipping up to land behind her.

Kyza!

Sam swung her staff.

He countered, blocking, and brought around his own staff. He was quick, his movements almost too fast for her to keep up with, and she focused on an augmentation for speed, needing to move even more quickly. As it washed over her, she breathed out, flicking the staff around using techniques that Elaine had taught her.

What did it mean that she was now using the teachings of the Kavers against them?

Sam could feel worse than she did, but she had a hard time mustering the necessary sympathy. She needed to escape, which meant she needed to knock this Kaver from the roof.

What of the other?

Had the woman lost sight of her, or could the other Kaver have circled around? Sam needed to position herself in a way that didn't expose her too much, but allowed her a look below.

She turned and moved so that she was able to spin around, looking to see if the other Kaver was near her. As she did, the man swung his staff around and nearly connected with her leg.

If he were to connect, she would surely fall off the roof, and dropping from this level would be fatal. She had nearly suffered that fate once already.

It was obvious that she wasn't going to escape, but that didn't mean she couldn't slow them.

Sam jumped.

With the augmentation she had, the jump carried her high into the air, and she spun, rotating around, so that when she landed, she was almost behind the other Kaver. She flipped her staff around and jabbed it at him, connecting with his chest.

The man grunted and fell back.

Sam spun again and swept his legs out, forcing him backward. He tumbled, sliding down the angled roof.

Movement out of the corner of her eye cause her to spin.

Without her augmentation, without the speed that she had placed on herself, she wouldn't have been able to turn quickly enough. Another staff swung at her. The older woman. Despite her age, she was fast—almost too fast for Sam to keep up with.

Sam spun her staff, blocking, and was forced back. Each step took her closer to the edge of the rooftop, and each step brought her closer to falling.

Sam managed to block another attack, but her foot slipped, and she nearly fell.

She managed to bring her staff up, but it wasn't quick enough. The other woman brought hers down, and collided with Sam's staff, forcing her back.

Kyza!

Sam was on her knees, her staff gripped in her hands, and needed to move, but she couldn't.

Anything she did put her in danger of falling.

But could she control her fall?

She jumped.

As she did, she flipped backward and jabbed down with her staff, centering it in the stones of the street below.

When it centered, she slid down. As she nearly reached the street, the man smacked the top of Sam's staff, sending it toppling.

Sam landed in a tumble and went flying forward. She barely managed to maintain her grip on her staff. She got to her feet and started running.

The sound of pursuit came from behind her.

Sam focused on an augmentation, trying to hold on to it so that she could use speed, but the type of speed she needed was more than what she had.

And she didn't want to draw too much attention as she went into Caster. She didn't want the Kavers to know where she traveled and didn't want them to catch her too close to where they held Marin. She needed to try a different path.

But where?

Sam raced forward, hurrying toward the distant

section. If nothing else, she would go where these Kavers couldn't follow her.

But where would that be?

She didn't want anyone to know where she had Marin, not wanting to let Elaine and Lyasanna know that she had her captive, but in order for her to get away, she needed to take a circuitous path, moving away from where they might think she was heading.

There was another possibility.

It would be risky, and she wasn't sure she would be able to pull it off—not without Bastan—but if it worked… Maybe she could distract the Kavers long enough that she could get back to Bastan's and question Marin. And she might be able to use the diversion for another purpose—especially if what she began to suspect was true.

But could she reach the Shuver before the Kavers pursuing her reached her?

19

A LOWBORN SECTION

T he streets were busier than she was accustomed to, though maybe it was the eastern sections that were busier. Sam wasn't as familiar with the streets here she was in other sections, not accustomed to fighting through crowds at this time of day. She kept her canal staff assembled, no longer caring about drawing unnecessary attention, deciding that it was better to be prepared for the possibility of an attack at any moment rather than fearing someone questioning her about her staff.

She didn't quite know how to find the Shuver. All she knew was that he worked in the eastern sections, but little else. Then again, she understood how the underbelly of the city worked, likely better than the Kavers. They worked outside of the city and with the blessing of the palace, nothing like the way Sam operated. She had street smarts and stealth, and a healthy fear of getting caught at all times.

Kyza, but she wished she had asked Bastan more questions about the Shuver.

All she knew was that he was a man similar to Bastan, which meant he would have to have a similar network. Sam had seen his men, and Aelus had mentioned which section he'd come from so if she could figure out where he based his operations, she might be able to use him.

She chose a tavern at random, presuming that would be the likely place for others in the underworld to congregate. When she entered, she took in the surroundings and the customers. It was cluttered and dirty—not all men had Bastan's compunction for order and tidiness—and full of seedy-looking characters.

Sam took a seat near the back wall. While she waited for one of the servers to make her way around, she scanned the room, looking for signs of anyone who might be helpful. She saw groups of men, mostly in twos and threes, sitting at tables, though there was one table of nearly a half-dozen men. Some were louder than others, and she immediately ignored them. Anyone who would be working for someone like the Shuver would not draw attention like that, needing to keep a lower profile.

"Do you work on the barges?"

Sam turned her attention to the young servant boy who appeared at her table. He couldn't have been more than fourteen, and he stared at her canal staff, the tray balanced on his hand almost tipping to the side as he started to reach for it.

Sam grabbed the staff and pulled it back toward her. It was the only weapon she had. If someone were to take it, and if she were to lose her connection to it, she would feel helpless.

"Sure. I work on the barges. When have you ever seen a female captain?"

"I didn't say you were a captain. You could be crew. There are plenty of female crew."

Sam grinned and shook her head. "Really? I'm not sure you can tell the difference between male and female if you think that."

The boy stepped back and shifted the tray on his hand. "I can tell the difference," he said.

"I'm just teasing you," Sam said. "I'll take a mug of tea."

"Tea?"

"Is that a problem?"

"It's not a problem. It's just that most who come in here want ale or something even stronger."

"Well, I'm not most who come in here."

"Yeah. I can see that. I don't know that I've ever seen you in here before."

"I'm just passing through the section."

"Why would you pass through Redsnal?"

Sam at least had the section name now. Short of a carrying a reputation, the name of a section wasn't that important to her. Her work for Bastan didn't typically take her far from Caster, and she knew that area well enough. But here in the eastern part of the city, the name would be good to know, especially if she needed to send word to Bastan. As far as he knew, she was going back to where they held Marin. When he learned she never arrived there, he'd worry and wonder where she went.

"I'm looking for someone."

"Yeah? That can be dangerous in Redsnal."

Sam chuckled. "I think I can manage."

"You need to have someone who can protect you here."

Sam arched a brow at him. "And you think you can offer someone protection?"

The boy shrugged. "For the right price."

Sam breathed out, trying not to laugh. "And what price would that be?"

He didn't get the chance to answer. A fight broke out at one of the nearby tables, and two men stood and began pushing each other. One of them threw a punch, and the other man fell back, nearly slamming into Sam. She grabbed her staff and slipped out of the way. As the punching man moved in on his opponent, he caught sight of Sam. As one, both men turned and glowered at her, almost as if the fact that she had moved out of the way angered them.

"I don't need any trouble," Sam said.

"You don't need it, but it looks like you found it. Maybe you come with us…"

Sam groaned. "Really? First, this boy thinks that he can offer me protection, and now, you think you're going to drag me off to wherever you will? I don't think so."

One of the men lunged for her, and Sam spun her staff, smacking his arm. It snapped with a sharp crack.

He jerked back and slammed into his buddy.

"Like I said, I don't need any trouble."

The men scrambled up, the one with the broken arm clutching it to his body but still trying to come close to her.

Sam glanced over at the boy who was watching, and she only shrugged. "Looks like they want trouble."

She darted forward, spinning her staff, connecting with the broken-arm man in the side of his head, and he collapsed in a heap. The other man tried to get behind her, but Sam spun, jabbing him in the chest with her staff. She didn't push quite as hard as she had with the Shuver's men, not wanting to crush his chest, only wanting to knock him down. The man went staggering into the wall and crashed, falling back. He gasped for air, clutching his hands to his chest as he attempted to catch his breath.

Sam took a seat at the table and looked up at the boy. "Now. About that tea?"

"Who are you?"

"No one. At least, no one that you need to worry about. What you should know is that I'm looking for the Shuver."

"That's quite a way of trying to get his attention," the boy said.

"Yeah, well, I don't have a whole lot of time, so I didn't really want to get caught up with some idiot thinking he would take advantage of me." Sam scanned the tavern as the boy scurried off, watching the injured men. Neither of them got up, and a few of the other men reached for them and pulled them away, propping them against the wall. They glanced at Sam, but none of them said anything.

When the boy returned with her mug of tea, she looked up at him. If he worked at a tavern like this, it was possible he would have some information, and maybe given what he'd seen from her—and her age—she might be able to convince him to share more than others would. "What do you know of the Shuver?"

The boy shook his head. "I don't know much. Please…"

Sam shook her head. "I'm not going to try to attack the Shuver. I just want to find him."

"He's not here. He doesn't come to Redsnal all that often."

"Then which section is his?"

"Oldansh has a place where he stays, and…"

Sam frowned. Oldansh was a dangerous section on the eastern edge of the city. She knew of it, much as many in the city knew of Caster. It had a reputation, though it wasn't nearly as frightening as the one Caster had.

"What kind of place does he have?"

"I don't want to be the one who tells you too much about the Shuver. If word gets back to him that I was the one who told you where to find him, I might be targeted."

"Like I said, I don't have any intention of going after the Shuver and causing any trouble."

"I don't know that you could." When Sam arched her brow, he shrugged. "You knocked down these two idiots, but they were half into their drink and aren't all that impressive even when they're sober. He's got others that work for him—others with real skill. I think you'd have a much harder time with them."

Sam grinned. "You might be surprised."

"What's that supposed to mean?"

"It means that I've got some experience with the Shuver's men." She wasn't sure whether it would be to her benefit to reveal that she had attacked—and killed—two of his men, or if it would only make things more difficult. Considering this boy likely didn't know much, she decided that it didn't make any sense for her to share too much with them.

"Fine. You go. And when they finish you off, don't come blaming me."

"If they finish me off, I won't come blaming anyone."

The boy frowned, as though trying to work through what she'd said. "That's true enough."

"Where is he?"

She took a sip of her tea and found that it was bitter. Had he poisoned it? After what she'd done, she shouldn't put it past him, and considering everything that she'd seen over the last few months, it wouldn't be terribly surprising to see a tavern like this poison her.

She decided to leave the tea alone. If it was poisoned, she wasn't going to be foolish enough to continue to try to drink it. If it wasn't, then it was just terrible, and she didn't want to drink it anyway.

"I already told you. He has a place in the Oldansh section."

"I need you tell me how to get there and how to find his place."

"I'm not going to tell you how to find his place."

"No? Then maybe I just bring you with me, and when he asks who helped me find his location, I'll just throw you out there."

The boy took a step back, and his eyes darted from side to side as though he intended to run.

"All I want is a chance to talk with him," Sam said.

The boy licked his lips. "Fine. If you make it into Oldansh, you'll find him along the outer canal. He has a massive building. Looks sort of like a warehouse, but when you get close, you'll see men watching it. That's how you'll know it."

"And how is it that you know it?"

"Because I came from that section. I got away from there. I got away from everything with the Shuver. He's a bastard."

"Yeah, I've known a few like that before too." Sam fished a coin out of her pocket and set it on the table before grabbing her canal staff and heading out of the tavern.

Once outside, Sam hurried along the street, moving between the crowds and keeping her canal staff clutched tightly. She always believed Caster to be one of the most dangerous sections in the city, but if the attack in the tavern was any indication, not to mention the fear she saw in the boy's eyes, maybe Redsnal was as dangerous as Caster. But because it was unfamiliar to her, because she didn't know any of the faces surrounding her, it seemed even more so.

Sam hurried along the cobbles, clutching her cloak tightly around her, wanting to stay obscured in the shadows as much as possible. She reached an intersection and did a quick survey, trying to determine where she needed to go. All she had to go on was the boy's directions. So, she headed toward the outer edge of the city, which meant following the canals.

She wasn't as familiar with the northeastern edge of the city, other than knowing that it abutted the periphery of the swamp. She found the canal and hesitated. The buildings lining the canal in this section were pushed away, leaving something of a shore next to the canal itself. There were people strolling along the water's edge, and she caught sight of someone who was actually fishing. That was something she never saw in Caster, and she was surprised to see that here.

There were too many people here for her to jump the canal, at least openly.

Sam looked for a better place to cross. All along the canal she saw more people.

The only option she had was crossing at the bridge.

When she made her way to the bridge, she wasn't surprised to find two men guarding it, preventing easy access. What did surprise her was that they didn't wear the colors of the Anders, not the way that many others who served as the bridge guards did.

Likely, they would work for the Shuver.

"What's your business heading to Oldansh?" one of the men asked.

"It's personal," Sam said.

"Personal? Everything is personal. Either tell me your business or turn around and head back the way you came."

Sam took a look over her shoulder. She might find it easier to jump the canals, at least in this instance, where she might be forced to answer more than she wanted to.

"I'm coming to see the Shuver."

The two men looked at each other and then began laughing. "You? A girl like you is risking herself against the Shuver?"

"I don't know that I'm risking myself so much as I am going to pay him a visit."

One of the men looked at her and eyed her canal staff. "What's that?"

"This? It helps me balance. It's sort of a walking stick."

"You can't have that here."

"I can't?" Sam said.

The first man shook his head. "Not here."

"What do you think I'm going to do with it?" Sam asked.

"It doesn't matter. Something like that is a weapon. The Shuver doesn't allow weapons."

Sam grinned and considered stepping back, but when

she turned around, she saw a flicker of movement in the distance. It was too fast and soaring to hide to be anything other than a Kaver.

Kyza. She needed to move quickly.

She would let the Shuver deal with the Kaver.

But first, she had to cross the canal, and she was getting frustrated, tired of the people attempting to delay her.

She flipped her staff, sweeping it toward the legs of the two guards. Both of them were knocked down, and Sam tapped them both on the chest, holding them to the ground briefly, enough to knock the wind out of them.

She jumped over them and went running across the bridge.

One of the guards recovered more quickly than the other, and she heard his wheezing shout.

Sam smiled to herself, ignoring him as she streaked onward, heading into the section.

There weren't as many people out in this section, and she didn't know if it was because the Shuver restricted access or there was some other reason. Sam slowed her pace, but only a little. If she went too slowly, she ran the risk of the Kaver reaching her. That person was out here and had managed to keep pace and had clearly waited for her during her brief stop at the tavern, which troubled her.

If the Kavers actually caught her, what would Master Helen—and Elaine—do?

Maybe the better question was what would Princess Lyasanna do?

That had to be the reason the Kavers were after her.

Sam hurried toward the far side of the section. If what

the boy said was true, she would find a massive building with men watching it.

As she made her way through the streets, she realized the people all had a certain appearance to them. They all had solid builds, and more than a few seemed to carry weapons beneath their cloaks. So much for not letting anyone through who was armed.

Unless the people who were here all served the Shuver. She wouldn't put that past him. It was the sort of thing Bastan would do, ensuring that those around him were only people who he could trust.

Maybe she had made a mistake coming here. It was possible that she was risking herself against far more than she realized.

She needed to move quickly.

There was a shout behind her, and Sam glanced back and saw the Kaver knocking someone down.

Kyza, but if they were willing to openly attack, she needed to move even more carefully.

Sam streaked along the street. It had been long enough since she had placed her last augmentation that she decided to attempt another one. She focused on her typical augmentations, thinking of strength and speed. It was difficult doing so while running, but the slow wash of cold came over her as she reached the canal.

Sam slowed and took a quick moment to take note of everything around her.

The Shuver had nearly a dozen men watching the building. Most were hidden in the shadows of alleys, and some were on building tops, and only a few were standing guard in front of the door, openly blocking the entrance.

Had Sam not had the same experience working with

Bastan and trying to keep an eye on how many men he had guarding his taverns any given time, she wasn't sure she would have even noticed the sheer number of people the Shuver had standing guard, but her time with him had taught her to make such assessments.

There was a flicker of movement behind her, and she spun in time to block a staff swinging toward her midsection.

Sam grunted and flicked her staff out, using a sharp attack. She was thankful she had managed to take the time to place in augmentation. If she hadn't, would she have been fast enough?

This person was quick, and she was highly skilled with the staff, far more than Sam. She wasn't terrible, and given the time that she'd spent working with it, she had managed to become more than serviceable, but many of the Kavers had been studying for years, far longer than Sam.

"You don't need to fight me," the woman said through gritted teeth.

"You came after me. You thought to attack me." Sam swept toward the woman's feet and then brought her staff back up, attempting to distract her.

"I didn't think to do anything. We are trying to bring you back."

"Back where?"

"Back to the palace. Elaine has asked that you come with us."

Sam shook her head. "If she wanted me to come back with you, she would have come herself."

"She did."

Almost too late, Sam realized that Elaine was on the

other side of her. She swung around, jumping at the same time, and realized that Elaine was there, her canal staff spinning.

"What are you doing, Samara?"

Sam frowned and jerked her head from Kaver to Kaver. Would she be fast enough to get free?

Against a single Kaver, she might, even if the other was more skilled than she. Sam thought she could use the Shuver's men to help her distract the Kaver, but against two Kavers?

And one of them her mother?

Sam wasn't sure that she could.

"Where have you been, Samara?"

"I am not your captive, as you assured me. I am free to go where I please."

"Not a captive, no, but Master Helen has reported that you were involved in an attack."

"I have? What sort of attack was I involved in?"

"From what Master Helen tells us, something happened at the university."

Sam continued to move back, not wanting to let the other Kaver get too close. So far, Elaine had made no attempt to swing her staff, and Sam wasn't about to launch herself at her. Doing so would only lead to an immediate battle, and Sam wasn't sure that was what she needed. If she could take a few moments, if she could sort this out…

"That wasn't an attack. Helen poisoned Alec."

"She wouldn't have done that."

"You might not think so, but I was there."

"What was he doing?"

Sam glanced from Elaine to the other Kaver. Her

answer now would have to be somewhat measured. If she revealed too much, then she risked exposing what Alec had been working on. Then again, maybe she could pull the other Kaver to her side. "He was attempting to make easar paper."

The other Kaver hesitated.

As she did, Sam noticed Elaine tensing.

Practicing with Elaine had taught her many things, not the least of which was learning what Elaine did when she was preparing to attack. The way she tensed now was her preparation, and Sam could tell she was readying an attack.

She used the hesitation from the other Kaver and swung her staff around, sweeping the woman's legs out from under her and jabbing her in the chest as she had the men on the bridge. It wasn't a fatal blow—and really only would knock the wind out of her—enough to buy her time.

"You want to attack me?" Sam asked.

"I don't intend to attack you at all."

"You sent them after me."

"I sent them to bring you in."

"No. I think you and Master Helen are trying to help Lyasanna conceal what she did."

"You can't believe Marin."

"Marin might be the only one who has been forthright with what she wants, especially lately. You, on the other hand, have shown me nothing other than a desire to delay me from going after Tray."

"Because you can't go after Tray. You have no idea how difficult such a journey would be."

"No? I know all about the forest beyond the swamp as

well as the plains beyond the forest. All I need is the guidebook, and I would be able to make my way to the Theln lands."

Elaine hesitated, and her eyes narrowed. The tension remained in her muscles. "You've spoken to Marin."

Kyza. Sam had said too much. She should have been more careful. She didn't need Elaine knowing that she had Marin captured, or that she and Bastan intended to use Marin to guide her to find Tray.

"Where is she, Samara?"

"I don't know."

"You have never been a good liar."

"Unlike you?"

"That's not what I'm saying. I can see it in your eyes. You're hiding something from me. If you know where Marin is, you have an obligation as a Kaver to reveal what you know so we may bring the traitor in."

"What if I'm not convinced she's the traitor?" Sam asked.

"You can't say that. After everything you've been through, how can you not believe that Marin is a traitor?"

"After everything that I've been through, I have a better understanding of the layers involved in making decisions. If Marin has been honest with me—and I suspect she has been—everything she said about Tray has been true. Everything she said about Lyasanna has been true."

The other Kaver attempted to get up, and Sam flipped over to her, jabbing her in the chest once more. It knocked the wind out of her again, enough that she couldn't keep attempting to come after Sam. Each time she did, she worried that Elaine would get close enough to attack.

"That's why you need to come in, Samara. If what Marin has said is true, then we need to understand what Lyasanna was thinking."

"You still defend her."

"I am her Kaver."

"That doesn't mean that you have to blindly follow her. I wouldn't ask Alec to follow me if I was doing something stupid."

"Such as what you're doing now?"

"What I'm doing now is trying to understand better what those who attempt to use me might have been planning."

"No one is trying to use you."

"Then why don't you leave me?"

Elaine's gaze drifted past Sam.

Sam jumped to the end of her staff, balancing there. Something struck her staff, and she wobbled, but flipped into the air, swinging her staff around. She managed to catch someone else who had appeared out of the shadows. Another Kaver.

"I'm afraid that I can't simply leave you," Elaine said. "There is too much that we don't yet know."

"How many more are you going to send at me? How many more do you intend to get hurt?"

"What makes you think that any of them will get hurt?"

Sam looked around the street as she unscrewed the ends of her canal staff. She quickly hung them on her belt and pulled her cloak tight around her.

"It's good that you've decided not to fight."

"Oh, that's not what I'm doing."

Elaine arched a brow at her. "Then what are you doing?"

Sam smiled.

As she did, chaos descended.

20

KAVERS ATTACK

Men appeared out of the shadows of alleys and from the rooftops, dozens of men, converging on Elaine and the other Kavers. Most were armed with swords, though a few had crossbows, brutal weapons that would fire quickly.

"You," one of the men said as he approached. "You're the one who attacked our people at the bridge."

Elaine turned toward him and spun her staff. She jumped forward, attacking with a brutal efficiency, but there were many men, and they converged on Elaine, surrounding her.

Sam could almost see the debate warring in her mother's mind as she tried to decide whether she would attack or whether she would turn and run. As the men converged, Elaine made her decision. She jumped to the end of her staff and flipped into the air and toward the nearby rooftop. She hesitated, crouching near the edge, and looked down at Sam for a brief moment before she scurried off.

The men changed their focus to the Kavers that were down. They were the ones Sam had immobilized, but they were starting to come around, getting to their feet and realizing they would have a challenge.

Rather than waiting, Sam hurried into the nearby building. This was the distraction she needed to get to the Shuver.

The inside of the building was a massive warehouse. Lanterns hung on hooks from posts scattered around, giving a weak light, not enough to fully illuminate the entire space. A few men were inside, and Sam tried to stay in the shadows as she hurried forward, keeping an eye on them as she did. She didn't want to draw the attention of the Shuver before she reached him.

The sounds of fighting continued outside on the street.

The Kavers must have recovered enough to at least put up something of a fight. Sam smiled to herself. How many of them were augmented? How many had any ability with augmentations?

Probably not enough.

She hurried along one wall. Two men raced past and paid her no mind. She wasn't sure if it was because her cloak obscured her presence, or just the shadows giving her cover.

She approached slowly and reached a better-lit section of the warehouse. There was a hearth here glowing with a bright, warm fire. A table had food stacked on it. Chairs circled the table, and all were empty. Someone huddled in a corner, a young girl who glanced at Sam with wide eyes.

Not at Sam. Past Sam.

She spun.

A wiry man approached. His weathered face looked like it had been in the sun his entire life, and he was dressed in gray—almost the same color as what Alec wore at the university. He carried a sword, and it was unsheathed, pointing at Sam.

"Who are you?"

"You don't need that," Sam said.

"Don't I? Someone appears in my building without warning, and I don't need to be able to protect myself?"

"If you want to fight, I'm happy to oblige, but that's not why I'm here."

"Then why are you here?"

"Because Bastan said he works with you."

The man frowned and flicked his gaze past Sam.

She shifted, noting that two men stood off in the shadows. One of them disappeared. She suspected he went off to find out whether Bastan knew anything about her. At least Bastan would hear she was unharmed.

"How do you know Bastan?"

"He's something of a father to me."

"I don't know whether to congratulate you or console you."

"There are times when I don't, either." Sam nodded to his sword, and she shook her head. "I told you. You don't need that."

"I haven't decided what I'll need."

"Fine. If you're going to have your weapon, then I get to have mine." She quickly pulled her canal staff out from underneath her cloak and screwed the ends together. She tapped it once on the ground.

The Shuver stared at it for a moment. "That? What kind of weapon is that? I have a sword."

Sam grunted. "Ask your men at the apothecary whether their swords did any good."

The Shuver glared at her. "You. You're the one who attacked them?"

"They will be leaving Aelus alone. As will you."

"Bastan has never sent anyone to dictate the terms of my business dealings before."

"This isn't Bastan coming to you. This is me."

"And you said you worked for Bastan."

"No. I said that I know Bastan. I didn't say I worked for him."

The Shuver grunted. He shoved his sword into its sheath and motioned for her to join him at the table. He stood behind one of the chairs, his hands gripping the back of it, and his gaze looking around the warehouse. "I suppose I have you to thank for this attack?"

"It's not my fault. Well… maybe it is a little."

"Why are you here? Is it only about the apothecary? He is of little use to me, especially since he's been so delayed with preparing the poison that I need."

"Bastan said you had worked with him before. I thought I could see if you would have any interest in working with him again."

"I thought you said you didn't work for Bastan."

"I don't."

"Then how can you offer what you have presented?"

"All I am offering is the possibility of you and Bastan working together. I thought that might be valuable to you."

"And how would you have us work together?"

"I know you and Bastan don't work in the same sections. That's why you've been able to get along."

"Bastan and I have managed to get along, as you would say, because Bastan has not made a move on my territory. If he ever did, I would have no choice other than to attack."

Sam smiled to herself. Bastan had made a different argument, and from what she had seen of the Shuver, he might be well protected, but not so well protected that Bastan wouldn't be able to eliminate him if it ever came to that. Then again, men like Bastan and the Shuver were nothing if not arrogant in their belief of their ability to be protected.

"Fine. You and Bastan have some sort of truce between you. There will come a time when you will need to work together."

"On what?"

"You control your section similar to the way Bastan controls his section."

"I don't control only my section, daughter of Bastan."

"Fine. And Bastan doesn't control only Caster. I think we can both agree you have enough influence in your sections of the city."

"So?"

Sam glanced around. How much time did she have before the Shuver's men returned from the battle in the street?

When they did, Sam would either have to fight her way out—and she didn't like her odds, even with augmentations, and especially not with augmentations that were fading—or she would have to escape before they appeared. That would be easier, but she needed to finish this. She needed to get the Shuver to agree to help.

She wasn't sure whether it would be necessary, but

with Elaine appearing in this section, Sam began to suspect that it might be even more important to have his cooperation than she had believed at first.

"I'm willing to overlook your attack on the apothecary," she said.

"You're willing to overlook it, are you?"

Sam nodded. "I am willing to overlook it. If you attempt another attack on Aelus, then I will not overlook it. Consider him under my protection."

"Bastan's reach does not extend to Arrend."

"No. It might not. But mine does."

"And who are you?"

"I'm no one. Nothing but a lowborn."

Sam heard movement behind her, and she knew it was time to act, especially if she was going to do anything. She shifted, sliding so that she could see behind her, getting closer to the girl cowering in the corner. She glanced over and realized that the girl was young—possibly six or seven—and she shivered.

What was the Shuver doing with her?

"You didn't come here just to threaten me. You came for something. Tell me, why are you here?"

"Because there will come a time, possibly sooner than Bastan would like, when he will need those in the outer sections to take action."

"What kind of action?"

"The kind of action that will ensure that the highborns no longer have the same authority they do now."

The Shuver smiled. "You would like me to believe Bastan wants to take down the highborns? Let me tell you what I know about Bastan. He has always been content with remaining on the periphery of the city and has always been content with the differential between high-born and lowborn. How else would he be able to steal wealth?"

"You can believe whatever you want about Bastan, but I'm telling you he will send word. If you don't want to run afoul of him, then you will answer when he calls."

"Run afoul? I think you mistake my concern for Bastan and his—"

Sam leapt forward and swung her staff, sweeping the man's legs out from under him. She raised her staff up and brought it down toward his chest but decided not to strike him.

"Just remember I work with Bastan. I got to you. If you don't want him to take over your section, then you will answer when he calls. And when he calls, be prepared."

"Be prepared for what?"

"Be prepared for a fight."

Sam slipped back, and as she did, she grabbed the girl cowering in the corner and headed toward the door along the back wall. She kicked it open and wasn't surprised to see two men standing guard. They fell with a quick crack to the skull from her staff.

"Where's your home?" she asked the girl.

"I'm... I'm from the Dorand section."

"Why are you here?"

"I don't know. I think... I think my father owed him something."

Sam glanced back at the warehouse. Was this the kind of person they would need to work with? Was she really willing to risk that?

But then, what choice did they have?

A FRIEND'S HELP

Alec hurried through the university as quickly as he could, the weakness from his illness making speed difficult. He could no longer move nearly as fast as he once had, and as much as he tried, he felt wiped out.

How was it that he was this weak?

He needed to find Sam, which meant he needed to get to Caster, but he wasn't sure he had the strength to do so. A part of him wished he would have gone with Sam when she had left with Bastan, but then, he hadn't known. And had Master Eckerd not shared, maybe he never would have known.

That had to be the secret that Master Helen had been keeping from him. It was a secret Master Eckerd had kept from him, trying to prevent him from understanding what it meant for Alec to be a Scribe. But now, he knew the key: Master Helen was the king's Scribe. Which meant what? Why wouldn't the king want them to come up with some way to make easar paper?

And why would Master Helen have attacked him?

None of it made sense. All of his experiences at the university had led him to think that everyone there was helpful, interested in bringing along the future generations of healers. But having been attacked by Master Helen, Alec no longer felt that way. He no longer felt the university was a safe place for him. And if the university wasn't safe for him, it meant it wouldn't be safe for anyone.

He stopped in his room and grabbed the books he could, stuffing them into his pockets. He would get to Caster, and he would ask Bastan to keep him safe, at least until they made their journey after Tray.

Yet as he bundled everything up, he saw notes on the table made by Beckah.

He paused and looked them over. They were notes she had made as she prepared for her testing, preparing to be promoted to junior physicker.

Where *was* she? After everything he had been through, he had expected her to return, but the fact she hadn't bothered him.

Having collected what he thought he'd need, he stepped out, closing the door and making certain to lock it. The lock wouldn't stop someone like Samara, but it would stop the average person from getting in. That was all he cared about. He started down the hallway and kept his eye out for anyone who might be dangerous to him.

There should be no one along the hall. It was late enough that everyone should be in bed—at least everyone except him. Alec had been out at this time of night before and rarely encountered anyone, except a few who chose to study late at the library.

Footsteps pounded along the tile.

Why should there be footsteps? Who else would be out and making their way through the university?

He tried to hurry. He wanted to get to Beckah's room before anyone came across him. Alec reached the student section. He found Beckah's door and checked it. He was not surprised when it was unlocked. He stepped inside and quickly surveyed the room. Beckah wasn't here. And likely wasn't anywhere in the university. Sam said they had searched everywhere. Had she been on the grounds, he suspected she would have come to check on him.

When Alec stepped out of the room, Stefan greeted him in the hallway.

"Alec? What are you doing in Beckah's room?"

"Have you seen her?"

"What? Beckah? I thought she was with you? She told me she was studying with you to prepare for her physicker exam."

"She had been until I got sick."

"You were sick?" Stefan looked at him and frowned. "You don't look sick."

"I'm better." Mostly, but Stefan didn't need to know that. "Have you seen Beckah this evening?"

Stefan shook his head. "I haven't seen her in several days, but then I haven't seen you in several days. I thought I would share with you that I came across—"

Alec grabbed his arm and pulled him with him as he continued down the hall. It might be helpful to have someone with him, especially a friend. Stefan and he had grown apart since he'd been promoted to full physicker, but he was still a friend.

"I need your help," he said the Stefan.

"With what? Is there something you can't figure out? Is there another healing that you need help with?"

"Maybe," Alec said.

"What is it?"

Alec looked along the hallway. He thought he heard the sound of footsteps, and he wanted to head down, but he needed to avoid drawing any attention to himself or Stefan. He nodded toward the end of the hall, to the stairs that would lead down to the hospital ward. Stefan went with him, and Alec leaned on his friend far more than he thought he should.

"Alec?"

"I'm fine," he said.

"I don't think you are. What happened?"

Alec swallowed, pushing back the dryness in his throat. When the weakness came on, that was when the dryness was worse. He needed to find his father, or Bastan, so he could get more of the eel meat to help take the edge off the illness. "An experiment that went wrong," Alec said.

"What kind of experiment? I heard you were working with my grandmother…"

Alec breathed out. He'd forgotten that Stefan and his grandmother had begun speaking more often, especially since…

Alec looked over at Stefan. "How well do you know your grandmother?"

"You've seen the relationship we have," Stefan said. "She can be difficult. I think your friend is closer to her than I ever have been."

"My friend?"

"The girl you often see. I think she and Grandmother Helen are pretty close."

Alec sighed. "I don't think they are, at least not anymore."

"What happened?"

"I don't know what happened. All I know is that I was working with your grandmother, and now she's disappeared. Do you think you could help me find her?"

Alec hated using Stefan this way, especially since he had never shared with Stefan the fact that he was a Scribe. Then again, Stefan might not understand. It could be that Stefan had the capability to be a Scribe. Was he aware of that? If he was related to Master Helen, maybe he had the same bloodlines, which meant it was possible he could have the same connection to power as Master Helen.

As they made their way down the stairs, Alec glanced over to Stefan. "Has Master Helen ever worked with you directly?"

"You've seen the extent of how much she works with me," Stefan said. "She has always preferred to keep me out of her research and hasn't given me any more attention than any of the other master physickers. Probably less than most."

Stefan sounded bitter, and Alec couldn't blame him. Having Master Helen's attention might be helpful, especially for someone like Stefan who wasn't nearly as naturally gifted as Beckah, or who didn't have the same experience as Alec. Often, having a master physicker who could serve as a mentor would benefit, but she hadn't chosen to mentor any of the students. Alec had been surprised and excited when she seemed to be willing to work with him, and in hindsight, that should have served as notice that something was amiss.

"I was just wondering if, even as a child, you knew much about your grandmother."

"Other than the fact that she goes to the palace more often than many master physickers?"

"Why do you think that is?" Alec asked.

"Probably because she is the most skilled physicker. Why else would they summon a master physicker?"

Alec studied Stefan and sighed. "That's probably it." They reached the bottom of the stairs and headed to the hospital ward. "Can you help me?"

"I think I should find you someone to talk to, Alec. If you're this sick, you need the help of a physicker."

"I am a physicker."

"Fine, then you need the help of a master physicker."

"I've already talked to Master Eckerd."

Stefan's eyes widened. "And? What did he say?"

"He said there isn't a whole lot that he can do to help."

"Why? What's wrong with you?"

"I don't know, and that's why I need to find your grandmother."

No one was on duty in the hospital ward. Alec looked around, looking for even the junior physickers, but there didn't seem to be anyone here. That bothered him. There was usually at least one, often times two, even though it was late at night. Could they have abandoned their posts?

Then again, it wouldn't surprise him. He'd seen the level of attention given to the patients in the ward after hours. The overnight physickers often used that time to relax, and many of them preferred to sleep when they should have been paying attention to the patients.

"Go wake the junior physicker on duty," Alec said.

"I thought you said you didn't need the help of a junior physicker."

"That's not why you need to wake him."

Stefan's eyes widened. "Alec, I don't want to get in the middle of something like this. I know it annoys you—"

"It doesn't annoy me. It angers me. They shouldn't be leaving the patients alone like this."

"I thought you needed to get help?"

Alec breathed out heavily. He did need to get help, but at the same time, there was no way he could leave here without correcting this. Something had to be said. "I do, and I will. But, go wake the junior physicker and tell him to come to the ward immediately."

Stefan shrugged and started off, leaving Alec standing —barely—in the ward by himself.

He started toward the closet at the back of the room. It was a set of wide doors that opened into a second room that held rows and rows of shelves, all stuffed with different medicines. He searched the shelves, looking for something that would help keep him more alert, and came up with a few items. All he needed was a little strength, and perhaps something else.

He grabbed a few vials and stuffed them into his pockets. He wasn't certain when he would come back, but he needed to have supplies until he was able to get the necessary help.

When he was done, he staggered back out into the ward and looked around. Stefan still hadn't returned with the junior physicker. Alec leaned on one of the cots, looking down at an elderly woman lying immobile. He was tempted to grab for the record hanging at the end of the cot but decided against it. He had to trust that the junior physickers were doing something for this woman, and didn't need to double-check everything, especially since he would be leaving. His insights wouldn't have any influence over what they might do.

He waited for Stefan to return, feeling increasingly fatigued the longer he waited. He shouldn't be this tired.

When Stefan still didn't return, Alec frowned and started toward the physicker room. It was a small alcove set off from the rest of the hospital ward, a place where the physickers could go to have a moment of reprieve from their duties. He thought it unfortunate that one of the junior physickers had long ago brought in a cot, which gave them a place to sleep, something he still didn't think was appropriate—or necessary.

The alcove was empty.

The cot looked like it had been slept in, and there was a sheet bunched up at the end of it. The desk had a stack of books, all references from the library he doubted were ever scrutinized nearly as well as they should be.

Where was the junior physicker? For that matter, where was Stefan?

"Stefan?" Alec said.

His voice came out weak, and he coughed, covering his mouth so he didn't potentially contaminate anyone else here. Could that be from the illness, or was the cough nothing more than his breathlessness?

Alec needed to shut his mind down, ignore everything else, and focus on getting out of the university and making his way to the Caster section, but he couldn't.

There was a light down the hallway. It was a back hall that led away from the hospital ward, and up into the physickers' quarters, but was also a secondary access to the master physickers' quarters.

Could one of the master physickers have come down?

Alec started toward the light, the weakness almost too much for him. He hated the way he felt and hated that he could barely keep himself up. He wished he had Sam's canal staff, something to lean on for support, anything that could help him stay upright and make his way more quickly.

Alec paused at the stairs. Stefan wouldn't have come here, would he? The only reason he would've gone up the stairs would have been if he had seen someone he knew... or if the junior physicker had taken him up.

Could the junior physicker have wandered away?

That seemed unlikely, even for some of the lazier junior physickers.

What was that light for?

Alec sighed and started up the stairs. If there was a master physicker here, maybe he could ask if they had seen Master Helen. Alec doubted they would have, especially if she *had* poisoned him. She would have disappeared—at least until she knew he was gone—dead. There wouldn't even be anything suspicious about her disappearance since she was often gone from the university for long stretches of time.

At the top of the stairs, Alec sank to his knees.

The effort of climbing the stairs had just been too much. He could no longer hold himself up. And now, he wouldn't even be able to get back out of the university and get to Sam. His only hope was finding someone like Master Eckerd—someone who might be sympathetic to him. He would take some of the medicine he'd just "borrowed" and hope he could recover enough to get out of the university.

There was movement. He saw it distantly, and at first, he wasn't sure what he was seeing, but then there was the steady thudding of feet along the floor. Alec twisted his head, barely able to look up, and when he did, he saw Stefan.

"Stefan?"

He frowned. "Alec, I'm sorry."

"Don't be sorry, I just need your help."

"No. I'm sorry."

Alec frowned, wondering why Stefan would be apologizing, and it still didn't register, even as hands grabbed him and lifted him, too strong for anyone at the university, which meant they were from the palace.

"Stefan?"

His friend shook his head. "As I said, I'm sorry."

Alec was dragged away from the masters' quarters, to the stairs, and out of the university.

22

CAPTIVE

Awaking in a bed, Alec did his best to sit up and look around the room he was in. It was not a cell, though he felt trapped. He was in the palace—he was sure of it—though they had covered his head during the journey here, making it difficult for him to see where they had taken him.

The room was far nicer than what he'd expect anywhere but the palace. There was a thick carpet, patterned in blue and red stripes, that reminded him of the colors of the Anders, and a dresser along one wall. Surprisingly, paper and a pen were stacked on the dresser. Alec lay back down, his head heavy, his body like lead. Even if he weren't locked in this room, he wondered whether he would be able to go anywhere. Would he even have the strength needed to escape?

He doubted it. He couldn't even get out of the bed.

Stefan had betrayed him.

But why? What had Alec done to deserve such betrayal?

Stefan was his friend, wasn't he? But then, Alec had begun asking about Helen, and probably had asked far too many questions. Stefan had probably gone to his grandmother to share what Alec was asking.

He had been a fool.

What now?

He rolled onto his side and tried getting up again but couldn't. His body didn't respond as it should.

Alec let out a frustrated sigh. He was trapped here, and Sam had gone off to Caster, and would never know what had happened to him. Would she come looking for him?

He suspected she would. Sam had proven that she was devoted to him, but in this case, he didn't know that he wanted her to come after him. If she did, she put herself danger.

He heard murmured voices through the door, and Alec debated whether to pretend to sleep or not. When the door opened, he didn't react in time. He was lying with his face to the door, his eyes staring at it, and he jerked back involuntarily at the person who entered.

He had never seen the prince, but everyone in the city knew enough about him to recognize him. The man was dressed in crimson and deep blue, stripes of color that demanded his attention. He was a striking man, taller than Alec, with wavy black hair that only had hints of gray streaked through it. His eyes sparkled, and he stared at Alec, seeming to weigh him for a long moment.

"You are he?" the prince asked.

Alec swallowed. His mouth was dry, and his lips were beginning to crack, signs he suspected were tied to the illness.

"I am who?" Alec asked. His voice came out in a croak.

The prince moved past the bed and out of Alec's view for a moment. When he returned, he was carrying a glass of water and handed it to Alec. Alec tried taking it, but his hands weren't steady enough.

The prince frowned and brought it up to Alec's lips, tipping it back. "Drink. You need water."

Alec took the offered water, trying to drink, but not sure whether he should trust the prince. What if he was working with Master Helen? What if they worked together to poison him?

But then, he was already weakened, so there was no point poisoning him further. If she wanted to harm him, then all she had to do was wait.

Alec drank, letting the water run down his throat. It was soothing, and he took a deep breath, trying to keep his mind focused. It was easy for him to feel overwhelmed, and to feel run down, and struggle with what had happened to him.

"You are the one. The one who has been working with Helen."

The prince pulled the glass away, and Alec looked up at the prince. He knew him by reputation only. But if what he had learned about the Anders was true, then he would be a Kaver. That meant he would have to have a Scribe, wouldn't it?

Who would be his Scribe?

Maybe it was one of the master physickers. With Alec's luck, he would be connected to Carl.

"I have been working with Master Helen," Alec admitted. There was no point in denying it, given that it seemed the prince already knew what Alec had been up to.

"Did you discover the way to do it?"

"To do what?"

"To make easar paper. That was what you were doing."

Alec took a deep breath, trying to infuse oxygen into his weakened lungs. "We weren't able to come up with the key to the paper," he said. "We tried, but nothing we did seemed to work, and the most recent attempt…" He took another breath. The most recent attempt had left him nearly dead. Did he share that with the prince? Maybe it would be how he could escape. Maybe he could find some way of using what had happened to him against those who would try to keep him confined.

"Kyza," the prince whispered.

Alec smiled to himself. It was the same sort of thing Sam said, the same type of swear. Maybe it was something of the Kavers, and he suspected that Marin had taught her to swear that way. Bastan didn't bring in the name of Kyza, not in the same way.

"Why?"

The prince stared at him for a long moment. Then he shook his head. "It doesn't matter, not anymore. What happened to you?"

"I don't know."

The prince frowned. "Don't know, or you don't want to say?"

Prince Jalen was next in line to the throne, though now that Alec had spoken to Master Eckerd, he no longer knew what that meant. What did the throne mean, especially when there were so many others who seemed to have power? If the university—at least the masters in the university—had a certain level of power, maybe even that which rivaled the palace, then what would it matter if the prince was next in line?

"I don't know what happened to me," Alec said with a frustrated sigh. "I think Master Helen added something to the mixture that poisoned me, but I can't be certain."

The prince studied him for a moment and said something under his breath that Alec suspected was another swear. "How certain are you of this?"

"I don't know how certain. All I know is that I was working on the recipe, and nothing in it should have been toxic."

"Are you certain?"

Alec stared at him. "Quite."

"How long have you been at the university?" the prince asked.

"A year or so."

The prince glanced over and looked to Alec's jacket. "Not even a year, and you're a full physicker?"

Alec nodded. "I had training before I came. I was a little older than the average student."

"Evidently. What kind of training did you have?" he asked as he turned back to Alec.

"My father. He studied at the university and left many years ago. He has been an apothecary in—"

"The poisoner."

Alec swallowed again and nodded toward the water, waiting until the prince tipped it to his mouth, allowing Alec to take a long drink. "It seems that way."

The prince frowned. "You didn't know?"

"Know that my father is a poisoner? Know that he has been using the knowledge he gained at the university to harm others? No, I didn't know."

"But he has been working on our behalf. You didn't know that?"

"What do you mean your behalf?"

"There have been assignments doled out from the palace. The poisoner has been given most of them, and he has been quite skilled at seeing them to completion."

"What sort of assignments?" Alec was starting to feel a little stronger and wondered if maybe it was just the water he needed, or if there was more. Had it been one of the medicines he took that was helping?

"The kind the king's poisoner would have been given," he said.

"King's?"

"As far as I know. I know my father has many poisoners, and they are often tasked with difficult responsibilities. They are assassins."

Alec shook his head. "My father should never have been an assassin. He's a healer. An apothecary."

"Can you not be both?"

"How?"

"I can tell you from my experience that there are people who pose a threat to the city and need to be removed. Should they remain and risk the city?"

"I don't think that's for me to decide."

"Then your father has decided. And he has determined the answer to the question is yes, at least for him."

Alec rested his head back on the pillow. He stared up at the ceiling for a long moment. "Is that why you brought me here? Did my father ask you to bring me?"

"No. I brought you here because I heard you had success with Helen."

"I don't know how much success I had. I thought I was following the right recipe."

"And how would you have known?"

The prince took a seat on the bed next to Alec. Even seated, there was something of power to him. He seemed coiled, as if he was prepared to strike, and Alec suddenly realized it was likely that the prince was augmented, even sitting as he was next to Alec.

"Who is your Scribe?"

"You're quite forward."

"How is that forward?"

"If a Kaver were to reveal their Scribe, that is considered quite forward. It would allow you to know the best way to challenge me."

"Do I look like I would challenge you?"

The prince chuckled. "It wouldn't be the first time."

"I don't understand."

"I suppose your time in the university has been too limited for you to gain an education like that. That is perhaps fortunate. At least for me."

"Why is that fortunate? And why would there be any sort of danger to you?"

"The Scribes have often thought they could gain more power. Some resent the position they are in."

"What position is that?"

The princess looked at Alec and stared for a long time. "Who is your Kaver?"

"You're quite forward," Alec said.

The prince laughed. "You won't share that with your prince?"

"My prince just told me that I was supposed to keep that information to myself."

"No, he said that it would allow another to challenge you. Do you think I might challenge you?"

"I don't know you. Maybe."

The prince grinned. "You are an interesting one." He stood and faced Alec. "Now. Where is the Scribe Helen?"

"I don't know."

"If you're keeping something from me—"

Alec shook his head. "I don't know. You could ask your father."

The prince frowned. "My father? Why would I ask my father where the Scribe… She's his?"

Alec licked his lips, his mouth suddenly dry again. "You didn't know?"

"As I said, it's not often that we get to know who is Scribe to whom."

"What about your sister?"

His face twisted in a distasteful frown. "My sister? She is the first Scribe in the Anders family in generations. She thought it was best to reveal that so that everyone knew, and has made a point of flaunting that, as well as flaunting her Kaver."

"You don't care for Elaine?"

The prince shrugged. "It doesn't matter, at least not to my sister. She already lost one Kaver and feels they are replaceable. She doesn't have the same connection, the same bond, that many of us do."

"And who is your bond to?"

"You continue to ask, but that won't make me any more likely to tell you."

"I only thought—"

"I know what you thought. I'm just telling you that I won't be any more inclined to share simply because you continue to ask." He glanced toward the door before turning his attention back to Alec. "You don't know where Master Helen is?"

Alec shook his head. "I don't know. I was trying to find her. She disappeared after poisoning me. No one has been able to locate her. I need to get to her and ask her what she added to the mixture so I can try to restore myself."

"Restore yourself?"

"I told you. While I was attempting to make easar paper, Master Helen added something to it that poisoned me."

"Ah, yes. I will see if there's anything I can offer to help you."

"I know what would help," Alec said. How would the prince react?

"And that is?"

"Eel meat."

"Eel? As in the canal eels?"

Alec nodded. "Their meat has restorative properties. I just need a little bit, and it can help."

"The eel has restorative properties? I find that hard to believe."

"It doesn't matter whether you believe it or not, it's whether or not it works, and I can assure you it does."

"How do you know this?"

Alec hesitated. "I've already used it. It was needed to help restore me when the poisoning first took place. I don't know how often I'll need to take it, but until I find a treatment that is permanent, I might need to use the eels."

"I will see what I can do."

The princess started to leave, and Alec sat up. "You haven't told me why you brought me here."

"Because you've been working with Helen."

"So?"

"I'm determined to know what she intends. If she has

figured out the key to easar paper, I would learn that for myself."

"She hasn't discovered the key. We've tried, but we've failed."

The prince frowned. "That's too bad."

"Why?"

"Because if you can't help me learn the key, you are otherwise useless to me."

With that, he headed out of the room, leaving Alec staring at the door.

23

CAPTURING THE CAPTIVE

S am reached Caster, taking a roundabout way so that even were Elaine to have followed her, she would still have been unlikely to know where Sam was going. She'd first had to take the young girl back to the Dorand section, and that had taken some time. She wasn't sure whether she should have, but the girl was too young to be involved in any activity of the Shuver. Maybe she felt that way because she was nearly the same age Sam had been when Bastan first involved her in his world. Whatever it was, Sam was determined to ensure she didn't stay involved.

Dorand was another peripheral section. The people there reminded her of those in Caster, and she suspected there was a Bastan-type in the section too. Maybe it was the Shuver. Maybe it was someone else. Either way, if what they suspected of Princess Lyasanna and the royals was true, it might be that Bastan would need to consolidate the outer sections, especially if the inner sections—

the palace and the university—decided to make things difficult.

It was late, and she was tired, and a part of her was concerned that she had made a mistake returning to Caster, especially knowing that Elaine was possibly following—and especially since she suspected that Elaine knew that Sam had Marin.

If she discovered her location, what would Elaine do?

How many Kavers would she send after Marin?

It wasn't really about how many Elaine would send, it was more about how many Lyasanna would send. Sam had little doubt the princess would bring everything she could to bear on Marin, especially if it meant protecting her secret.

She climbed to a rooftop and started across the familiar buildings as she made her way through Caster, trying to remain hidden. From here, she watched the streets, looking for signs of anyone who shouldn't be here. There had been another time when Sam had seen Kavers in this section, though then it had been for a very different reason. They had sought her then, as well, but only because they wanted to help her learn what it meant for her to be a Kaver. This time was different. This time, she needed to avoid them because she now knew what they were after, and if they found her, it would put her—and possibly Bastan—in danger.

She reached the alley that held the entrance to Bastan's cells, and she dropped down right in front of the door and knocked.

It took a moment before the door opened, and Jonas glanced out. He had the same massive build as every other man that Bastan had watching the door, though quite a bit of a gut along with it. A wide smile greeted Sam. "Samara."

"It's Sam."

"But Bastan always calls you—"

"I know what Bastan always calls me. That doesn't mean that's what I want to be called."

"Fine. Sam. I think Samara is pretty."

"You can think it, but don't say it. Is he here?" She pushed past him and entered the room, waiting a moment until she was sure he closed the door. He replaced the bar barricading the door, and Sam waved to him as she made her way to the next door. She wasn't sure he would be back yet, since he'd gone off to find one of his connections. But at the bottom of the stairs, Bastan was coming out from the cells.

"Samara. I understand you decided to go confront the Shuver?"

"I had two Kavers after me. I needed some distraction."

"So, you decided to use the Shuver as your distraction?"

"There was a little bit more to it."

"You shouldn't have gotten involved with him. You placed yourself in between him and his business with Aelus."

"I already put myself in between him and Aelus when I attacked his men. I just wanted to make sure he didn't come after him again."

"That's not the only reason you went."

Could the Shuver have already sent that much word to Bastan? She thought he would have sent some notification, but only because he had sent off one of his men. That would have been mostly for confirmation, and nothing else. The Shuver wouldn't have anticipated that Sam would have attacked him.

"I'm only making some preparations."

"And those would be?"

"Those would be making sure that we have some way of defending ourselves if it becomes necessary."

Bastan studied her. "Samara, we don't need civil war in the city. Whatever else is happening, we don't need to create more difficulty. There are those of us who have worked on the edges for a long time. We want to remain working on the edges of the city."

"Bastan. What have you told me about how you defend Caster?"

He frowned. "Why are you asking?"

"Only because you made it clear that you will do anything necessary to defend the people you care for. Those people include all of the people of Caster, isn't that right?"

"I think *all* of the people would be a bit of a stretch."

"Fine. Maybe not all of the people, but you care about most of the people in this section. I've seen it. You may want to pretend that you don't, but you have done everything you can to ensure that this section is as safe as it can be."

Bastan breathed out heavily. "Samara, one of the things I learned long ago is that when you live too far from the palace, they don't care about what happens in your section. I've learned that if I want to keep the section somewhat safe, I need to be involved in that."

"Which is all I'm trying to say," Sam said.

"And what does the Shuver have to do with it?"

"I thought I could see if the two of you could work together."

"We already work together often enough."

"Not like this. I think if things happen the way I fear they might, there could be a different outcome in the city."

"And this is all about the princess?"

Sam nodded. "Which is why I need to speak to Marin."

Sam headed toward the cells, and Bastan went with her, nodding to the man standing guard. It was a measure of respect—a surprising one—that Bastan didn't attempt to stop her. He didn't seem to care that she was coming to visit Marin or that she moved so freely through his hidden areas.

"What do you intend to ask her?" Bastan asked.

"We are going to ask about what Master Helen might have done."

"And then?"

"I don't know. It might involve me breaking into the palace so that I can find the guidebook so that I can go after Tray."

"Even though this Master Helen might have attacked your friend?"

Sam hated that it might come to that, but it was possible that it would. "Did you get him?"

Bastan frowned. "I tried, but…"

She rounded on him. "But what?"

"He wasn't there. I assumed Aelus brought him out. He would know enough to keep his son safe."

"And if he didn't?"

"I will help you find him." When they reached the door leading into the cells, Bastan took her hand. "You were careful making your way here?"

"Bastan, you taught me better than that. I made sure that I took the most roundabout way that I could. Kyza, that was why I went to the Shuver's section. I needed to draw the Kavers away so that they didn't know where I was heading."

"But Elaine knows of your connection to Caster. If she comes here…"

"She won't know how to find this place."

Bastan frowned. Sam suspected there was something he wasn't telling her, but maybe it didn't matter.

When Sam pushed the door open, Marin stood at her cell, hands gripping the bars. A smile crossed her face. "Bastan. You have decided to question me again so soon?"

"It's not Bastan who's questioning you. It's me."

"Samara. Eventually, I think you're going to grow tired of all of this questioning. Eventually, you're going to come to a decision about how you feel about me. Maybe you'll even begin to trust me."

"I don't know that I can trust you, not ever again, but that doesn't mean that I don't believe you."

Thunder rumbled.

Bastan glanced toward the door, and he frowned. "Was it raining when you came?"

Sam shook her head. "No, but it was dark, so if a storm was coming, I wouldn't have been able to tell."

"Was there lightning?"

"No."

Bastan let out a frustrated groan. "I think we need to move."

"Why?"

Thunder rumbled again, and this time, it had enough

force that some debris and dust trickled down into the cell.

"She found you," Bastan said.

"She?" Marin asked. "You brought Elaine here?"

"I didn't bring Elaine here. I—"

There was another peal of thunder that rumbled, sending the walls shaking.

Sam glanced over to Bastan. "We can't leave her here, not if Elaine is coming. We need to bring her with us."

"That's dangerous, Samara."

"Not as dangerous as if the Kavers get her. I don't know what they'll do, but I'm sure they will question her much more vigorously than what we have done."

"Is that a problem for you?"

Sam glanced over at Marin. It shouldn't be, not after what Marin had done to her, but Sam didn't want to leave her here and didn't want to lose out on any way that Marin might be able to help her when she went for Tray. And then there was the fact that Sam felt Marin was fonder of Tray than her. She needed the woman's help.

"If I bring you with me, you won't make a run for it?" Sam asked.

Marin looked at Sam and then at Bastan. "Where would I go?"

"There are plenty of places in the city for you to hide," Bastan said. "I seem to recall that you have nearly as many contacts as I do."

"I *had* those contacts. Most of them are lost."

"It hasn't been so long that you would have lost your contacts," Bastan said. Everything rumbled again, and Bastan stood there, calmer than Sam felt. "If you decide to run, I will ensure you don't go far. I will use my network to find you, and trust me when I say that I won't be nearly as accommodating the next time I get ahold of you."

"You haven't been accommodating this time," Marin said.

"You've been fed. You've been kept inside. You haven't wanted for anything during your capture," Bastan said.

"Other than freedom."

"Had you wanted to maintain your freedom, you wouldn't have done what you did to Samara."

"If I hadn't done what I did to Samara, then Trayson would already be dead."

Sam glanced at Bastan. "Come on. Let's bring her with us."

The door opened behind them, and Sam turned, pulling her staff out and readying it. Sayd stood there, his eyes wide and a sword in hand. "Bastan. We're under attack. There is pressure at the door, and I don't know how much longer we'll be able to hold it. You need to get out before they break through the door."

"There's no other way out," Sam said.

"There's another way," Bastan told her. "Haven't I taught you anything? You should always plan so that there's another way out."

Bastan pulled a ring of keys out of his pocket and unlocked the cell door, pulling it open so that Marin could come out. She hurried from the room, practically falling out. Bastan grabbed her arms and jerked her upright. "Don't think of trying anything."

"The only thing I will do is help," Marin said.

"Don't even try that," Bastan said.

They hurried back to the main door, and she expected him to take them up the stairs, but he veered away and down another hallway. It was a narrow hall, one that she didn't remember seeing before, and he reached a flat section of wall where he stopped. Bastan pressed on one of the stones, and the entire thing swung in.

"A hidden door?" Marin asked. "You and your secrets, Bastan."

"I have kept Samara safe all this time because of my secrets," he said.

"You were never asked to keep Samara safe."

"No? And you would have kept her safe by yourself? You were absent all the time. It was almost as if you had no interest in her."

"Then you weren't paying attention. My interest has always been in Samara and ensuring that she was safe. If she wasn't safe, how could Trayson be safe?"

Bastan led them into a room, and on the other side, there was a narrow stair that twisted around. Bastan started up it, and Sam motioned for Marin to go in front of her. Marin glanced back at her, a frown on her face. She followed Bastan up the stairs. At the top, Bastan stood behind a plain, stout door. His hand gripped the handle, and he remained frozen, waiting.

"What is it?" Sam asked.

"I'm just making sure there's nothing on the other side," Bastan said.

"And if there is?"

He glanced back, and his gaze fell on her staff. "Then we need to be ready for whatever we encounter," Bastan said.

Marin pushed forward and attempted to get in between Sam and Bastan, as though she was going to force her way into the next room, trying to fight so that Sam didn't have to.

"Step back," Sam said.

"Samara—"

"No. If there's something there, then I'm going to be next to Bastan, helping him."

"You don't think I would help?" Marin asked.

"I don't know what you might do."

Marin glared at her for a moment before stepping to the side and letting Sam pass.

Bastan considered her for a moment before pushing the door open.

He ducked and rolled, sliding aside as something streaked past Sam's head.

She turned and saw that a crossbow bolt had stuck into the wall behind her.

Marin smiled darkly. "You wanted to be the first one in," she said.

Sam glared at her.

She focused on an augmentation, thinking about strength and speed, but this time attempting to make her skin impervious. She was only intermittently successful with that, but anytime she attacked somebody who had the ability to hurt her, she tried to use this augmentation.

As it washed through her, she ran into the room.

Violence greeted her.

There were probably a dozen soldiers, common soldiers, and likely from the palace. Along with them were three people who had to be Kavers. Bastan was fighting with a sword, confronting three of the soldiers and managing far better than Sam would ever have expected. Maybe he *was* a djohn as Helen had suggested.

"Samara, get out of here."

"Not leaving you behind, Bastan," she said as she darted forward, the augmentation allowing her great speed. She swung with the staff, knocking down two soldiers before they could turn to her. Others approached, but Marin grabbed a sword and began to fight, knocking back the soldiers. Sam had only a moment to register that she should be more troubled by the fact that Marin was so skilled with the sword.

Then she came face-to-face with one of the Kavers.

She didn't recognize the man. That bothered her. She didn't recognize many of the Kavers she had seen, which meant that Elaine had kept them from her. Why would she have prevented Sam from knowing other Kavers? The only answer that made sense was that she didn't want Sam to know about them.

The man glanced to her staff, and then he swung his down toward her.

It collided with her shoulder, but with her augmentation, she felt nothing.

His eyes widened slightly. "Yeah. I'm augmented." Sam swung. She brought her staff around as rapidly as she could and caught him in his side. He grunted as he fell forward, and Sam allowed herself no remorse for the way that she knocked him down. How could she, when he had been so willing to harm her?

She darted to the side, coming toward the other Kaver. This one was an older woman, and she glared at Sam, giving Sam a moment to swing and bring the staff around, connecting with the woman's staff. She was better prepared than the man had been. It was almost as if the man had been startled by the fact that Sam was not bothered by his staff connecting with her shoulder.

"You're the one we're after," the woman said.

"Am I? Did Elaine send you after me?"

"Elaine? No. The princess sent us after you."

"I have no intention of going back to the palace with you."

"The princess doesn't want you brought back the palace. She wants you removed."

Sam frowned. Had she made a mistake with Elaine? Could she have been trying to help Sam avoid what Lyasanna might intend for her?

It would be something to think about when she had more time. Right now, she had to focus on getting out of here before these Kavers hurt her—or managed to grab Marin.

She pushed back, driving the Kaver toward the far wall. The room was not large, but it had high ceilings which was an advantage for her—but also for the Kaver. They were able to swing their staffs, and they attacked with a steady rhythm, one that Sam had not experienced before. The woman was quick, and she fought with a certain brutality. Sam felt her staff against her arm and then her leg, and was thankful for her augmentations, because if she hadn't placed them, the staff would have hurt her quite a bit more.

Eventually, the augmentations would fade.

Having placed them herself, without Alec's assistance, she knew they would fade soon. Alec's augmentations seemed to have a lingering effect, though Sam wasn't sure if it was her focus, or her strength that caused them to fade.

The woman seemed to be augmented, as well, though Sam wasn't sure if the augmentation was the same. Did she use strength and speed the same way that Sam did? Or could she be impervious much as Sam was?

Maybe it was neither.

It would be beneficial if the woman wasn't augmented at all, but the way that she attacked, the speed with which she was able to move, made it seem as though she was.

Sam spun and jabbed her staff forward.

The woman blocked, knocking Sam back with a kick to her stomach.

Even with the augmentation, it took the wind out of her. She focused, trying to keep her thoughts steady, trying to keep her mind on the attack, but it was increasingly difficult when facing someone like this.

Around her, she heard the sounds of fighting, and someone grunted, though she wasn't sure whether it was Bastan or someone he was fighting.

She wanted to look, but she had to keep her attention focused on this Kaver.

Sam tried to bring on another augmentation.

What would she choose? She still had strength and speed, and she thought she still had the impervious protection, but there had to be something more that she could do to stop this woman.

She looked up at the ceiling.

The room was big—big enough for her as a giant.

She had never tried to augment herself that way, though Alec had. Sam had been annoyed when he had, but now? If she had speed, along with her strength, adding size shouldn't be a problem.

Sam tried to focus on what Alec had written. It came

to mind slowly, and she focused on the way he had written about her being too short, and things that he might have tried to make her bigger.

The augmentation washed through her.

With it, she grew.

The other woman stepped back and tried to bring her staff around, but Sam grabbed for it. She was quite a bit taller than the woman now, and with her longer reach, she grabbed her arm and tried to lift her, but the other Kaver tried to kick her back.

Sam spun her staff. It felt considerably smaller in her hands, and she moved it much more rapidly. She flicked it at the Kaver, and though she missed, it forced the woman to move off to the side.

Shifting her steps, Sam tried to keep herself low. If she were hit on the legs, she would go down hard. She was thankful that she hadn't made herself *too* big. She thought about when Alec had made her into a giant, she had been enormous, and that would have been difficult for her to handle in such tight quarters.

Sam reached for her again and grabbed the canal staff away from her.

"Why is Lyasanna doing this?"

"Does it matter? I've learned not to question when it comes to the Anders."

"You should always question. What if she's wrong?"

"She's the princess. She can't be wrong."

Sam jabbed at the woman with her staff, and she jumped away, her back slamming into the wall. "Everyone can be wrong."

The woman glanced past Sam then turned and ran.

Sam turned to see what else might be happening in the

room. There were still four soldiers, and they were converging on Bastan. Sam darted forward, sweeping her staff at them. The augmentation started to fade, and she began to shrink, returning to her normal size.

Weakness began to work through. It was surprising. She had used augmentations before and hadn't felt quite as weakened when they faded as she did now. Maybe it was because she had done something she wasn't accustomed to doing. She wasn't sure she could fight again, were there the need.

Bastan made short work of the soldiers, finishing them off.

When he was finished, he turned to her, worry in his eyes. "Are you harmed?"

Sam checked herself her injuries but didn't think she had any. "I think I'm fine," she said.

"Good. We need to get moving. Grab Marin and—"

Bastan looked around, and his jaw clenched.

Sam followed the direction of his gaze and realized that Marin was gone.

Not only that, but the three Kavers were gone.

"I don't think she escaped," Bastan said.

"No. That's what I'm worried about."

Sam raced outside the building, and the streets were empty. In the distance, three people moved quickly—far too quickly to be anything but augmented.

Not three. Four.

The fourth was flung over one of their shoulders.

Kyza.

Marin was gone.

Bastan joined her on the street and looked over at her. "What are you going to do?"

"I have to get her back."

"You don't need her to get Tray."

"That's not it." Sam hated to admit what she said next, but seeing what Lyasanna had been willing to do, what other choice was there? "I have to get her back because I think she might be the only one to have done the right thing all these years."

Bastan sighed. "Then I'll help."

24

WORKING WITH ROYALTY

Alec leaned on the table as he stirred the pot, working with the combination of substances he had memorized. There was other information in the book that might have been helpful, and had his father not taken it, Alec might have tried to see what else he could learn, but he'd have needed someone to translate the Theln language.

As he mixed the combination together, he wondered if the outcome would be any different this time. Would he end up poisoning himself again? He didn't think the combination of items in the recipe for the easar paper were toxic, but how could he be sure? He'd never heard of items that were stable when separate somehow became dangerous when mixed together.

"I still need the svethwuud," Alec said.

The prince leaned over his shoulder, wrinkling his nose as he stuck his head toward the pot. "I have someone looking to see if they can find something called svethwuud."

Alec took a seat. He was still tired, and the time he'd spent mixing the ingredients and constantly stirring it together had made him even more aware of how tired he was. He had slept, the bed far more comfortable than any he'd slept on in quite some time, and he had been well cared for, the prince providing food and water and anything else he could ask for. Regardless of the fact that he felt something like a prisoner here, the prince made sure he had everything he needed.

It made him feel less like a prisoner and more like he was simply working with the prince.

"This is what it was like when you were mixing it with Helen?" the prince asked.

Alec shook his head. "There was something more irritating in it."

"Could it have been the maple?"

Alec doubted it. "It's possible…"

"But you don't think it likely," the prince said.

"No. The species of wood shouldn't make a difference. Maple in particular is a fairly benign wood. It doesn't interact with anything."

"And what of this svethwuud?"

"I've never heard of it. I don't even know what it is, or whether it's simply the Theln name for another type of wood. If I had the book…"

"I can't allow you to leave here until I know whether this is going to be effective," the prince said.

"I would come back," Alec said.

The prince grunted. "It's not so much a matter of whether you would come back as whether you would be allowed to return."

"Who would prevent me from returning?"

"I'm not the only one who is after this paper," he said.

Alec leaned back in the chair, looking around the room the prince had set up his makeshift lab. All around him were shelves packed with books and various leaves and roots and oils, all things that Alec had requested. The prince had gathered them without hesitation, managing to acquire them quickly and easily, far more quickly than Alec ever would have managed.

The table they used was made of metal and likely incredibly heavy. The pot sat on top of the table, and a fire burned beneath it, heating the contents. The pulp mixture steamed, but it did so with a quiet sort of burbling, and while there was a strange odor to it, it was nothing like what he had experienced when at the university.

He was even more confident that Master Helen had done something, and that she had poisoned him somehow, but why? He still couldn't understand why she'd have done that.

"I think the key will be acquiring the svethwuud," Alec said.

"You had thought the eel venom was a part of it."

Alec frowned. "Only because that was what Master Helen said. And maybe this recipe isn't for easar paper, so it could be I'm wrong."

"But you don't think so," the prince said.

"No. I think this is for easar paper."

There came a knock at the door, and the prince got up to answer it, pulling it open briefly before stepping back inside and closing it once more. When he returned, he carried a tray that he set down on the table. Chunks of some kind of meat were piled on the tray, and Alec frowned at it. It was a strange, almost silvery-looking meat, nothing like anything he'd ever seen before.

"What is it?"

"This is what you asked for. Eel meat. I thought you said you had partaken of it before."

"I had, but I was barely awake when I did. My father force fed it to me."

"I will tell you that it took some difficulty to acquire it. From what I could tell, this is not something many have ever fished for."

"The university claims it's toxic to prevent others from going after it. The meat has restorative powers, but they try to limit those who may go after it."

"Typical," the prince said.

Alec smiled. "Why typical?"

The prince waved his hand. "It doesn't matter. All that matters is that it's not the first time the university has tried to claim one thing when another is for their benefit."

"Such as treating only those who have the means to pay?"

The prince's face contorted into a scowl. "It's unfortunate the way they have sought to accumulate wealth. Had they only partnered with the Anders…"

Alec stared at the prince, not sure what to say. So, he said nothing and took a piece of the eel meat, tentatively putting it in his mouth. There was a foul flavor to it. How had he eaten this before? Maybe the foulness to it was enough to deter others from eating it. It certainly made it believable that it was toxic.

"It's not to your liking?"

"It's not good," he said.

The prince picked up a piece and slipped it into his

mouth, chewing it. He did so slowly, as though attempting to savor the piece. When he was done, he swallowed, a frown on his face. "It is interesting. I can see why you would be displeased with it."

"It's not so much that I'm displeased, it's more that it tastes terrible."

The prince stood for a moment, then his eyes started to widen. "Oh."

"What is it?"

"I feel... I feel a strange warmth."

Alec hadn't felt anything quite like that. Then again, he wasn't sure whether the poisoning he'd been subjected to prevented him from feeling the same warmth. "As I said, it's supposed to have a restorative property."

"This is different from restorative. This is almost... power."

Alec frowned. "Power?"

The prince stared at Alec. "You have never experienced this?"

He shook his head. "When I took the eel meat before, it was intended to help restore me after the poisoning. I don't remember anything else."

"Try some more."

Alec took another piece, and then another. Soon, he had consumed half the platter. Still he hadn't felt anything.

As he thought about it, he realized that wasn't *quite* true.

The more meat he consumed, the more he began to feel strength returning. It happened slowly and built up gradually. Thankfully, it seemed the eel meat still worked to restore his energy and his strength. Was that what would now be required to maintain his strength and stamina? Would he now need to consume eel meat on a regular basis?

He looked at the tray. If that was the case, it was a foul future for him.

"It's almost like an augmentation," the prince said.

"But?"

"But it's not. It's just... energy. I don't know how to explain it any other way, other than to say that whatever it is, I feel incredible." He glanced down at the tray and took another piece, chewing it just as slowly. "I can see why the university would have wanted to keep this from the Anders."

"I don't know that it's so much that they kept it from the Anders as they kept it from everyone else. The eels provide a certain protection to the city from the Thelns."

"And how did the eels manage that?"

"I don't entirely understand it. I think it's something to do with the way they encircle the city, creating an augmentation that pushes the Thelns back."

The prince took another piece meat. "You thought the key to making your paper was in the eel venom."

Alec nodded. "That was what Master Helen had suggested. I don't know whether it was true, and considering the way that she attacked me..."

The prince smiled. "What if it wasn't the eel venom, but the eel meat?"

Alec looked to the pot where the pulpy mix was slowly boiling. "I'm not even sure that is the answer," Alec said. "It might be that there is nothing of the eel involved in the mixture."

"Unless the Thelns called something involving the eels svethwuud."

"But what would that be?" Alec asked. He didn't expect the prince to answer and couldn't think of the solution himself. He had anticipated trying different types of woods, going through them one by one until he came up with the answer, determined to experiment. With the prince as an ally—at least an ally in creating easar paper—Alec didn't worry that he would run out of supplies. The prince seemed intrigued by the possibility, as if he thought they could work together to come up with this solution.

"Maybe the wood has something to do with the eels," the prince said.

It was an offhand comment, but it got Alec thinking.

What did he know about the eels?

He knew they were found in the swamp, and they had seemed to attack Sam and her canal staff. They seemed to congregate around the reeds, and were often found in greater numbers near the clumps of trees that grew in the swamp.

"What do you know about the swamp?"

The prince waved his hand, taking another piece of eel meat and popping it into his mouth. For a moment, Alec worried that there would be a problem with the prince consuming too much of the eel meat. He didn't know what side effects there might be, if there would be any at all. Maybe to someone like the prince—a Kaver who must have some skill—there wouldn't be any side effects.

"I know about as much as anyone can know. It provides a border for us and is practically impassable."

"It's not impassable."

The prince paused as he was reaching for another piece of meat. He looked over at Alec. "You have traveled through the swamp?"

"Only a little bit," Alec said. "When we were looking for the eels, trying to understand the venom, I went out on the swamp with a barge captain." He decided that it was best to keep Bastan's name out of it. It might not matter, but knowing Bastan, he would not want anyone else to realize that he had any involvement in it. "Besides, some of the Kavers have crossed the swamp entirely."

"That's only rumor," he said.

"It's no rumor. I've seen Kavers making their way across the swamp with nothing more than their canal staffs. It's impressive, and I think if they were to rest along the way, they wouldn't have any difficulty crossing the entirety of the swamp." And then there was what was beyond swamp, though Alec didn't know enough about what was there. He suspected that Sam might know—and most likely Marin did. He thought it possible that he could figure it out, but it would require the prince's help. "There's a place in the middle of the swamp, an island that Kavers can reach."

The prince steepled his hands together and frowned. "You have seen this?"

Alec nodded.

"Your Kaver?"

He hesitated. If he answered this truthfully, it might put Sam in danger, but if he didn't answer truthfully, it might prevent the prince from helping, and he wanted to see what the prince might be able to share with him. He might not know anything that could help, but what if he did?

"My Kaver was working on trying to see whether she could cross the swamp, but I don't think that she had mastered it, not completely."

The prince sat in silence for a while. "If it is possible, and if Helen was convinced the eels were required for creating the paper, it makes me wonder whether there is something about the swamp wood that would be a part of the creation of the easar paper."

Swamp wood.

Alec shook his head. The prince might have unwittingly put it together. That had to be the key, didn't it? It had to be that the swamp trees were part of the easar paper. And if the trees were a part of it, maybe they were granted their power by the canal eels, though not quite as directly as what Master Helen would have thought.

"We need to find a supply of that wood," Alec said.

The prince stared at Alec for a moment. "I think I can manage that."

"I have a friend, someone who can help—"

The prince shook his head. "No one else. Not until this is complete."

"And then what?"

The prince didn't answer, and it made Alec uncomfortable.

25

SVUTHWUUD

It was only now dusk, but moonlight already sent silvery shafts of light across the water. Alec tried to focus on the beauty of it, but the now all-too-familiar stench of the swamp overwhelmed his senses. He thought back to his two previous experiences out here, the first having been when he'd gone out to the island with Sam and Bastan in search of Tray, and then again when he'd come out eel fishing with Bastan. There was something strange about the swamp, something that made him uncomfortable, and regardless of the fact that he was with the prince and two completely silent soldiers, he felt nervous.

"You trust them?" Alec whispered.

"More than I trust you."

Alec swallowed. "I'm only asking because—"

"I know why you're asking. Just know that they are trustworthy."

The prince stood near the stern of the barge, and he pushed with a long, slender pole that forced them out into the swamp. He had a steady and rhythmic pattern that made Alec think he had done this before, which left Alec wondering what other secrets the prince might be keeping.

"How much farther do you think we need to go?" the prince asked him.

Alec shrugged. "I'm not sure. All I know is that we need to get deep enough that we can reach the trees. And I don't recall the trees growing too close to the edge of the swamp."

In those parts, it was mostly reeds, and none of the trees. He had grabbed a few reeds as they went past them, deciding that, if nothing else, they could try that also, but he didn't want to only use the reeds. He had a growing conviction that what the prince suggested about the trees was accurate. What if the swamp trees were svethwuud?

The idea intrigued him, and it was something he doubted Master Helen would have considered, especially given that she had been focused solely on the eels.

As they continued to make their way further into the swamp, the prince remained silent, steadily pushing them along. Alec pointed every so often, directing him, trying to remember where they had been when he had seen the eels before. There had been a spawning ground some-where deep into the swamp, and it was a place that his father had known about. Having come here only once before in search of the eels, Alec hoped he could find it again, but he wasn't entirely certain he could.

When full darkness fell, the moon was bright enough that it cast light, enough light he could easily see. "There," he said, pointing in the distance.

"I see it," the prince said. He spoke softly, and Alec saw

his whole body tense. How long could he maintain such effort?

They reached a clump of three trees.

"Like this?" the prince asked.

Alec looked at the trees. "There are clusters of trees like this all throughout the swamp. I think they are all the same, which would mean they are likely the ones we seek."

"I sense your hesitation."

"I think… I think we need to ensure there are eels found around the trees. It could be that there are other species out here. The presence of eels could be the sign that they are the right ones."

The prince nodded slowly. "You have an interesting thought process, physicker."

"I'm sorry. I don't mean to make this more complicated than it needs to be—"

The prince shook his head. "That wasn't meant as any sort of insult. I was commending you for the way you are thinking through this. You're right. If we are looking for trees that might be tied to the eels, we need to ensure eels can be found around the trees."

"There were spawning grounds in certain areas of the swamp."

"Do you remember which ones?"

"I thought this could have been one, but I'm not certain, not anymore. It's hard to know. At night, in the darkness, everything starts to look same."

"The only way to find out is to investigate."

The prince set the long staff on the deck of the barge and then peeled off his cloak. He pulled his boots off and stood at the edge of the barge… and jumped.

Alec barely had time to react.

The two soldiers remained silent and didn't do anything when their prince jumped in. What was the prince thinking? Could he really believe he could withstand eel bites, and if the eel managed to pierce him with its tail…

Unless the prince was augmented.

It was a possibility. The prince could carry an augmentation, could be protected from anything harmful happening to him because of that. Alec hadn't seen him place one, but Sam had proven she didn't need easar paper for the augmentations to be effective.

Alec could only wait.

He stood at the edge of the barge, looking down at the water. There were swirls, and a few bubbles that drifted to the surface, but there was nothing else. There was no flurry of eel activity, but there was no sign of the prince, either.

The water wasn't deep here. Looking at the long pole used to propel them through the swamp, Alec could gauge the depth of the water, and it would only be slightly above the prince's head, certainly not so deep that would be unable to resurface. Then again, if there were eels in the water, he would be in much more danger.

He glanced over at the soldiers. It shocked him that they seemed so nonchalant. This must be something they saw often enough that it didn't bother them, though it did bother Alec. He didn't want to be with the prince when he met his death.

There came a splash along the port side of the barge and Alec hurried over. The prince grabbed the bottom railing and flipped himself onto the deck of the barge. He shook water from himself and tried to press more water out of his clothes. His mouth wrinkled in a distasteful frown.

"That was unpleasant."

"What were you doing?"

"I needed to know whether there were any eels."

"By jumping into the swamp?"

"It seemed an easy enough way to find out. We could have swept a net through the water, but this was faster."

"I've seen people attacked by eels. I've seen the way they can pierce you with their tail, and the venom doesn't have an easy antidote." At least not without easar paper, and even that was a temporary solution. Without Sam's blood, Alec would have had no way of helping the prince. They would need access to both types of eel venom. What was the prince thinking?

The prince withdrew a small knife from his waist and jabbed it toward his stomach. Alec stared in shock until he noticed the knife bounce off the prince's stomach.

"You have an augmentation," Alec said.

"No. Feel the cloth."

Alec ran his fingers along the cloth that shrouded the prince. It was smooth, but it was firm. Almost metallic.

"Armor?"

"The finest I can buy. Who needs augmentations when a simple suit of armor can be just as effective?"

"What if the eels attacked your face?"

"I can see that coming," the prince said.

Alec shook his head. "I still can't believe you did that. That wasn't the most sensible plan."

"The next time you can jump in."

"No thanks." He glanced down at the water. "Did you find any eels? Is this the right place?"

The prince motioned to the trees. "There is a swarm of eels over near those trees. They are swimming in an out of the root system, disappearing." He turned back to Alec. "Yes. I think this is the right place."

The prince lifted his long barge pole and pushed them toward the trees. When they reached them, the prince grabbed a branch and started to break it off.

"We might need to get a section of the root also."

The prince frowned at him. "Why?"

"If the eels are swimming around the roots, we would want to make sure we're getting something that has most potency."

"Won't that kill the tree?"

"Not necessarily. In many plants, if you take only a section of the root, it will stimulate increased growth. It might even be that taking a section of the root would help these trees—and the eels."

The prince shrugged. "You're only saying that so that I have to jump back down into the water."

"You said you had armor."

The prince glared at him. He said nothing more as he jumped off the edge of the barge and into the water. He was gone only a few moments before he threw himself back onto the barge. He had a long hunk of slimy root that had a strange, glistening coating to it.

Something writhed near him.

"Prince? The man ignored him. "Jalen?"

With that, the prince turned to him. Alec nodded to his leg where an eel was chomping down on his calf, his tail attempting to flick up and penetrate the prince in the belly.

"That's interesting," the prince said. He unsheathed his knife and stabbed it through the eel. It took a moment, but the eel stopped moving. "How much of this do you think we need to be successful?"

Alec looked at the long hunk of root. "I don't know. If this works, it might be enough for a single batch, but we would need more to make a decent quantity of easar paper."

He couldn't believe he was actually thinking the recipe might be effective. If it was, did that mean they no longer would have a limited supply? Could he have finally discovered the key to making it so they weren't reliant on finding supplies from outside of the city?

Essentially, stealing from the Thelns.

"If it works, then at least we know where to come to harvest more."

They turned and started back toward the city. Alec took a seat on the barge, staring at the slick surface of the tree root, wondering whether this really was what the Thelns had used for their easar paper. How would they ever have thought to use this?

Unless they knew something more about the connection between Kavers and Scribes. Which they had to. Everything he had learned made it seem likely that the Thelns knew much more about what it meant to be a Scribe. That was the reason Scribes who went into Theln lands rarely returned. They were tempted, and that temptation kept them there, preventing them from returning to their home and the university.

"What is it, physicker?" the prince asked, taking a seat

next to Alec. They drifted, and Alec smiled, thinking that there was something almost peaceful about drifting through the swamp. As surprising as it was, he felt a connection to the prince, and thought that maybe, under different circumstances, they could have been friends. That, despite the fact the prince was who he was and Alec was the son of an apothecary.

"I'm just thinking about the easar paper. I'm thinking about how difficult it has been to make, and I'm thinking about—"

Alec frowned. In the distance, he swore he saw movement.

The prince leapt to his feet and peered out into the night.

Alec stood and took a position next to the prince, looking into the darkness, though his eyesight wasn't in any way enhanced. With only the moonlight, he could barely make out whether anything—or anyone—was out there. If there was someone, it meant were likely a Kaver. That was the most likely explanation, though what Kaver? And what would they want?

"We need to hurry now," the prince said.

He began to push off with the pole, moving as quickly as he could, sending them streaking through the swamp. Alec couldn't tell whether he was augmented, or whether it was simple determination that propelled them as quickly as they went.

He stared behind them, watching the swamp, searching for signs of movement.

When it came again, it startled him.

It was a flicker of activity. It had to be a Kaver. Nothing else would move like that. Nothing else would flip and soar into the sky and land with little more than a quiet splash.

"It's a Kaver," Alec said.

"I'm aware of that," the prince told him.

"Is there anything you can do?"

The prince glanced over at him briefly. "I'm not so much of a... proficient... Kaver. Let's say that I prefer more practical approaches."

"Such as the armor?"

The prince nodded. "I've never taken my position quite as seriously as some. Perhaps that was a mistake, but it is what it is."

He made a motion, and the two soldiers stood and took positions at the back of the barge.

Alec couldn't help but wonder what use they would be if a Kaver appeared on the deck of the barge? He had seen Kavers fight, had seen the way they could spin and move and use their staffs to deadly effect. If there was a Kaver coming after them—or even more than one—there might not be anything that these two soldiers would be able to do to counter, especially if the Kaver was augmented.

The city gradually came into view. It happened slowly —far too slowly—and the prince continued to push, moving with a rapid, almost frantic, energy.

Alec turned his attention to the rear of the boat, looking back. The movement he saw that told him there had to be at least two Kavers. It was a flicker of shadows, and little more than that. There came a soft splash when they landed, their staffs parting the water so smoothly that they made little sound. Was that what Sam was to become? Was that what she already was? Could she flip and fly across the swamp with the same grace?

And then someone appeared on the deck.

It was an older man, and he had graying hair and a solid build. His canal staff stood three feet taller than his height, and he spun it around, sending a spray of water off of it.

The soldiers converged on him, swords unsheathed and slicing at the Kaver.

They were pushed back, the Kaver too fast with his staff and movements.

Still, the soldiers maintained their focus, seemingly not intimidated by the much longer reach of the canal staff.

The prince continued his focus, sending them through the water, not distracted by the battle taking place at the rear of the barge. For that, Alec was thankful. If he changed his focus, he would delay them. All Alec wanted was to get back onto land, and then...

Then he would make a run for Sam.

He would take the piece of tree root with him, and he would see if he could make easar paper with it, even if it wasn't completely effective.

Another Kaver landed on the deck. This one came close to the prince.

He swung his barge pole out of the water and at the Kaver.

The pole was too long, and he didn't have the same augmentations as the Kaver, so the Kaver was able to spin her staff quickly, knocking the prince down.

She struck his arm, and Alec feared it broke a bone, having seen the way the staffs could injure people, but with his armor, the prince seemed unharmed.

He swept the barge pole beneath the Kaver, forcing her to jump.

As she did, Alec moved into position where she would land, and shoved, sending her flying out into the swamp. Her canal staff went flying, and she landed in a splash.

The prince stared into the distance, an angry look on his face, before lifting up the barge pole and quickly using it to push them forward again. "Thanks."

The sound of fighting behind them caught Alec's attention. He turned to see the two soldiers attempting to push the Kaver back, but he was quick. How many augmentations did he have? Or did he even need augmentations? Could he be like Sam and Marin, able to control them without needing a Scribe to help?

One of the soldiers fell into the swamp.

Alec tried to reach for him, but the barge moved way too quickly. He thrashed in the water and then went under.

Alec squeezed his eyes closed briefly. He didn't want to think about what fate the man might face. He didn't want to think about the way the eels would attack, piercing his flesh, the poison taking hold. When it did, he would drown, especially if there was no one there to pull him back up and provide an antivenom.

Now there was only one soldier facing off against the Kaver.

It was an uneven fight.

The soldier attempted to push him back, but the Kaver was skilled and used his staff to his advantage, keeping the sword from reaching him. He played with the soldier, tapping his staff every so often on the barge, flipping from place to place as he did, kicking the soldier, and then flipping again, kicking him once more. It sent the soldier staggering from side to side.

Alec glanced forward and saw they were near the city. The prince had pushed them as quickly as he could, and land was in sight. It was one of the outer sections, and not near enough to the palace for safety, but at least it was land where they could run, and possibly find other soldiers.

And then what?

If the Kavers were fighting the prince, that meant there was some sort of discord within the palace.

Alec turned his attention back to the Kaver. He tried to push him the same way he had pushed the woman, but the Kaver flipped the staff toward him, forcing Alec to jump back to avoid getting hit.

With another flicker, the Kaver's staff struck the soldier, sending him flying out into the water.

The Kaver flipped, soaring over Alec to land near the prince.

The prince brought his barge pole around, but as before, the pole was too long, and he was too slow with it. It wasn't an even match, not against an augmented Kaver and a shorter canal staff that was easier to manipulate.

Still, the prince managed better than Alec would have expected. He got a strike in, and then another, and then still another. With each one, the Kaver gritted his teeth and continued to spin.

The barge drifted. Land appeared, and they crashed into it.

The prince staggered. The Kaver managed to correct himself before the prince, and he swung his staff, connecting with the side of the prince's skull.

Alec grabbed the piece of slippery swamp wood, stuffing it into his pocket. On a whim, he grabbed the eel before jumping off the barge and raced into the city.

He glanced back and saw the Kaver with the prince slung over his shoulder, but the Kaver didn't pursue.

Because he didn't have to.

Movement appeared out the corner of his eye, and Alec turned, seeing another Kaver.

It was the same woman from before.

26

ESCAPE FROM THE KAVER

T he Kaver. She was soaked and covered in filth, and a rivulet of blood streamed from the side of her face, but she moved with the same fluidity she had before, likely augmented.

How had she survived?

Alec ran into the city, thinking that if he could get ahead of her, he could disappear into a crowd, or maybe into a building, and then he could make his way gradually toward Caster and to Bastan.

Had he not recently had any eel meat, he wasn't sure he would have had the necessary energy, but the effects seemed to linger longer than they had the last time. Maybe the key for him was to keep eating eel meat.

He held the eel tightly in his hands, not wanting to let go of the creature in the event he began to weaken. He could eat more of the meat to regain his strength and maybe get away, though against an augmented Kaver, Alec wasn't sure if any amount of strength would help.

He looked around, but nothing about the section was

familiar. He didn't know the sections that abutted the swamp as well as he should. He probably should have taken time to learn them, especially knowing how important the swamp was, but he simply hadn't.

He turned down a main street. It was late, and there weren't many people out. Were there more people, he thought he could hide more easily. Most of those that were out and about staggered, clearly intoxicated.

He would have to find a place to hide.

But where could he hide that would be safe? Where would he be able to hide that could provide him any sort of protection? Without knowing anyone in this section, he didn't know that he could.

He tried to think the way that Sam would. She would find a place with people, and the only place that would have people at this time of night would be a tavern.

Alec surged forward and reached a stretch of the city where there was row upon row of taverns.

Had he not had the same experience with Sam in Caster, he might not have felt nearly as comfortable coming to a place like this. Before, he would have felt incredibly uncomfortable in these sections, mostly because they were so different from his home section.

He glanced back. The Kaver moved behind him.

She was slowing, and he doubted it was because of an injury. It was more likely she figured he was caught, with no place to go. And she would be right. He *was* caught.

He chose a tavern at random and jumped inside.

The building smelled stale, mostly a mixture of ale and sweat, though there was an attempt to cover those stenches with something else, either that of baking bread or roasted meat. Neither seemed to be completely effective.

He moved to the back of the tavern, wanting to use the people inside to mask his presence. There were probably a dozen people, and a few of them glanced up when he entered, staring at him strangely. It took a moment before he realized that he still clutched the canal eel.

He had no choice but to hold on to it. It was too big to stick in his pocket, but he had to find some way to hide it.

He made his way past a table and spotted a stack of napkins. He grabbed several and quickly wrapped them around the eel, hoping it would look more like any fish in wrapping.

The front door opened, and he ducked, taking a quick seat near the back of the tavern. Alec glanced back as the Kaver entered. She scanned the tavern, and he tried to tip his head down, trying to be as inconspicuous as possible.

She started through the tavern, looking from table to table. He was frozen in place, not able to move, and afraid of what would happen when she reached him. Would she attack? Or would she try to take him with her?

Most likely, the latter, especially if Master Helen had decided he needed to be brought in.

She took a seat across from him, and Alec tensed.

"You are the Scribe I was sent to bring to her."

"I'm not going."

"No? What makes you think you can refuse? Do you think you can fight your way past me?"

Alec looked around the tavern. There would be no help for him here, though that didn't stop him from casting a glance around the room. The people here were either drunk or caught up in their own business, and it was unlikely that any of them would be interested in helping an outsider. Alec couldn't even blame them. Why would they help?

"Why does she want me?"

She shrugged. "That's not any of my concern. I was told to bring you in, so I intend to bring you in."

"And the prince?"

She sniffed. "He made a mistake getting involved in something that he should not have."

"What happens when the king finds out?"

"Do you think the king doesn't know?"

After learning about Master Helen and how she was the king's Scribe, he decided that it was likely the king did know. And if that was the case, then it meant the king had allowed the Kavers to attack his son. But why?

"I'm not going with you," he said.

He gripped the eel, preparing to unwrap the tail. If nothing else, he thought he could stab her with the barbed end, thinking maybe it would secrete some of its venom. That would at least slow the Kaver, maybe even kill her, and he could get away.

"You're going to come with me, either way. But you can choose whether you come awake or unconscious. One way will be less painful for you than the other, but it matters not to me."

There was commotion near the back of the tavern, and Alec looked up. A silver-haired man entered and looked around. He had sharp eyes, and there was something about him that reminded Alec of Bastan. He wore a gray jacket and pants, the quality much finer than what Alec would have expected to find in this section, and he made his way toward Alec.

Alec glanced over to the Kaver. Was this man with her? If he was, did that mean he was her Scribe?

If so, she would be more dangerous than he realized. Facing off against a Kaver alone was bad enough, but involving her Scribe…

Maybe there was nothing he could do. Maybe he truly was going to get dragged back to the palace, either to Master Helen or to the king. Now that he had the swamp wood, he feared what Master Helen might do. How might she use it? Would she simply take it from him and begin to make easar paper on her own?

The man took a seat next to Alec and the Kaver. He ignored Alec completely, focusing only on the Kaver. "You should not have come here."

She shot the man a look. "This is none of your business. I am here on business of the palace."

"Is that right? Well, the palace is a little far removed from this section."

The woman flicked her gaze around the tavern before settling back on the man. She sat there calmly, one hand resting on her canal staff, and Alec knew from his time with Sam that she would be only a moment from twisting her staff and attacking, able to use it against the man in little more than a heart beat's notice. Did he even realize what trouble he was in?

If Alec said anything, would it matter? It wasn't as if he could help. Then again, maybe he could use the distraction. If he could take this time, and if he could slip away before she managed to get to him, then he could disappear and hurry over to Caster and find Bastan and Sam.

"You would contest the authority of the throne?"

282 | D.K. HOLMBERG

"I would contest anyone's authority in Oldansh other than mine."

"And who are you?"

"I'm someone who has dealt with your kind before. You thought to come in here and challenge me?"

The woman's demeanor seemed to change ever so slightly, seeming to take the man seriously for the first time. She positioned herself in such a way that she could move quickly, and Alec noted the tension in her hands and the way that she readied her staff. All it would take would be a single jump, and she would be up.

Then again, she didn't seem to realize there were men moving in behind her.

They did so with subtlety, and though they appeared intoxicated, the way they moved told him that was unlikely to be the case. They walked with less of a stagger than he would've expected had they been intoxicated.

"What do you mean that you've dealt with my kind?"

The man glared at her. "You thought to come to Oldansh and attack."

He made a motion with his hand, and men converged on her.

It happened in little more than a blink of an eye, and as they converged, Alec kicked, sending her staff flying across the room.

The man looked over at him, and Alec shrugged.

The man reached for her, but she jumped, spinning, and lashed out with her feet, kicking and sending the nearest attacker back. She spun again and punched, her fist connecting with another man's chin, and he went staggering backward.

Even without her staff, the Kaver was formidable. She

was far more than Alec would have been able to manage, but there were simply too many people. Everyone in the tavern seemed to get up, and all converged on her. They swarmed her, unmindful of injury, and restrained her, grabbing her arms and legs, and holding her down. One man punched her repeatedly in the face until her nose was bloodied and her lip was split, and her head sagged forward.

"What do you want us to do with her, Shuver?" the man asked.

"We will tie her up until we get answers." He turned his attention to Alec. "And now. What about you? Why were you with her?"

Alec shook his head. "I wasn't with her. I was running from her."

"Why would she have been chasing you?"

What would a man like this respect? What kind of answer could he give that would help him and protect him?

"Because I took something from her," Alec said.

The man—the Shuver—frowned. "What would you have taken?"

Alec pushed the eel across the table. "This."

The Shuver frowned for a moment before he grabbed the bundle and began pulling napkins away from it, revealing the eel within. He looked up at Alec, an almost incredulous expression on his face. "This? This is what she was after? An eel?"

"Do you know how difficult they are to catch?"

"No one tries. There would be no point, because the eels are useless."

Alec decided to take a gamble with what he said next.

"They could be useless, but I was asked to bring an eel to someone, he wanted the barb at the end, thinking it would make an interesting trophy." The barb would be useless, at least it would be unless there was poison still in it. He was sure the man knew nothing of the venom the eel carried, and even if he did, harvesting it was difficult, even for Alec. And he wasn't about to reveal that the eel meat was beneficial, not to a man like this.

"Who asked you to bring the barbed tail?"

"Bastan."

The man stared at him for a long moment before he let out a heavy sigh and turned to one of his men. "Send word to Bastan that I have his prize."

"What else do you want me to tell him?" the man asked.

"I don't care."

Alec looked over at the man. If they were going to send word to Bastan, that might be better than anything he could hope for. "Tell Bastan the apothecary has his tail," Alec said.

The Shuver looked over to Alec and frowned. "Apothecary?"

Alec nodded.

A twisted smile formed on the Shuver's face. "Interesting."

He motioned, and two men grabbed Alec's arms and lifted him, dragging him away.

27

THE PALACE

The palace gleamed in the moonlight. Sam stared at it, debating whether she should approach, or wait for Bastan. After the attack in Caster, he was coming, angry at what had happened and determined to help rescue Marin. The only problem was that Sam wasn't sure if they would be enough.

And she still didn't know what had happened to Alec.

Something had happened. She wasn't sure what, but she was determined to figure it out. Alec had disappeared from the university. After leaving Bastan, she'd searched the university herself, only confirming that he was missing, as Bastan had said. He wasn't in Arrend, either.

She didn't dare search for answers, not wanting to expose the connection between them and raise questions, but skulking around the university hadn't revealed any information about what had happened. With the poisoning that he'd been subjected to, Alec shouldn't be able to disappear, not quite like that.

That meant something had happened to him.

Kyza, but she'd been a fool to leave him. She should have known better, given that he wasn't just sick; he'd been attacked, and that meant he was still in danger. Someone should've stayed with him to protect him, but she had been determined to go with Bastan to find out what else was going on. But where had that gotten her? They still didn't know where Master Helen was, and Marin had escaped. They were now all paying for her mistake.

There was movement outside the palace. It was more than what she was accustomed to seeing, and with the way they patrolled, and the staffs that were carried, it appeared the Kavers were patrolling.

That was unusual. Typically, only the palace guards stood the watch, routine soldiers who might be skilled with the sword, but didn't have any capacity to be augmented, and certainly wouldn't be carrying canal staffs.

What was taking place? Were they concerned about her? Or was something more going on?

Sam wanted nothing more than to jump across the canal, race into the palace, and see what was taking place, mostly because she wanted to know what the princess might have planned. She didn't have any hesitation in going to Lyasanna, other than the concern that Lyasanna might have her detained. If Elaine was there, it might be too much for Sam to get away.

Sam turned away from the palace. Attempting to cross the canal and enter the palace would be a difficult mission now, especially with the Kavers that she saw. Not to mention the Kavers she didn't see.

She started back toward the Caster section, winding

through the streets. There was a solemn pall to the air, almost as though the people of the city realized something was amiss. Did they realize the Kavers had become active? For so long, the Kavers had remained hidden. Then again, Sam hadn't realized there were nearly as many Kavers as what she had seen recently. Why keep them from her? From the city?

She reached Caster and Bastan's tavern and went inside. There was nothing off about the tavern. There was normal activity, with people sitting at tables and drinking and gaming, with a musician singing near the back of the tavern, the song a mournful one that she had never heard before. Sam took a seat, looking around, and began tapping her hands on the table. When Kevin came out of the kitchen and saw her, he made his way directly toward her, grinning.

"You know, you could simply just come back to the kitchen if you're that hungry."

"It's not that I'm hungry, it's that I'm…" She looked around the tavern. "I'm waiting for Bastan to return."

"Well, I don't know when he might return from Oldansh."

Sam's eyes widened. "He went where?"

"Kyza, maybe I shouldn't have shared that with you."

"Why wouldn't Bastan have told me?"

"Probably because he didn't want you to do anything stupid and go after him?"

She glared at Kevin. "When have I ever done anything stupid?"

"I know well enough not to answer that," Kevin said. "Besides, take a minute, eat, and be ready for whatever he's got planned."

288 | D.K. HOLMBERG

"What makes you think he has anything planned?"

Kevin's tone turned serious, something that was atypical for him. Kevin was usually jovial and joking, and despite his size and ability to defend himself, seemed content to simply run the kitchen. "Because he was attacked, Sam. Bastan is not going to let that go by without a response. All of us are prepared for whatever Bastan has in mind."

"Kevin, I'm not sure this is the kind of fight that he can win."

"You know Bastan," he said.

"I know Bastan, but that doesn't mean that he needs to attempt something that will get him in trouble." What could he do, anyway? Attacking the palace was beyond them, even with the resources Bastan could summon. Somehow, she needed to sneak into the palace, which would be one of the most difficult tasks she ever attempted, and without any augmentations, she wasn't certain she wanted to take such a risk. Even for Marin. Even knowing what Marin meant to the her successfully getting Tray back.

Kevin tapped the table and stood, then went back into the kitchen, returning a few moments later with a tray of steaming food. He leaned in and smiled. "Eat, Sam. If Bastan is going to plan an attack, you need to be ready."

She took a spoonful of food and looked up at him. "What makes you think I'm going to be involved in anything stupid that Bastan might do?"

"Because you care about Bastan as much as he cares about you."

Kevin turned and began to make his way through the tavern, stopping to visit with various tables. Sam took heaping spoonfuls of food, shoveling it into her mouth as quickly as she could, looking around the tavern. How many of these people would Bastan call into service? Probably too many. More than would be able to return.

Something like that would only end up with people getting hurt.

No. Sam couldn't let Bastan do that. She couldn't let all of these people put themselves in danger.

She finished her food and nodded to Kevin as she left the tavern. She began to make her way through Caster, looking at buildings, feeling the sense of home that she had always tried to avoid. Caster was her home, despite every attempt of hers to move beyond it. She was a lowborn—and she no longer cared. There had been a time, well, a lot of times, when she hated the idea that she was a lowborn, and hated what that meant for her, but now, she appreciated the fact that the people in the section had cared for her as well as they could. She had never been in danger—not really—and Bastan had made sure she had not wanted for anything and had used his considerable influence to ensure she was safe. Even Marin, in her own way, had protected her.

Could the same have been said of Elaine?

Sam no longer knew. She didn't really know all that much about Elaine, nor about what she might have done or not done. She had remained a mystery, almost intentionally so, and with everything that Sam had gone through, maybe that was for the best. Maybe it was better that she not know Elaine as her mother. Maybe it was better that she know Elaine only as a Kaver who attempted to train her, and now, the one who would betray her.

She found herself making her way toward Alec's section. She veered away, not wanting to head there, not wanting the memories. Wherever Alec had gone, he was likely taken by Master Helen, which was even more reason for her to go to the palace. Not only could she go after Marin, but she could go after Alec. Once she got to him, she would break them free, and…

Then what?

She would be hunted as long as she stayed in the city. Bastan could protect her up to a point, but for how long? How long could she remain undetected in a city this size? Probably a long time, but at some point, she would run into a Kaver, and she would be forced to fight.

Maybe it would be best if she left the city entirely.

If she did that, she would be leaving Bastan behind. She couldn't drag him with her. He'd worked many years to establish his business and his network. She couldn't ask him to give that up and put him in a new environment where he couldn't really defend himself. If she could get to Marin, she would have another Kaver, someone else who could place augmentations, and they could hopefully work together, but what of Alec?

He was the one that she struggled with the most.

She couldn't take him from the city, not into the swamp and across the forest and then beyond. Scribes didn't return from Theln lands.

That meant it would only be Sam and Marin.

Was that what she wanted?

She didn't want to leave Alec behind; she knew that. But she also didn't want to put him in danger and taking him with her across the swamp would certainly do that.

The swamp itself was deadly enough, and if what Marin said about the forest was true, that would be even worse.

First, she had to make sure he was safe. Then she could make additional plans and come up with her final decision. She wouldn't even have to tell him what she was doing. She could sneak off, disappearing in the night, and explain later why she had done it.

He would hate her, and she would hate the fact that he would hate her, but...

Sam found herself back at the university. As she watched, she saw movement in and out of the building, though that surprised her at this time of night. There should be no movement. There should be nothing, other than darkness.

Sam started forward without thinking about what she was doing. She jumped, pushing off with her canal staff as she cleared the canal, and reached the university lawn. She streaked across the lawn and intercepted the figure heading into the building.

Sam swung her staff around, blocking their entry.

The person turned.

She had hoped it would be Master Helen, but it wasn't. It was the fat physicker—Carl.

"You."

"What are you doing out?" Sam asked.

"Does it matter? I am a master physicker, and I have every right to—"

Sam jabbed him with the end of her staff. "Where is Alec?"

Even asking was bound to get him into trouble, but at this point, she no longer thought that was the most concerning thing. She needed to find out where he was so that she could help him, and then she would break him free.

"I haven't seen Physicker Stross since you decided to break into the classroom."

"He doesn't have any right to use the classrooms? I thought as a full physicker, he would have those rights."

Carl frowned. "You don't know anything about the university."

"I think I know plenty. Where is he?"

"I don't know."

"Then where have you been?"

Carl looked over his shoulder, and his gaze darted to the palace.

"The palace? What are you doing at the palace this time of night?"

"It doesn't matter."

"It does."

"Do you really intend to attack a master physicker at the university?" Master Carl asked, putting his hands behind his back and thrusting his belly forward.

Sam sniffed. She thrust her staff forward just a little, enough that it connected with Master Carl's considerable belly. "I think I just did."

"You would risk your friend's position at the university?"

"How are my actions risking Alec? If you think to bring any charges against him because of what I have done, you will find yourself facing a *very* different threat." She jabbed him again. "Does it make you mad that he knows more than you?"

Master Carl glared at her. "Physicker Stross does not know more than a master physicker."

"No? There are plenty of things Alec seems to know. He's told me quite a bit about the limits of the master physickers, and most of them are limits he has not had. Does it bother you that an apothecary knows as much as he does?"

"If he still identified as an apothecary, then it would. But Physicker Stross has embraced his role of the university. Though he might find it more difficult now that you have chosen to attack me."

"Again, if you intend to take revenge on him for my actions, then we will have a very different conversation." Sam tapped him on the belly again. "I am not without abilities, and I'm not without resources, so even if you think to do something to Alec, know that my father will make certain that no harm comes to Alec."

"Father? Should I be concerned about him?"

She smiled. "You met him earlier. It seemed you were quite impressed by him. Bastan is his name."

His eyes widened. Master Carl looked around, glancing back at the palace again. "I was only visiting with a colleague."

"Which colleague?"

"Why should you care?"

"Because I do. Which colleague?"

"Helen."

Sam clenched her jaw. "And where is she in the palace?"

This time, Master Carl chuckled. "You can intimidate me all you want, but there is no way you will reach her in the palace."

"No? Considering that I live there, I think I would have no difficulty getting in to see her."

His eyes widened slightly. "You live there?"

Sam grinned at him. "For now."

"She is with the princess."

Sam lowered her staff and let Master Carl go. He glared at her for a moment before hurrying forward and into the university.

Sam turned her attention back to the palace. If Helen was there, and if she was with Lyasanna, then what about Alec? Where would they have taken him?

Her only option was to attempt to reach the palace, and to do that, she had to be prepared for a fight.

But perhaps not at first. Maybe she could approach and make her way in before she had to fight.

Crossing the bridge had been far easier than Sam had expected. She flashed her ring, the sigil of the palace, and was granted quick access. Once on the other side, she paused, looked around, and waited for the patrols to move past. She headed straight toward the main entrance of the palace, walking with a confident step, trying to make it look like she belonged. If she showed any hesitation, she would be challenged.

She reached the doors without anyone stopping her.

She started to relax.

As she pulled the doors open, she glanced behind her.

A pair of either guards or Kavers started toward her. If guards, Sam could manage them. If Kavers…

She closed the door behind her and debated but finally set the lock. The palace doors were never locked, typically relying on the guards on the bridge and the patrols on the grounds to keep the palace safe. It would draw attention, but at this point, Sam no longer cared about that.

She hurried along the hallway and up the stairs. She

would start with Lyasanna. She would demand that she release Alec, and then demand to find Marin, and then…"

Someone grabbed her arm, and Sam spun.

Elaine stood behind her, watching her.

"Samara. You should not have returned."

"I thought I was welcome in the palace?"

"You were welcome until you began to protect Marin."

"I didn't protect her. I simply kept her captive so that I could ask her a few questions."

"Is that not the same?"

"It's not the same at all, and Lyasanna's reaction to it was unnecessary."

"And what reaction was that?" Elaine asked, guiding Sam along the hall. She held on to her arm, squeezing with a little force, just enough to keep Sam from jerking free. She relented, allowing Elaine to drag her along, choosing not to fight—not yet. That might have to come later, but she didn't relish the idea of fighting Elaine.

"Attacking Bastan and his home. Sending Kavers to kill me."

Elaine paused and looked back at Sam. "I didn't attack Bastan."

"Kavers did. Entire buildings within Caster were destroyed. Places that were my home."

"This should be your home, Samara."

"The palace? The palace will never be my home. I'm lowborn, and I'm fine with that." It had taken her a long time to come to that conclusion, but now that she had, Sam felt good about saying it.

"You can never be lowborn," Elaine said, pulling open a door and dragging Sam inside.

"No? I was raised in Caster. That's about as lowborn as they get."

Elaine shook her head. "No. No Kaver is ever lowborn."

"Why?"

"Because you are a descendent of the Anders."

THE CELLS

S am held Elaine's gaze, not able to look away. "Anders?"

"You didn't think that you could simply come to the palace because you were a Kaver, did you? You didn't make the connection before?"

"I didn't think that it mattered. I thought the Kavers protected the Anders."

"The Anders don't need protection. The Anders are protection."

Sam looked around. They were in a small storeroom, and Elaine positioned herself so that she locked the door, keeping Sam confined. "Are you going to hold me here? Do you intend to keep me captive indefinitely?"

"I don't have any intention of holding you captive, Samara. I needed a chance for us to talk, and this seemed about as good a place as any for us to do that.

"Where is Alec?"

"Your Scribe? Why should I know?"

298 | D.K. HOLMBERG

"Because Master Helen poisoned him."

Elaine shook her head. "I sincerely doubt one of the master physickers would be involved in poisoning another physicker."

"You can doubt it all you want, but that's what happened."

"Why?"

Sam debated whether she should be honest with Elaine or keep her in the dark. Honesty meant that she might reveal the fact that Alec knew—or possibly new—the recipe for easar paper. Then again, all it would take for Elaine to know would be for her to ask Master Helen.

"Because he thought he had found the way to make easar paper."

Elaine tensed. "There should be no way for anyone to know that secret."

"Why?"

"Because the Thelns would never allow that secret out. It's too dangerous."

"I don't know whether the Thelns would allow it to get out or not. All I know is that he had access to a book that contained a recipe he was trying, working with Master Helen, when he was poisoned. Were it not for his father's help, Alec would have died." She didn't say anything about the fact that Alec may still be poisoned, and that their efforts to save him may have failed. That was part of the reason she needed to get to him, so that he could have eel meat, so that he wouldn't get any weaker.

"Kyza," Elaine said.

"What?"

"There has been a flurry of activity over the last few days. I haven't understood it, but perhaps that's what it's about. If the secret to easar paper is going to come out, it would explain the activity, and it would explain the movement that I have seen."

"What movement is that?"

Elaine shook her head. "It doesn't matter."

"It does matter. If the Kavers intend to attack the Thelns, then it matters. The Thelns haven't done anything, other than try to get revenge for what Lyasanna did."

"You can't believe Marin."

"And why can't I? It makes sense. It fits with everything that we have seen. The Thelns only wanted to attack Lyasanna, and those who they thought worked on her behalf. They blame the Kavers for stealing their prince."

It felt strange referring to Tray and that way, but that was what he was, especially with who his father was.

"Samara—"

"No. You have to think about other possibilities, Elaine. Don't be so blindly beholden to what Lyasanna has told you that you ignore the other possibilities. And if Alec has managed to come up with the recipe for easar paper, and if it means that the Kavers intend to attack, then shouldn't you know?"

Elaine took a deep breath and sighed. "Come," she said, grabbing Sam's arm and dragging her from the room. They hurried through the hallway and went down a flight of stairs to Lyasanna's rooms.

Elaine knocked and when the door open, Master Helen greeted her.

"Helen," Elaine said. "I am looking for Lyasanna."

"She is unavailable," Master Helen said. She glanced to

Sam, and her gaze hesitated for only a moment, but enough that Sam saw the tension in her eyes.

"Unavailable? Is it because she is sleeping or because you would keep me from her?" Elaine asked.

"Because she is unavailable."

"And yet, I am her Kaver," Elaine said.

Master Helen stood in the doorway, blocking entry.

Sam took a deep breath, focusing on augmentation, letting it wash through her. Each time she did it, it happened more easily. This time, it was a flash of power. She darted forward, slamming into Helen and into the room.

When she was inside, she glanced over at Elaine. "Are you coming in?"

Elaine studied her, but said nothing, stepping inside the room and closing the door.

"What is this?" Master Helen asked. "What do you think you are doing? Don't you understand my position here?"

Sam held on to Master Helen. She was heavier than she looked, but with the augmentation, Sam was able to keep her firmly in her grip and prevented her from moving. "What did you do to Alec?"

"Is that what this is about? You blame me for something happening to your Scribe?"

"You were working with him. You're the only one who could have done anything to him. Tell me what you did, and—"

"And what?"

"And then you will help me find Marin."

Master Helen glanced from Sam to Elaine. "I think you have it wrong," she said.

"Release her," a voice said from the darkness.

Sam looked over and saw Lyasanna standing in the doorway. She was small, similar of stature to Elaine, and for that matter herself, and she had eyes that flashed with irritation. She took a step into the room, and there was something about the way she moved that surprised Sam.

She gasped, sudden understanding hitting her. "You're not a Kaver. You're a Scribe."

Lyasanna frowned. "That's not new news, Samara. You know I am Elaine's Scribe."

"Perhaps I do, but maybe that's wrong." She looked from Elaine to Lyasanna. "She's augmented. That's why Master Helen is here. I don't understand what's going on, but look at her, watch the way she moves. She has an augmentation."

"If she had an augmentation, I would be aware of it," Elaine said.

"Not if someone else placed it. And not if she is using someone else's blood and their Scribe," she said, looking at Master Helen. "Who is your Kaver?"

"That is a personal question," Helen said.

"The king," Elaine said. "Her Kaver is the king."

If she was the king's Scribe, and if they used the king's blood to augment Lyasanna, what did it mean for the king?

"Where is he?" Sam asked.

"You have no right to ask about the king," Master Helen said.

"I don't? I thought that my being a Kaver gave me some right."

"I think you overestimate what that means," Master Helen said.

Sam turned to Elaine. "Something's going on here. I told you that it was. I don't care if you believe me but look at your Scribe. Look at the way she moves. Tell me she's not augmented."

Elaine turned her attention to Lyasanna. She stared at her for a moment, and as she did, her eyes widened.

"No. For a Scribe to be augmented, it takes considerable Kaver blood. It would take…"

"Elaine. It's time that you depart. Leave Samara here," Lyasanna said.

Sam snorted. "And with your augmentations, do you think you can hold me?"

"I don't have to be the one to hold you."

The door opened, and three others entered. They were Kavers, and Sam thought she might have seen one of them before, but she wasn't certain. If she hadn't, that meant they were all people who were new to her. More Kavers who had been hidden.

"Where have they been?" Sam asked.

Elaine glanced at the Kavers. "They were in the Theln lands. They were supposed to keep an eye out for movement."

"And did you know they were returning?"

Elaine shook her head. "No."

"Samara, I think it's time you—" Lyasanna started.

Sam took a deep breath. As she did, she focused on more augmentations. She worked through them, thinking about what she needed, and power flooded into her.

She jumped back and spun her staff, connecting with two of the Kavers before they had a chance to react. The third swished his staff around, but Sam was ready and brought hers down, sweeping his legs and knocking him to the ground.

She turned back to Lyasanna, facing her and Master Helen, not certain what Elaine might do. How might she react?

"You have to decide," she said to Elaine. "Something's taking place and it's not right. Don't follow blindly." She turned her attention to Master Helen. "What did you do to Alec?"

"What needed to be done. Once he provided the recipe, I couldn't have him aware of it. It would create too many problems."

"And yet, the recipe was incomplete," Sam said.

"It was close enough that it won't take long for me to determine the rest of it. Once I do, and once we have the adequate supply of easar paper, then we can finally fully infiltrate the Theln lands and be rid of them."

Was that what this is about? Was this about Master Helen planning her attack? And why would Master Helen be the one to plan the attack anyway?

"You allowed this?" Sam asked Lyasanna.

Lyasanna stared at her. "The power has always been at the university. And now, with a presence within the Anders family, we can consolidate the two arms of power. With that, we can finally make short work of the Thelns."

Sam glanced over to Elaine. She could see her mother was struggling with how to respond.

"You're not going to do this. Even if you thought you could, the Kavers—"

"The Kavers will fall into line," Master Helen said. "They will do what their Scribes instruct, and seeing as how I lead the Scribes, there is little else that you can do to stop this. It's a shame that your Scribe proved to be so challenging. Had he only been a little more compliant, he could have been a part of this. You could have been a part of this. If anything, you should blame him."

Sam shook her head. "Blame him? I agree with him." It was time for her to get moving. "Elaine?"

"I'm sorry," Elaine whispered, apparently still unwilling to go against the princess.

Sam gritted her teeth. She wasn't ready to fight her mother, not like this, but what choice would she have?

Surprisingly, Elaine spun and struck Master Helen with her staff.

She grabbed Sam, and they darted from Lyasanna's room, running along the hall.

"We need to find Marin and Alec," Sam said.

"Once we do, we will be traitors to the Anders," Elaine said.

"Apparently, I already was." Elaine guided them along the hall, heading down the stairs to a section of the palace where Sam had never been. "What made you decide to agree with me?"

"You are my daughter. If nothing else, that connects us. I know I haven't been the mother that you deserve, but I wasn't about to let them harm you simply because you disagreed with them."

Elaine reached the door. A man was blocking it, and she nodded to him. He stepped to the side, and Elaine passed through, revealing rows of cells on the other side.

She found Marin quickly, and Elaine opened the door, releasing Marin, who glanced from Sam to Elaine.

"What is this?"

"Apparently, treason," Elaine said.

"No. The real treason is Lyasanna."

Elaine frowned. "Why would you say that?"

"Look down there," Marin said, motioning to a cell at the end of the row. Elaine frowned as she made her way over to it. When she reached the door, she peeked inside, and she gasped. "Jalen?"

29

ONE MORE ATTEMPT

A lec stared out at the bars of the cell. This was an actual cell, nothing like when he'd been confined by Prince Jalen. At least then, though he might have been confined, there was never the sense that he was truly a captive. He had been well treated and fed, things the Shuver didn't seem interested in doing. Instead, Alec had nothing more than a wooden mat and a bowl of mush. There wasn't even a place for him to void.

Two men stood guard outside the cell, as if Alec could somehow break his way free from the barred confines that he was in. At least they hadn't taken his cloak, and they hadn't taken the svethwuud inside. If they had, he didn't know what he would have done. He prayed Bastan would come, or better yet, that Sam would come, but considering the reaction that the Kaver got from the Shuver, Alec wasn't sure he wanted Sam to come. Would the Shuver have his men attack her the same way he had them attack the Kaver?

The reaction suggested to him that the Shuver had

encountered Kavers before, and he wondered what might have happened.

Had Sam been here? Had she somehow done something that had angered him?

He wouldn't put it past her, especially if she thought she could gain something by coming here.

It had been hours since they had placed them in the cell, and he wondered how long they intended to hold him.

His mind raced through everything that had happened. The prince was now captured by the Kavers. Helen had poisoned him. And now he was captured, unable to even get word to those who might be able to intervene.

The prince had been kind to him, at least as kind as someone who held him captive could be. The door opened, and the Shuver entered, leading in a few others.

"Bastan," he said.

Bastan looked over at the Shuver. "Let him go."

"Let him go? You realize he came in here with someone who intended to attack."

"I don't care who he came in here with. All I know is that he is one of mine."

Bastan spoke with a dark menace to his tone, and Alec appreciated the sentiment. He never really knew where he stood with Bastan. Bastan understood his connection to Sam, though not much else.

"Not until we come to an agreement."

"There will be no agreement, Chester."

The Shuver glared at Bastan. "You know how I feel about that name."

"I don't care how you feel about it. I know who you

are. And don't begin to think that because I have come into your section that you have any sort of hold on me. Do you really want to attempt to confine me?"

Bastan shifted, revealing the sword hidden beneath his cloak. Alec had seen him fight with the sword once before, and it had been a terrifying sight. Bastan was incredibly skilled, and he wouldn't be surprised if the man could intimidate a man like the Shuver, even though Bastan had come into his section.

"Fine. He's yours."

The Shuver motioned to the two guards, and one of them turned and pulled a key from his pocket, unlocking the cell. Alec hurried out and took a place next to Bastan.

"Tell me about the person he was with," Bastan said.

"I don't know," the Shuver replied.

"She worked for the palace," Alec said. "There is some sort of turmoil there."

Bastan frowned at him. "Turmoil?"

Alec nodded. How could he phrase it in a way that would let Bastan know what was going on? Maybe he didn't have to. Maybe he only needed to help get out of here, and then he could explain to Bastan what was taking place.

"I don't understand it. It's complicated and beyond my ability to comprehend." If he played stupid, maybe Bastan would realize that there was something to it and that he needed to be cautious.

"I shared with you, and now you need to share with me," the Shuver said.

"You did. You brought one of my people back to me. For that, you have my gratitude."

"Gratitude? I want something a little more substantial than gratitude."

"Fine. There is an attack taking place within the city. I would warn you to be ready."

"What kind of attack?" the Shuver asked.

"The kind that unsettles power."

The Shuver's eyes widened. "The palace? The woman we confined claimed she was with the palace."

"You confined her?"

The Shuver waved his hand. "What choice did I have? She, like the others, came here and attacked."

Bastan started to smile. "Interesting. Perhaps we will be better prepared than I realized."

"What do you mean?" Alec asked.

Bastan glanced over. "Marin is gone. They've taken her."

Alec hurriedly tried to think through the complications. If Marin was gone, then the help Sam had hoped to have with making the crossing over the swamp and then beyond to reach Tray would be gone. And then there was the strangeness to Master Helen's attack on him, as well as the attack on the prince.

"Bastan, I think we need to return to my father's shop."

"Why?"

"Because I need a few supplies. And, if I'm right, we may need to stop this attack."

"Stop it? I want nothing to do with it until it plays out."

"I think we *need* to be involved."

Bastan watched him, saying nothing for a long moment, but the Shuver laughed. "Why would we care whether there was an attack? Let the royals destroy themselves."

310 | D.K. HOLMBERG

Bastan was watching Alec, who almost squirmed beneath the weight of his gaze. There was something about the way that Bastan looked at him that made him uncomfortable.

"I don't know everything that's taking place," Alec said. "But it's all connected."

"What does it matter?" Bastan asked. "Even if they destabilize, it's not like we don't have any ability to ensure stability of our sections."

"I don't know that it's all about stability. I think this is about something else. I think this is about what's happening where Tray has gone."

Could the princess have been angling for more power? If she intended to remove the prince, then it was possible. If she did remove Jalen from power, Alec wouldn't be surprised to see Lyasanna push an attack on the Thelns.

Any attack that she caused would lead to greater instability within the city. It would lead to violence. It would lead to even more danger for those who lived here.

Bastan had to see that.

"Help me get to my father's shop, and then I might be able to help Sam. We can rescue Marin."

"I'm not convinced I want to help rescue Marin," Bastan said.

"Even if she can help Sam?"

"With everything that Marin has done, I don't know that I can trust her, not anymore."

"You keep saying that name. Is this Marin, *the* Marin?"

"It's the same," Bastan said.

"Kyza," the Shuver said. "If Marin is involved, I have to help."

Bastan frowned. "You have to help with Marin?"

"Marin helped ensure I had my position. Without her, none of this would be possible."

Bastan frowned. "She's been playing me."

"What do you mean?" Alec asked.

Bastan shook his head. "It doesn't matter, not anymore. All that matters is that perhaps Marin has been more deeply involved than I've ever realized."

He nodded to the Shuver, and they headed out of the cells, back through the tavern, and out onto the street. As they went, Bastan glanced over. "What really happened?"

Alec told him about the prince and everything that had taken place, and described the Kaver attack, including how he had escaped.

"All of this because you went after one of the trees in the swamp?" Bastan asked.

"It might be the key to making easar paper."

"I thought you said the key was the eels?"

"The eels might be part of it, but I don't think they're all of it. And if the prince is right with what he saw, the eels swam around the trees." He touched the section of swamp wood in his pocket, hoping that it was what they believed.

"What if the prince is the one who intends to attack?" Bastan asked.

"What do you mean?"

Bastan shrugged. "I think you have focused on only one possibility. What if there's another? What if the prince intends to use the easar paper to attack the Thelns?"

Alec hadn't considered it. What did he *really* know of Jalen? It was possible he'd been played, but from the little he knew of the man, he didn't think it likely. "I don't know."

"And you still think you should make this paper?"

"Bastan, if we can understand it, if we can begin to use the power of the easar paper, that is incredibly valuable. Even if we're the only ones who know the secret."

Bastan grunted and started to smile.

They quickly crossed through the city, heading toward Arrend. When they reached it, they stopped at his father's shop, and the door was locked. Bastan pushed him aside and picked the lock, forcing his way in.

"We should hurry," Bastan said.

"Why?"

"Because your friend has it in her head that she needs to make a move soon."

"What kind of move?" Even as he asked, he thought he knew. Sam would be the kind to go after Marin, thinking she could rescue her. And it was possible she could, though it would be dangerous. Anything she might do would potentially put her in significant danger.

"Considering that Kavers attacked my hideout, I think Sam is determined to go after them." Bastan looked over at Alec. "Any loyalty she once had to them is gone. I doubt that was their intention, but…"

Alec hurried into the shop. The other ingredients to mix the easar paper were all common, and he found them easily on his father's shelves, then headed to the back of the shop where the hearth was and the big pot. Once again, Alec filled the pot with water and began to add the same ingredients he'd mixed before, quickly bring it to a boil. He withdrew the piece of swamp wood and held it in hands, twisting it. How would he add this? It would need to be cut up, turned into something that would be added to the mixture, but how?

He began to cut off sections of the root, and as he did, he added them to the boiling water. He was surprised when the water seemed to dissolve the root entirely.

"What is it?" Bastan asked.

"It's the water. I think the other ingredients are the reason this works. I didn't know what the purpose of some of these would be, but when mixed together, they seem to dissolve the section of root."

"Then keep going," Bastan said.

Alec made quick work of the rest of the root. He had no idea how much to use, so he added all of it to the boiling water and continued to stir. The smell was not nearly as pungent as it had been with other woods, and it wasn't awful in the same way it had been when he had been at the university attempting the same thing. This was almost sweet.

"What now?" Bastan asked.

"Now I have to strain it and stretch it," Alec said.

He went to find the proper supplies, then returned and strained the water from mixture, setting it aside. The effort of mixing the thick pulp was tiring, and Alec started to sway on his feet.

Bastan grabbed him. "Eel meat?"

Alec nodded. "I had some when I was at the palace with the prince. It helped, but I think it's starting to wear off."

"The prince brought you eel meat?"

"I told him it would help."

Bastan shook his head. "I'm still not sure that this is the right plan. But… I will trust you in this. Finish what you're doing, and I will return with something that can help."

"Return with Sam," Alec said.

Bastan snorted. "Fine, I will return with Sam, as well."

When Bastan left, Alec turned his attention back to the paper mixture. He still didn't know whether it would work, and whether the recipe was accurate, but if it was, it was possible he would be the first one in the city to have made easar paper. That idea should excite him, but instead, it made him nervous. Having an abundant supply of easar paper was powerful, and he could only imagine the lengths others would go to in order to get it.

Maybe Bastan was right. Maybe the prince didn't have a benevolent intent. Maybe he wanted something else.

Either way, Alec was determined to have the supply of paper. He trusted himself and Sam to use it appropriately. He might not trust others, but he and Sam...

And once they had enough paper, then they could go find Tray. They could go to the Theln lands without fear of not having adequate augmentations for Sam. And he wouldn't have to fear his illness consuming him.

30

THE REAL DECEIT

The door to the prince's cell was difficult open. Sam grabbed the bars, trying to pull on them, but she just wasn't strong enough to rip the bars off. Had she an augmentation, maybe it would've been different, but without one—at least more than what she could supply to herself—she needed the keys.

"Can you pick the lock?" Elaine asked her.

"It's not quite the same as breaking into someone's home," Sam said. "A lock like this…" She pulled out her lock-pick set and began to work on the cell door, but it wasn't the same. Trying to break in here was much more difficult than simply trying to break into a house, or any of the locked buildings that Bastan had sent her into over the years.

"Let me have a try," Marin said.

Elaine glanced at Marin. Sam could see the levels of distrust in her eyes, distrust that had built over years.

"Gods," Sam said, handing the lock pick over to Marin. "It's not as if you don't know what you get when you have

Marin here." Marin glanced at Sam, took the lock pick, and began to work on the cell door.

"We need to hurry," Elaine said.

"There is only so much I can do to expedite this. If we had the keys…"

Sam raced back down the hall, thankful for the augmentation that still held, but wishing she had something more, enough that she could have some strength. She pulled the door open and saw the guard standing there. She grabbed him, yanking him into the room. It startled him enough that he couldn't react, not before she managed to smack him unconscious with her staff.

Sam searched him and found a ring of keys. She brought them back to Elaine, who pushed Marin out of the way and began to work at the lock, going key after key, trying them in the lock, and failing to find the right one to open it.

Marin glared at Elaine and pushed her aside, once again working at the lock.

"I need to find Alec," Sam said.

"The Scribe?"

This came from within the cell. The prince.

Sam grabbed the bars and leaned close. "Do you know him? You know what happened to him?"

The prince shook his head. "He was with me on the barge in the swamp when we were attacked. You must be his Kaver." When Sam nodded, he smiled. "I have seen you around here before. What are you doing with her?" he glanced at Elaine.

"Trying to break you out," Sam said.

"Out? She's the one who put me in here."

Sam glanced over to Elaine. Her mother just shook her

head. "I wasn't the one who placed him here. I didn't know he was a prisoner."

"You would have to have known. They wouldn't have acted without your permission," the prince said.

Elaine started to argue when Marin looked up at her. "Enough! I'm trying to figure out how I can open this cell, and with the two of you bickering, I'm not going to be able to do it effectively."

The prince looked down at Marin, and there was a strange expression in his eyes. "I had heard you were dead. That's what they told me."

"That's what I wanted them to believe," Marin said.

"Why?"

Marin paused before finally looking up. "Because of your sister."

"What did my sister do that made you want to be dead to me?"

"Later."

"Later," the prince said, shaking his head. "With you, it was always later. And now? If you fail to rescue me, will it be later once more? Will you tell me again that you don't have time to share what happened to you all those years ago and what you've been doing?"

The lock clicked, and Marin stood, handing the lock pick set over to Sam. She took it and slipped it into her pocket and helped Marin as she pulled the door to the cell open, letting the prince out.

"Like I said, later."

"Are there any others?" Sam asked Jalen.

"There was another from the university, but…"

Could that mean Beckah? Alec would want to know what happened to her, even if it wasn't the outcome he wanted to know about. For his sake, she needed to learn what happened.

They reached the end of the hallway, and Elaine glanced down at the fallen guard. "He's a good man," she whispered.

"There are going to be a lot of good men you're going to have to deal with," the prince said. "Most of them were pulled into something that they might not have wanted to be pulled into."

"Your sister has it in her mind that they are going to attack the Thelns. What is your position on that?" Sam asked.

"That is my sister's plan, not mine," the prince said. "She's angry about their attempt on her and has managed to convince my father that now is a good time for us to turn our attention back northward, and back to the Thelns." He knelt next to the fallen guard and pulled a sword out of the man's sheath, and then stood, swinging it briefly, as if getting a feel for the weapon. "I've been trying to figure out a way to counter her desire. She has convinced the university the attack is necessary for us to have an adequate supply of easar paper, and I have been trying to prove that if we had a supply of our own, we wouldn't need to attack."

"That's why you know Alec," Sam said.

"When rumor came that there was someone at the university who had discovered something about the easar paper, I thought I could find out what he might know."

"He was poisoned by Master Helen," Sam said. "He wouldn't have been able to help you that much, not in that state."

"He was still weak when he was brought to me, but he asked me for a restorative that I helped provide."

Sam frowned a moment before nodding. She glanced at the prince, realizing he had made a point of not saying it out loud, not in front of Elaine and Marin. Was that coincidental, or was that a sign that he didn't trust one— or either—of the women?

But then, who did Sam trust? Did she trust the prince? She'd already seen the way that Lyasanna could lie and had learned the extent to which she would go to cover up something that she wanted to hide, attempting to deceive not only her Kaver, but everyone. Marin had been unwilling to murder a child to cover up her mistake.

"We need to go to the king," Elaine said. "He needs to know about this."

They were taking too long, and Sam was uncomfortable with that. "I don't think that going to the king is going to matter."

"Samara, you haven't been in the palace long enough to understand the dynamics. Lyasanna might have convinced the king, which has given her an element of authority, but if he understood what she was doing, and if he knew—"

Sam shook her head. "Think about what you saw, Elaine. Lyasanna was augmented, and she used Helen to help her with those augmentations. The only way that happens is if the king has either allowed himself to be used, or—"

"Or they have forced him," Elaine said softly.

"Kyza!" The prince grabbed the door and glanced out before racing down the hall.

Sam followed, staying close behind him. "I want to know what happened to Alec."

"You were captured, and it's likely the Kavers that attacked us on the swamp managed to get your friend after they got me. He would have been in one of these cells though, so perhaps he managed to escape. He isn't without his own talents, and he might be one of the brightest Scribes I've ever met."

"Did you figure out the secret to making easar paper?"

The prince frowned. "I don't know. It's possible we did, but we didn't have time to test it, not before they managed to capture me. I had intended to do a trial, but there just wasn't the time."

They hurried through the hallways, and Sam could tell they were making their way out of the palace. She stopped, and the prince glanced back at her. "I need to find Alec."

"You don't know that he's here," he said. "I already told you—"

"I know what you told me, but if he is here, I can't leave him."

"And I can't leave the king," Elaine said. She looked over at the prince. "And you shouldn't, either."

"He wasn't willing to listen before. What makes you think he will listen now?"

"How do you know he wasn't forced, coerced?" Sam asked.

"I have a hard time believing that would be possible," the prince said.

"Oh, trust me. Many things are possible. Even having your memories erased."

"It wouldn't be possible without... The Book? The Thelns used the Book on you?"

"Not the Thelns. Someone else."

"Now is not the time, Samara," Marin said.

"I realize that. I don't know that there's ever going to be a time, but that doesn't make it so that I will forgive you for that."

"Even knowing why?"

"Even knowing why."

Boots thundered down the hall, and the prince jerked his head around. "We waited too long."

"Samara, how augmented are you?" Marin asked.

"I'm augmented as well as I can be. They aren't as strong as when Alec places them.

"It's not about the strength of the augmentation, it's about having the benefit of it. The ones you place yourself will be longer-lasting, and you will be better able to resist an attack."

"I won't have an augmentation," Elaine said.

"Because you never managed to master those skills," Marin said. "If Samara can do it, then you can do it."

Elaine looked at Sam. As she did, a dozen people appeared in the hallway. Some of them carried swords and would be palace guards, though others didn't. Kavers.

"I'm not as strong as Samara," Elaine said.

"If they capture me, they will make certain the attack happens," the prince said.

Sam grunted. "Then I guess we can't let them capture you."

She tapped her staff on the ground and surveyed the people in front of her. As she did, she focused on adding her own augmentation, and it swept through her slowly, a warning that she was already growing fatigued. How much longer would she be able to last?

She glanced over to the prince. If he was trying to prevent Lyasanna from attacking the Thelns, then she had to work with him. She had to help him.

Even if he wasn't, she needed to get Marin out of here. Marin was the one who would be able to help her reach Tray.

Sam tried to prepare herself, and as she did, the Kavers attacked.

Four of them surged forward, their attention focused on Elaine.

"If I could get a staff—" Marin said.

Sam jumped forward, twisting in the air, and landed in the middle of the four Kavers. She drew their attention to her and flicked her staff, twisting it, catching one man on the wrist, the other on the ankle, and both of them staggered, but they didn't fall.

They were augmented.

She spun, twisting again, bringing her staff around in a blur, needing only to separate one of them from a staff. If she could, she could even the odds a little.

Elaine was fighting near her, but without augmentations—and without the same ability as what Sam had developed—she wouldn't be of nearly as much use. She would be skilled—Sam had seen exactly how skilled Elaine was, even without augmentations—but she wouldn't be as terrifying as these other Kavers were.

Steel clashed with steel, and out of the corner of her eye, Sam saw the prince fighting, flashing through a series of movements with nearly as much skill as what she had seen from Bastan.

Sam flipped her staff up, and she connected with an arm of one of the Kaver's.

She flicked her wrist, bringing her staff in so that it connected with his flank, and then she kicked. The kick separated his staff from him, and it went skittering over toward Marin.

Marin darted forward, twisting through a series of movements, and joined Sam, standing side-by-side with her as they fought, pushing back the Kavers.

"You really are quite skilled, Samara," Marin said.

"Is now really the time?" Sam asked.

"I just thought you should know." Marin grunted, spinning her staff. She was amazing to watch. Even augmented, Sam wasn't sure that she would be able to defeat Marin. There was something about the way she flowed through the movements with her staff, the way she worked it through the air, that was almost otherworldly. She was able to do that without the same sort of augmentation that Sam relied upon. That amazed Sam, but she had to keep herself from staring for too long.

One of the other Kavers smacked Sam in the back. She was thankful that it was her back, as she was able to stagger forward, catching herself before she fell, and spun her staff around, managing to defend herself.

"I really do think it was good I began training you. If I hadn't, can you imagine what might've happened?"

"Can you imagine what would have happened had you only told me the truth?"

"I told you, you never would have felt quite as devoted to Tray."

Marin flipped her staff around and caught two Kavers on the side of the head, and they crumbled.

She slipped forward, positioning herself in the middle of the Kavers, and twisted her staff. Each time she did, she connected. More than how she was able to connect, taking down Kaver after Kaver, it was the way that she was able to evade the others and avoid attack.

More people appeared.

These were soldiers, but with the numbers that arrived, there wasn't a way they could fight back.

"We need to get out of here," Elaine said. "We can't fight off this many."

"Maybe you can't," Marin said.

"No, she's right. We need to find another way," Sam said.

"Besides, we need to get to the king."

"Kyza!" Marin flipped, landing on the other side of a row of Kavers, and twisted her staff, pushing them back. "Go. I will hold them off."

Elaine grabbed Sam's arm and pulled her away. They reached for the prince who joined them, and they backed along the hall, heading toward a wide staircase at the opposite end. Marin stayed in front and single-handedly gave them time to retreat. Every so often, Sam felt compelled to join her, and when she did, she found that Marin already had things taken care of.

They reached the stairs, and as they climbed, Sam could hear Marin continuing to hold off the Kavers. With Kavers in front of them, it was difficult to retreat with any speed.

"You need to turn and face forward," Marin said to Sam. "I don't know what we will encounter at the top of the stairs—"

As they rounded a landing, she came face-to-face with Lyasanna.

"Samara. I don't know what you think you're doing—"

"Sister," the prince said, "I have you to thank for this?"

"Jalen. You are a fool for getting them involved."

"Getting them involved? They were already involved. And what have you done with father?"

"Father has ruled long enough."

"Father doesn't rule. You know that."

"Helen has decided that father has been the figurehead long enough," she said. "And considering that I have trained at the university, and that I am a Scribe, it is time for one of the Anders to truly rule in the city."

"Why you and not to me?"

"Because I'm a Scribe."

Sam got in between Lyasanna and her brother, positioning herself so that she could keep the princess from harming him. She didn't know what augmentation Lyasanna had, but if it was strength or speed, she needed to be able to block her from attacking.

"Don't make me strike you," Sam said.

"The moment you attack me, is the moment that your treason is complete," Lyasanna said to Sam.

"My treason? I'm not the one who sent a Kaver to murder an infant."

Lyasanna glared at her. "You know nothing, Samara."

"I know what you did. I know the kind of monster you are, and I know you will never lay a hand on Tray. Not as long as I have anything to do with it."

"What is this?" The prince step forward and jabbed at Lyasanna with his sword, but she simply stepped off to the side, twisting out of the way. Speed. At least Sam knew one of the augmentations she had. Perhaps not all of them, and perhaps she didn't have the same level of speed that a Kaver might manage, but she avoided the prince's sword easily.

"Oh, Jalen, don't act as though you have never done anything immoral."

"What is this about a child?"

"It doesn't matter."

"Does father know?"

Lyasanna grinned. "Why would it matter if father knows? Now that he will soon be abdicating the throne, handing over the rule to me, it makes no difference what father knows."

"We need to get to him," Elaine hissed.

"And you," Lyasanna said, facing Elaine. "You are the greatest disappointment. You were supposed to ensure my safety. That is your task as my Kaver."

"My task? I have served the Anders a long time, and I have always done everything in my power to ensure your safety, but if what Marin said about you is true, I can no longer serve as your Kaver."

"You don't get to *decide* to simply stop serving as my Kaver."

"I can choose. And I choose not to serve someone who would slaughter a helpless child."

"Even a Theln?"

"Even a Theln."

The conversation was taking too long, and Sam realized almost too late that was the point. Guards appeared above them, dozens of them, and mixed in with them were a few more Kavers. They were on the stairs below and now on the stairs above. Attempting an attack on either front would be difficult. They were trapped.

Lyasanna smiled. "You see, there is nothing you can do now." She turned to the prince. "And you, brother, will need to come with me. I think that once you share with me who your Scribe is, I will have another way to set augmentations, and another way to ensure my position. It really is too bad you never wanted to train as a Kaver. If you had, perhaps you would be more formidable."

The Kavers on the stairs above and below surged toward them almost simultaneously, and Sam realized that they were trapped, and that there might be nothing that they could do to escape.

She turned and saw the prince take a deep breath and pull a sheet of paper out from his pocket.

Easar paper.

He glanced past the princess and then looked at the Kavers approaching, before turning his attention down the stairs, to the hall below.

"Have you ever wondered why I never trained with the Kavers?" he asked his sister. When Lyasanna frowned, a hint of a smile twisted his mouth. "Because you aren't the only Scribe in our family."

With that, he pulled out a vial, and Sam realized that it was blood. He dipped his finger in it and quickly scrawled a few words on the paper.

"You're a Scribe?" Lyasanna asked. "Who is your Kaver?"

"I thought she was dead for so long, only to learn recently that she still lives."

The sound of shouts beneath them rang out.

Sam's eyes widened. "Marin? I thought Jessup was her Scribe?"

"I was the first." The prince smiled at his sister.

"Do you think that one Kaver is enough to stop all of this?"

"I don't know that we need to stop anything," he said. "We merely need to get past you."

The Kavers began to push forward.

Sam came to a decision.

She flipped her staff and smacked Lyasanna on the side, sending her staggering. She twisted but didn't fall. Sam flipped over her, landing amidst the oncoming Kavers. "I will buy time. Go check on your father," she said to the prince.

"You can't do this, not alone," he said. "Even the two of you." He glanced back to where Elaine stood ready.

"I have to. If you can stop an attack on the Thelns…" It wasn't so much that Sam cared about the Thelns, it was that she cared that an attack on the Thelns meant an attack on Tray. If they attacked, if the Kavers made a push into the Thelns lands, it meant that Tray would be in even more danger than he already was.

She started to work through movements, twisting with her staff, fighting against a pair of Kavers whose names she didn't know. How many of these hidden Kavers had the princess summoned back home? How many had already been in the Thelns lands, positioned for an attack? How many more could still be in the palace?

The Kavers she faced were skilled. They forced her back, and she was struck along the side, and then struck again, this time thrown forward.

Kyza, but she wasn't going to survive this.

She hated the idea that she would die in the palace. There would have been a time when coming to the palace, and being here, learning what she had learned, would have seemed like all she would've wanted, but now? Now she would rather die in Caster. She would rather have Alec and Bastan and Tray with her.

Sam fell, dropping to her knees.

A staff struck her, and then another, the blows raining down.

She heard a shout behind her and realized Elaine cried out.

She had come all this way only to fail.

31

GATHERING TROOPS

After straining the pulpy mix, Alec flattened and stretched it across the table. It didn't look like easar paper, but then again, he didn't know what easar paper would look like when it was raw and unformed like this. Would it work?

There wasn't much of the swamp wood remaining, so in order for him to make more, they would have to find and harvest more of the roots, but for now, it might be enough that they tried this. He put what he'd stretched on a tray and headed out of his father's shop, locking the door behind him.

He needed to get back to Caster.

He ran, hurrying through the streets, hoping he could find Sam and could get to Bastan. He needed eel meat so that he could feel a little stronger. The effort of working on the easar paper had drained him, and he was feeling run down, mentally tired and physically fatigued, and he wasn't sure he would have the energy necessary if he needed to make even more paper.

The city blurred past him. He kept himself focused on only one thing, and that was keeping upright, making his way toward Bastan and the others.

Figures came toward him.

Alec knew he should be concerned, especially with how quickly they were moving. They were storming toward him, dozens of them. As they approached, he realized most of them carried swords, not bothering to hide them.

His tired mind had a hard time keeping things straight.

He stepped off to the side of the street, not wanting to be jostled by these men—the soldiers—and someone grabbed him.

Alec blinked and looked up. Bastan stared down at him, his silvery hair seeming to gleam in the early morning light.

"Did it work?" he asked.

"I don't know. I'm... I'm..."

"You are tired," Bastan said.

All Alec could do was nod.

Bastan took hold of Alec and helped lower him down against the wall, giving him enough space so that he could lie back. Alec kept the tray resting on his lap, not sure how long it would take for the mixture to dry. Bastan grabbed his face and pried his mouth open and shoved something in there. Alec tried to fight, forcing whatever it was out of his mouth, but then realized what it was Bastan was doing.

He chewed.

The eel meat was bitter, and each time he ate it, he felt the same way, but even with the first bite, he felt a growing warmth washing through him.

"More," he said.

Bastan shoved another piece in his mouth.

Alec chewed and began to feel more alert. He looked up and saw that dozens of men waited in the street, all of them armed.

"What are you doing?"

"It seems Samara has decided to break into the palace on her own."

"And you're going after her?"

"I'm at least going to make a show of going after her. With enough threat of force, I will—*encourage*—the palace to release her."

"Why would she go in there?"

"The gods only know. She's either after Marin or you, or she's simply too stubborn to know she should've waited."

Alec took a deep breath and grabbed another piece of offered eel flesh. "Probably all of the above."

"That was my thought. Now, we need to hurry, before the other arm of the attack takes place."

"The attack?"

"It's time for the palace to realize that those of us in the outer sections have some strength remaining. And considering what Sam has experienced, I am determined to do this now. Were it not for her, I might have waited. The timing isn't quite right, but…"

Bastan grabbed Alec's hand and jerked him to his feet.

"How much more do you need?"

"All that you have," Alec said.

Bastan handed him a jar. Alec glanced at it and then looked up at Bastan. "You had this?"

"Since you were injured, I made certain to have a

supply on hand. I told you, I will look out for those who are mine."

"Am I now one of yours?"

"Sam claims you, so I claim you."

Alec took another piece of the eel meat and chewed it slowly. He looked down at the tray and checked the paper. It was drying, but it wasn't quite dry.

"Is that it?" Bastan asked.

"This is what I was able to make. I don't know if it will work, but…"

"But it is all that we have. I've tried finding more, but it seems there is no more to be found, at least not in the city."

"I think the university sources it from outside of the city. I think the Kavers bring it out of the Theln lands."

Bastan guided them through the streets, hurrying across bridges. As they went, Alec realized the bridges were unguarded. They went across them without having any challenge.

"Bastan?"

"I have removed most of them. I have advised them to return to their homes for their safety."

"Most of them?"

"Some of them disappeared," he said.

"Where did they go?"

Bastan shook his head. "All I can guess is that they were recalled to the palace."

As they neared the university section, the building gleaming in the distance, Alec felt a growing sense of trepidation. The physickers inside would not fight, and maybe they wouldn't even be aware of a fight but going with Bastan like this meant that he was throwing himself in with people willing to go against the throne—and the Anders.

Was that what he wanted?

He wanted to help Sam. That thought, more than any other, stayed in his mind. And if she was in the palace, and if she was in danger, he was determined to go after her and do whatever it took to help and ensure she got to safety.

"You don't have to come with us," Bastan said.

"I think I do."

"When this is over…"

"When this is over, I will not likely be able to return."

Bastan clapped him on the shoulder, pausing long enough to turn to him. "You are a physicker, regardless of anything else. From what I've seen, you are a damned good physicker. You don't need the university to prove that to yourself."

Alec tore his gaze away from the buildings rising up. He didn't. Bastan was right. He had gone to the university to learn, to study, but what had he discovered? He had learned some things from the master physickers, mostly about surgical skills, but when it came to treatment of illness, and the various approaches, his father had taught him most everything that he knew. The only thing the university had that his father did not was access to the library, all of the records that the physickers had acquired over the years.

He didn't need the university. He didn't need to become a master physicker.

He turned his attention toward the palace. On the other side in the section adjacent to it, there was movement.

"Do you see that?" he asked Bastan.

"I see it."

"What is it?"

"That is Chester answering my call."

"Chester?"

Bastan shrugged and started forward, crossing the bridge leading to the university section. When they reached it, soldiers suddenly swarmed out of the university.

Bastan made a motion with his hand, and the men with him hurried forward, engaging the soldiers in sword combat.

It was war.

There was no other way to describe what he saw.

Alec had never expected to see anything like it, and certainly not within the city, but as Bastan's men attacked the guards, men cried out, screaming as swords cut into flesh, and as men fell. Blood sprayed, filling the air with its coppery smell.

Alec couldn't take his eyes away. With each injury, he assessed how he would heal them, ways that they could be helped.

"Wait for me," he said to Bastan. Alec ran around a side door and inside the university. "We need physickers!" he shouted, uncertain whether anyone would respond. He ran up the stairs and reached the hospital ward. He threw the doors open, "We need physickers outside. Now!"

There were two junior physickers, and one of them started toward him.

"Find others," he shouted at the man. "Outside. Now!" Alec turned and raced back outside. When he rejoined

Bastan, the other man looked over at him. "I couldn't leave them all simply to die," Alec said.

"You can't save everyone," Bastan said.

"I can save as many as possible, even if I'm not the one to do it."

The fighting died down relatively quickly, with Bastan's men being the victors. Bastan guided him toward the palace section. As they went, other men joined them. There were more and more people coming, and it took Alec a moment to realize that the people joining them were with Bastan.

They reached the bridge and crossed over. It was wide enough for five people to cross at one time, and when they reached the middle of the bridge, they were met by a dozen soldiers, all armed with swords and crossbows.

Bastan stepped forward.

Alec feared that something would happen to him, surprised he would feel that way about Bastan. He watched as Bastan stepped up to the nearest guard and spoke something softly to him, his sword still sheathed. Were Bastan concerned, he would unsheathe his weapon, but the fact that he kept it sheathed, and that he approached so casually, left Alec thinking that perhaps he knew this person.

After a moment, Bastan turned back.

"We will continue," Bastan said.

One of the guards suddenly surged forward, and Alec cried out.

Bastan reacted even faster.

He unsheathed his sword and swiped around, cutting down the guard who ran at him.

He stood, his sword raised, glaring at the rest of the guards. Then he raised his hand and motioned.

The men with him surged forward.

They reached the guards and made quick business of taking them down. Many were thrown into the canal, and Alec watched in horror as they splashed around, fearing for what would happen to them. Would the eels attack?

Bastan grabbed his sleeve and pulled him along, and Alec had no choice but to follow.

They reached the palace lawn.

There were soldiers here, but Bastan's men and the others who had crossed from another bridge began to take them down. Bastan greeted a gray-haired man in the middle of the palace lawn.

Alec's eyes widened. The Shuver.

"This will be bloody," the Shuver said.

"Not as bloody as you think," Bastan said. "If my person inside has anything to say about it, this will be over quickly."

"And then? It will be as you promised?"

"It will be as I promised," Bastan said, glancing over to Alec.

The men made their way toward the palace. When they reached the doors, they found them locked. Bastan picked the lock and threw them open, surging inside.

Alec expected they would encounter guards, but there was no one.

"You have been here before. Is it always like this?" Bastan asked.

"There usually are guards—"

The sound of fighting came from down the hall.

Alec motioned, and Bastan made his way toward it. When they reached it, Alec nearly froze in place.

Marin was there, holding a staff, and she was moving so rapidly that she was knocking down soldiers before they even had a chance to turn toward her.

She was augmented.

He had seen Marin fight before, but he had never seen her fully augmented, not like this.

Marin seemed to take them in. "Apothecary. Sam needs your help."

Bastan's men hurried forward and joined the fight.

Alec stood there, clutching the tray that held the possible easar paper, knowing what Marin meant, but afraid the easar paper he'd made would not be enough. Yet, if he didn't try, if he did nothing, what would happen to Sam?

He reached into his satchel and pulled out a vial of her blood. He poked his finger with his belt knife and added his own blood to Sam's, sat down on the floor, and began writing on the paper.

A KAVER RISES

Pain flooded through Sam. She tried not to think of it, tried not to allow the thoughts of everything that she would lose to work through her in her last moments, but she couldn't help it.

She cried out.

She tried reaching toward her staff, but her arm seemed to be broken. It didn't work, and besides, even if she managed to grab it, there were simply too many. Even augmented—or, at least, even with the augmentations she could place on herself—she had not been enough.

And now...

Cold washed through her. Was that the sense of the end? Was that all she would know in her final moments?

It began in her feet, working its way up to her legs. When it reached her heart, she anticipated that it would stop. Why was her mind slowing like this? Why was everything seeming to happen slowly?

The blows continued to rain down on her, kicking her in the stomach, the back, something jabbing her in her shoulder. All of it was pain, and all of it was almost more than she could bear.

She wished she could see Alec, even if just one more time. Hopefully, he had gotten away as the prince had said. If he'd managed to make it out, maybe he could get help, use his father or Bastan to help him get the support he needed, to continue supplying eel meat for him.

The cold reached her chest and hovered.

The pain began to dissipate.

Her mind began to clear.

Was she not dying?

Could the cold that washed through her be something else? Could it be…

An augmentation.

Alec had found more paper… Or he had actually managed to *make* it.

Power flooded into her. Sam could scarcely believe it, and she grabbed for her staff, ignoring the blows raining down on her. Her body, her skin and bones, suddenly impervious to the attack. Strength filled her. Everything seemed to slow.

Sam attacked.

She hadn't felt the power of an augmentation granted to her by Alec in quite some time, and now, having it flooding through her, she welcomed that power, she added her own awareness of how to augment herself, and it allowed her to attack with more vigor than she had before.

The two Kavers standing in front of her fell.

Sam spun, ducking beneath the next attack, finding it almost easy to do.

What had Alec done? How had he placed in augmentation like this?

She would ask him later. She needed to work quickly. When the augmentation faded… she wasn't sure he had enough blood from her to continue placing augmentations, and she wasn't certain how much paper he had made, or how much strength she would have to hold on to these augmentations.

Her staff was a blur. She jumped, flipping into the middle of the attackers, and spun her staff around, knocking down soldiers and Kavers.

When they were down, she turned her attention to the others she had come with. The prince lay motionless on the ground, and she found her mother standing in front of Lyasanna, a sword piercing her chest.

"No!"

The princess held the sword, and she was saying something to Elaine, whispering softly.

Sam pushed off with her staff, swinging around and connecting with the back of Lyasanna's head, sending her staggering toward the stairs. Sam heard the sword fall to the floor as she spun her staff back around, connecting with Lyasanna's side, and then back around, knocking her leg, satisfied when a crack rang out as it broke under the force of Sam's blow.

Lyasanna screamed and fell to the floor. As she writhed in pain, Sam stepped up to her and jabbed her in the chest with her staff, knocking the wind out of her. Sam nudged the princess's body with her foot, and Lyasanna's head rocked to the side as her eyes closed.

Sam grabbed the sword and threw it off to the side, the she ran up to Elaine and pressed her hands on her belly, putting pressure on the wound, holding steady as the blood poured out from her.

"Elaine," she said.

Her mother turned her head toward her, and she blinked. "Samara. You are even more than I ever could have imagined."

"We need to get you help. We need to get you—"

Elaine shook her head. "There will be no help, not for me. This… this is the kind of wound that there is no coming back from."

"We can help. Alec must've found more paper, and we can place an augmentation, we can restore you, and…"

Elaine shook her head again. "Samara. I'm so proud… I'm so proud…"

Her eyes closed.

"Alec!"

Sam stood and turned to the stairs. She raced down them to find Marin finishing off a row of attackers. Surprisingly, Bastan was there with dozens of men she knew, and there was the Shuver, fighting alongside Bastan. What were they doing here together?

Alec sat on the floor, his head bowed, furiously writing.

Sam ran over to him. "I need your help."

Alec looked up. "Sam. You're okay."

"I am. Thanks to you. But now Elaine needs your help." She grabbed him and lifted. Her augmentations were fading as they climbed the stairs, but she didn't need the augmentations, not anymore. When they reached Elaine, Alec immediately took I the scene and crouched down next to her.

He quickly began to assess her injuries, first checking

for a pulse and putting his ear against her chest to listen for her breath sounds. Sam had seen him make assessments like this enough times that she understood what it was he was doing, but he wasn't moving fast enough. He wasn't checking her fast enough.

"There was a sword to her chest," Sam said. "Fix that."

Alec looked up at her, tears welling in his eyes. "Sam. There isn't any fixing this."

"No. You can augment her. Here," she said, holding out her hand, waiting for Alec to poke at it and draw blood. It didn't matter whether he took too much, not now, not if it was enough to help bring Elaine back. She didn't know her mother, but she wasn't about to lose her, not now.

"There are things that we can't fix," Alec said. He stood and took Sam's hand. "She was stabbed in the heart. I can't augment that. I can't repair that. She lost too much blood."

"What are you saying? Alec, with everything that we've done, what are you saying?"

"I'm sorry, Sam. She's gone."

Sam looked down at Elaine and grabbed the easar paper from Alec. She crouched next to Elaine, looking for something to write with. She reached over for Lyasanna's sword, wanting only to stab at her hand, wanting to draw blood so that she could try an augmentation herself. Alec had taught her enough that she thought that she might be able to help. She didn't need him to do this for her, especially if he refused…

Someone grabbed her and lifted her.

She turned to see Bastan.

"Samara. She's gone. You've seen enough in your days to know that she's gone."

"But, Bastan, she's…"

"I know what she was. I know *who* she was. But she's gone."

Sam sobbed, and Bastan pulled her close, wrapping his arms around her, hugging her, letting Sam rest her head on his chest. She beat on him, and he ignored the blows, ignored the pain he must feel as her fading augmented strength attacked him, content to simply hold on to her.

She shouldn't feel like this, not for Elaine, not for someone who had never really been there for her, but it was her mother, and she had not had the opportunity to know her, not as she wanted. And now, she never would.

"We need to finish this," Bastan said as her sobbing began to ease.

"I don't know how," she said.

"Whatever took place here needs to be done," Bastan said.

Sam took a shaky breath and pulled away from Bastan. "The princess," she said, motioning to Lyasanna where she lay motionless. She still breathed, unlike Elaine. Sam had half a mind to change that. "She intended to lead an attack on the Thelns. She had convinced the king," she said.

"And him?" Bastan motioned to the prince. Alec was checking him, and rolled him over, and given the way he didn't try to do anything, seemed content that his injuries weren't significant.

"He was caught up in it," Sam said.

"Why don't we go and check on the king?"

"Bastan…"

Bastan looked over at her, a hint of a smile on his face. "What?"

"What do you intend to get out of this?"

"Samara, what do you take me for?"

"I take you for a businessman. I take you for an opportunist."

Bastan chuckled. "Yes, well, that would be fitting, wouldn't it? Let's just say I have an interest in maintaining peace."

"You have an interest in ensuring your powers aren't disrupted."

"Is that so different?" he asked.

The prince groaned as he started to awaken, and he sat up, grabbing his head. "Apothecary," he said, looking over at Alec.

"He's not an apothecary," Sam said, grabbing the prince and jerking him to his feet. "He's a physicker. And he's my Scribe."

The prince glanced from Sam to Alec before his gaze settled on Bastan. He looked beyond Bastan, to the men gathered behind him, his eyes wide. "And it seems you have your own army."

"I have friends," Sam said. "We need to check on your father."

The prince nodded, and they headed down the hall after him. They reached some stairs, and they made their way in a direction that Sam had never been, though perhaps that didn't matter. They climbed the stairs, and at the top, they found a set of double doors closed. The prince pushed them open and led them inside.

A massive bed occupied much of the room. A thin man lay on the bed, his skin pale, and his arm stretched on either side. Needles were stuck in his arms.

Alec gasped. "They exsanguinated him."

He rushed over and examined the king, but even from

where Sam stood, she could tell that the king would not come around. He was gone. Lyasanna had drained him of all of his blood—and all of his power.

"Lyasanna did this?" the prince asked.

"She wouldn't have been able to do this, not by herself. This is..." Alec closed his eyes, swallowing. "This was surgical."

"That means the university," the prince said.

Alec nodded.

"It was Helen," Sam said, understanding what she'd said to her. "She did this."

"Then we need to go to her," the prince said.

THE MASTER PHYSICKER

A lec entered the university, trailed by Sam and Marin, with Bastan and a couple of his men along with them. Beckah remained in the palace, rescued after the attack from what had appeared to be Helen's private cells. There had been a few other students, which left Alec thinking they might be Scribes... or had the potential to be.

The prince walked at his side, and it felt strange having him with him. A few people they passed in the hallway paused and glanced at Alec, but when their gaze fell on the prince, they hurried away.

Master Helen had disappeared sometime during the fight, and though they now had Lyasanna restrained in one of the cells, Alec was concerned about what she might do. How long would they be able to hold her?

And how long would any of this remain quiet in the city?

Maybe it didn't matter. To most within the city, the ruling family was nothing more than that, and did little to influence their day-to-day lives, but he feared there might be a different sort of chaos within the city.

They reached the stairs leading up to the masters' section, and Alec hesitated only a moment. He swept up the stairs and began opening doors.

"What are you looking for?" Sam asked.

"Any of them."

"Why?"

Alec glanced back at her. Sam seemed remarkably well, especially considering what they had been through. He was surprised. He half-expected her to be suffering from the attack, but she didn't seem to be. The easar paper had worked.

He, on the other hand, still struggled with the effects of the poisoning. He was tired—incredibly so, especially after what they had experienced. If only the easar paper could take that away. He'd have to continue to study to determine what it was Helen had done to him if he ever intended to recover completely. *If* he could recover completely.

"Master physickers were involved. I don't know exactly what they were doing, but they were involved. And that needs to end now."

"Do you think you can end it by yourself?" Sam asked.

"I'm hoping to, but if I can't, that is why you are here."

A part of him wanted to go to the hospital ward to see if the other physickers had managed to help any of those injured during the battle outside the university, but that could come later. He continued to open doors and glance inside. In one, he came across Master Carl.

"Come with me," he said.

Master Carl looked up, and he started to say something until he realized that Alec was with the prince. He nodded quickly.

As they made their way down the hall, there were only a few master physickers present. He came across Master Harrison, and there was Master Carson and a few others.

Alec stopped at the end of the hall.

"Is this it?" the prince asked.

"What is this?" Master Carl asked, somehow finding it within him to summon a spine.

"We need to go down to the hospital ward," Alec said.

They started down the stairs to the back access to the hospital ward, and when he entered, he found chaos. There were dozens of junior physickers all scrambling around, all stitching or working on the injured soldiers. A few full physickers worked, though not as many as what Alec would have expected. For a moment, he thought there were no master physickers, but then he saw Master Eckerd, moving from bed to bed, and surprisingly, Aelus.

Alec breathed out.

Master Eckerd saw him and made his way over. "Alec. We could use your—"

"How many Scribes remain?" Alec asked.

Master Eckerd glanced from Alec to those with him. "What is this about?"

"This is about an attempt to overthrow the power in the city," the prince said. "This is about my father dying. This is about needing to create stability now."

Master Eckerd blinked. "Alec—"

Alec shook his head. "We need to know. How many Scribes are missing?"

Eckerd breathed out heavily. "I don't know how many

Scribes. There never were that many to begin with, and of those on the ruling council…"

"Who sat on the ruling council?"

"Only three. Helen, Brendel, and…"

"And who?"

Eckerd looked over at Alec. "And Lyasanna."

"She was on the ruling council?"

"She is one of the Anders," Master Eckerd said.

And though she was now being held in a cell at the palace, the two Scribes were missing.

"The council needs to be replaced," the prince said.

"It's not that easy," Master Eckerd said. "I don't know much about it, as I didn't sit on the council, but I know there are things that they were privy to that the rest of us were not."

"Easy or not, it must be done. If we can't trust them, we need to place those we can trust on the council." The prince glanced to Alec. "Who do you trust?"

"You're asking me?"

"I'm asking for your opinion."

Alec looked back. He disliked Master Carl, but that didn't mean he couldn't be trusted. He thought he could trust Master Eckerd, but could he? Which of the other remaining master physickers could be trusted?

The prince touched his arm. "I can see this is difficult for you."

"It's not that," Alec said.

"Then I will choose. It will be you, Master Eckerd, and myself."

Master Eckerd blinked. "The council is led by master physickers."

"From what I've seen, Physicker Stross has the intellect to be a master physicker," the prince said.

Eckerd considered Alec for a moment. "I won't dispute that. I suspect were he tested, he would easily pass to master level, but I'm more concerned about you."

"There is no need for you to be concerned about me."

"The council has always been comprised of master physickers and an Anders. That Anders was a Scribe. And from what I can gather, you are a Kaver."

"Not a Kaver, and though I haven't spent any time in the university, it's not as if I have no training. There is another who can vouch for me."

Alec frowned, wondering who might be able to vouch for the prince. It was shocking enough to learn that he was a Scribe, and it was even more surprising to learn he had studied, training as a physicker.

"I can vouch for him," Master Carl said. Alec turned, and Master Carl shrugged. "I've been working with him for the last ten years. He never wanted it known he was training with me, so I have kept that secret. I didn't know any other way to teach, so I trained him as I would any student physicker."

Master Eckerd glanced from Alec to the prince. "It seems we need to hold a testing for two master physickers." He turned his attention to the hospital ward, looking at all of the activity. "But first, there is something else we must do. We need to settle all of this down, and then we can talk."

Alec nodded. "I will help."

"As will I," Jalen said.

S am waited for Alec, sitting in his now cleaned room, staring at the wall, unable to do anything else. She hated waiting, but what choice did she have? When he returned, his hands stained with blood, his eyes weary, she stood. "You need eel meat."

He sighed. "Eventually."

"I can send Bastan for some."

"Thank you," he said. He sank into the chair at his desk and looked up at Sam, weary. "We helped as many as we could, and… It was good."

She smiled. She enjoyed seeing Alec like this, enjoyed seeing the way that he worked with the patients in the hospital, and she realized that this suited him.

"Bastan found something," she said.

"What did he find?" Alec asked, resting his arms on the desk and leaning forward.

"While trying to secure the palace, he came across a storeroom the princess had. Within it were stacks of easar paper."

Alec blinked. "Stacks?"

"That was why she had recalled all of Kavers. She had sent word that they needed to steal as much easar paper as possible and bring it back into the city. We knew she had, but I never imagined it would have been so much. She intended to use it to complete her attack. But that's not all," Sam said.

"What else?"

She handed Alec a folded sheet of paper, and he took it, blinking his weary eyes a moment until they cleared enough for him to read the contents of the page.

"All of them?" Alec asked.

"So it seems. I don't know how they managed it, but all of the Kavers we faced had been influenced. Master Helen was far more skilled than we realized. You need to see what she did, the way she documented."

"We need to find her," Alec said. "I don't know what more she can do, but if she manages to attack here again…"

"I can't stay, not in the city."

"You still intend to go after Tray?"

"I have to. He's been gone so long, and with what just happened…"

"I can't go," Alec said. "I'm needed here, at least until all of this settles down."

Sam smiled. "I know."

"Sam—"

She crouched next to him, taking his hands, trying not to think about the blood that had stained them. "I need to find Tray. I need this to be over."

"And what happens if the Thelns attack when you go?"

"I have a plan for that," Sam said.

"What plan?"

"I intend to offer a trade."

Alec blinked, and it was a moment before understanding came to his eyes. "Oh, Sam, you can't really intend to do that. You can't intend to use her like that. How is that any different from anything they have done?"

"She needs to pay for what she has done. We need to have a lasting peace with the Thelns. And…"

"And what?" Alec asked.

"And we need to understand why Scribes who go to their lands don't return. I think… I think it's better that you stay here. I would be too afraid of what might happen if you went."

Alec blinked, and it was a measure of his fatigue that he only nodded. "When do you intend to go?"

"I don't know. Probably soon. I need to make some preparations, and I want to make sure that everything is stable here, but then…"

Alec breathed out. "At least that will give us some time together before you go."

Sam smiled and pulled him close, hugging him. "I don't want to go. I don't want to leave you."

"I know."

"I wish we could just be together and understand what it means for us to be Kaver and Scribe."

"I don't."

Sam swallowed and pushed back. "You don't?"

Alec shook his head. "I want to know what it could be like for us to be Alec and Sam."

Sam pulled him close and embraced him again. "I want that too." She feared they might never know what that was like. She feared that, with everything they had to do, she would always be left wondering. She feared she wouldn't be able to return from the Theln lands.

She couldn't tell Alec any of that. Instead, she just remained in his arms, letting him hug her, and hugging him back. For now, they would have this moment together, even though both knew it wouldn't last.

Don't miss the final volume of The Book of Maladies: Exsanguinated!

Looking for another exciting fantasy read? Check out book 1 of The Dragonwalker: Dragon Bones

Dragons have been gone from the world for centuries, though their power remains.

A war fought a thousand years ago removed the destructive threat of dragons, allowing fire mages to use the magic stored within their bones to protect the empire for millennia. The empire has known a fragile peace, held together by that ancient magic.

Fes has always longed for stability. Raised within the slums of the empire, taught to steal and hurt others to make his way, when he's discovered by the emperor's chief fire mage, he's given a chance to use his particular gift for gathering lost dragon relics to become something more.

An encounter with a priest in possession of a dragon bone reveals the existence of a new power that threatens to return the long dead dragons to the world. Chased by the dangerous enemies, Fes travels into the bleak lands of the Dragon Plains before others can reach it. If he survives, what he discovers means the continued safety of the empire and a promise of wealth and freedom. If he fails, the deadly power of the dragons might return.

Yet, with a growing and unexplainable magic within him, it's the promise of understanding who he truly is that might be the most valuable, only it's the same power that leaves him with questions some within the empire don't want answered.

Dragon Bones is the exciting first book in an epic new fantasy series.

People:

- Aelus Stross: An apothecary and skilled healer. Alec's father
- Alec Stross: a physicker
- Bastan: a thief who essentially runs Caster
- Elaine: Sam's mother. Kaver.
- Hyp: a moneylender in the Arrend section who frequents Aelus's shop
- Kevin: Bastan's employee
- Lyassana Anders: Princess, Scribe to Elaine
- Mags: a painter with a unique talent
- Marcella Rubbles: owner of a stationary store in Arrend
- Marin: a Kaver who had a dangerous assignment
- Master Carl: Master Physicker, unpleasant to Alec

- Master Eckerd: Master Physicker, mentor to Alec
- Master Helen: Master Physicker
- Ralun: A Theln
- Rynance Vold: A dangerous man
- Samara (Sam) Elseth: a thief
- Trayson (Tray) Elseth: Sam's brother

Places and Terms:

- Arrend section: a merchant section
- Balan Day: a day to celebrate the festival god
- canal eels: possibly mythical creatures living in the canals
- Callesh section: a merchant section
- Caster section: a lowborn outer section of the city
- Central Canal: the canal that separates the lowborn sections from the merchants and highborns
- Drash section: a merchant section
- easar paper: magical paper
- Farnum section: a merchant section
- Highborn: a term for the wealthier living in the center of the city
- Hosd section: a lowborn section near the swamp
- Jaku section: a highborn section where easar paper was found.
- Kyza: one of the many gods worshipped in Verdholm

- Lostin section: a merchant section
- Lowborn: a term for people living in the outer sections of the city
- Lycithan: a southern nation. Known for their skilled artisans.
- Narvin Plains: east of the city, thin stretch of land
- Physicker: healers with specialized training at the university
- Piare River: connects to Ralan Bay and the canals
- Ralan Bay: a trading hub along the coast of Verdholm
- Sacred Alms: the healing religion Alec follows
- Sornum: Bastan's tavern
- Thelns: dangerous brutes
- Valun: a country known for various artifacts, including the stout rope Sam uses
- Verdholm: an isolated city situated near the coast with canals running through it separating it into different sections
- Yisl: one of the many gods worshipped in Verdholm

Printed in Great Britain
by Amazon